MURDER ON EMBASSY ROW

MURDER IN THE WHITE HOUSE

MURDER ON CAPITOL HILL

By Margaret Truman

MARGARET TRUMAN

MURDER IN GEORGETOWN

A CAPITAL CRIMES NOVEL

WITNESS

An Imprint of HarperCollinsPublishers

This book was previously published by Arbor House Publishing Company.

WITNESS
An Imprint of HarperCollins*Publishers*
195 Broadway
New York, New York 10007

Copyright © 1986 by Margaret Truman
ISBN 978-0-06-239178-0
www.witnessimpulse.com

First Witness mass market printing: December 2015
First William Morrow hardcover printing: August 1986

HarperCollins ® is a registered trademark of HarperCollins Publishers.

Printed in the United States of America

10 9 8 7 6 5 4 3 2 1

Chapter One

The broad barge creaked in the still May night as a team of mules on the towpath strained against their ropes to free it from its mooring. Six musicians in straw hats and red vests launched into a brassy version of "Rampart Street Parade." The mules' efforts finally overcame inertia, and the barge—and the music—slowly moved up the C & O Canal.

"Delicious idea for a party," the stout wife of Georgetown's leading banker shouted. She wore a gray robe over a crimson jupe in the style of seventeenth-century France. An elaborate lace collar defined the broad dimensions of her bosom.

"Who *was* Henry Fleet?" her friend—who wore a gown more appropriate to eighteenth-century Germany—shouted back.

"He was . . ." She laughed. "He was the Rosendorf Evans of his day." Her mention of Washington's leading furrier caused both women to shake with laughter.

The party had been conceived to honor the 1632 arrival of an English fur trader named Henry Fleet, who, history had it, was the first man ever to come ashore in Georgetown. (Captain John Smith reportedly sailed past in 1608 but never bothered to get off his boat.)

New Jersey senior senator John Frolich stood to the side of the bandstand with his friend, multimillionaire real-estate developer Marshall Jenkins. Both wore dark business suits; a sizable number of the nearly 100 guests had chosen not to costume themselves.

"Who persuaded the canal commission to hand over the barge tonight?" Frolich asked.

Jenkins shrugged and muttered, "Louise, who else?" Louise Walling was Georgetown's reigning social hostess. It was said she lived and breathed parties, woke up at 4:00 A.M. with ideas for them. She was partial to theme gatherings. When someone mentioned Henry Fleet over lunch at Le Lion d'Or, this night's party was only an invitation away.

Jenkins looked across the barge to where his wife, Elsa, stood with Frolich's wife, Henrietta. Henrietta Frolich, who was short and matronly, wore a beige linen suit. Elsa Jenkins's tall, shapely figure was nicely displayed in a yellow silk dress that clung tightly to every contour of her body. It was cut low, revealing the upper reaches of full, loosely bound breasts. The two women were closely watching a girl dressed in an Indian maiden's costume who was sinuously dancing to the band's slow version of "St. Louis Blues." Her partner was a young man with long hair cut in a punk fashion. Two earrings hung from his left ear. He wore only a leather loin-cloth, and his bare torso glistened with sweat as he and the girl gyrated their hips to the drummer's backbeat.

Jenkins nodded at the dancing girl. "She never runs out, does she?"

Senator Frolich smiled ruefully. His daughter, Valerie, suddenly intensified the movement of her hips, inching closer to the young man until their pelvises touched. Frolich's eyes met his wife's and they both grimaced. "Young people," Frolich said gruffly. He moved over to the bar and ordered vodka on the rocks.

The band finished the blues number and there was applause for the dancing couple. The pianist, a young woman whose femininity was concealed by her Dixieland outfit, began to play the "Royal Garden Blues," her delicate left hand creating surprising thunder as she created a rolling bass line that would have pleased Fats Waller.

"Precious, isn't it?" a tall, elegant man with silver hair said to Frolich.

Frolich turned, smiled at George Alfred Bowen. "A little too much so," Frolich said.

"Never too precious for Louise," Bowen said. "I just wonder what the poor thing will do after this gala. She's running out of worthwhile historical figures. Henry Fleet? What's left?"

Frolich laughed and sipped his drink. Bowen, America's most famous and influential columnist, ran his index finger over a pencil-thin white moustache, raised his eyebrows, and sighed. "Are you still planning to be there this weekend?" Bowen asked.

"Yes."

"I told Marshall we should try to make it earlier on Friday. Is that all right with you?"

"Fine," Frolich said. He moved away, casually snaking his way through the tight cluster of guests.

"Hello, George."

Bowen looked Louise Walling up and down and said, "A splendid costume, Louise, but a bit risqué for the period, isn't it?"

Walling glanced down at her bosom. "Of course not," she said with mock indignation. "It's Spanish and extremely authentic for the period. They began lowering the neckline early in the sixteen hundreds, although God knows they weren't fans of the bosom. They used to strap lead shields over young girls' breasts to keep them from growing. Harrison told me that." Harrison—it was his only name—provided costumes to Georgetown's elite partygoers, as well as to Washington's leading theatrical troupes.

Bowen smiled. "Be that as it may, Louise, I still find it shocking."

She guffawed. "You haven't the right, George, to find *anything* shocking, not with your reputation. Which young, innocent thing are you corrupting tonight?"

"I can't imagine what you're talking about, Louise. I'm here alone, anxious only to celebrate Mr. Fleet's historic arrival."

"You're impossible," she said, splaying a fan across her face.

"Difficult but adorable," said Bowen. "Excuse me. Lovely party. Mr. Fleet would have been proud." He walked away, his slender body aristo-cratically erect, gray eyes in constant motion as he cut a skillful path toward the bandstand. "Good evening, Valerie," he said to Frolich's daughter.

"Hello, professor," she said sweetly, then gig-gled. "Are you about to ask me for this dance?"

Bowen smiled. "No, although the idea isn't without appeal. I didn't realize you'd be here to-night."

"I hadn't planned to be, but . . . well, it was better than studying. The assignment you gave us this afternoon is dull."

"I'm sorry you found it so. I consider the ques-tion of libel and slander to be of primary concern to fledgling journalists."

" 'Fledgling.' It makes me sound like a tiny, wingless bird."

"Which is exactly what you are, you and your fellow students. I watched you dance before. It was very provocative."

"Was it? Good. I like to provoke."

"I'm aware of that, as is your father."

Valerie looked past Bowen to her father. He had slipped away from a knot of people and was heading her way. "Speak of the devil," she mut-tered.

"Hello," John Frolich said to his daughter.

"Hello." It was a flat, emotionless response.

"Could I speak with you for a minute?"

She glanced at Bowen, who raised his eyebrows and slipped away.

"Talking about the seminar?" Frolich asked.

"I told him it was dull."

"That's not very smart. He *is* your professor, as well as my friend."

"That doesn't make it more exciting."

"Valerie, I . . ."

Her face was awash with defiance.

"I want you at the house tomorrow. Your mother and I wish to talk to you."

"About what?"

"You know perfectly well about what."

"Dad, I . . . Look, this is silly. I see things one way, you and mom see them another. What I do with my life is my business. I just want to be left alone."

"To do what, to destroy . . ." He bit off further words. "Damn it, Valerie, you take what pleases you but won't return any kindnesses. It's because of my friend Marshall Jenkins that you have an apartment. You go to school because I foot the bills. Stop pretending you're a grown-up. You're anything but."

She started to walk away, but he grabbed her arm. "Let go. You're hurting me."

"Be at the house tomorrow at six."

She wrenched herself free and disappeared into the crowd. Frolich looked up at the piano player, who smiled at him. "Any requests, senator?" she asked.

"What? No, no thank you."

Standing alone near the bar, Elsa Jenkins had been watching the scene between Frolich and his daughter. It was obvious they were not engaged in pleasant conversation. She thought of the Frolich family: the senator, patrician features, clothes custom-made in London, power emanating from every pore, chairman of the Senate Select Committee on Intelligence, confidant to the president, presidential material himself, rich and privileged—and arrogant. Henrietta Frolich, on the other hand, was dowdy and dull, shapeless mousy brown hair, thin-lipped, and with the demeanor of a frightened sparrow. Their only child, Valerie, was twenty, with energy threatening to burst through her skin. Short like her mother but less boxlike, she was full-breasted and narrow-waisted, with huge brown eyes in a constant receiving mode, always laughing. Valerie was in her third year at Georgetown University, a journalism student, straight A's, the only junior to be accepted into George Alfred Bowen's twice-a-week seminar. But she was virtually estranged from her family. Elsa knew how much it upset John. He never could hide it.

Frolich came to Elsa's side.

"You're upset," she said, traces of her German heritage still evident in her speech. She squeezed his arm.

"No, I'm . . . she's a very difficult girl."

"Yes, and charming. She'll come around."

"Maybe. How are you?"

"All right. Marshall wants to go to Rome next week."

"You?"

"Yes, I'll go with him. Only a week."

The band began to play again—"The Muskrat Ramble." Guests started dancing. Frolich saw Valerie rejoin the young man in the loincloth on the dance floor.

"I'd better see to Henrietta," Frolich said.

"Are you coming back to our house later?"

"No. I have a heavy day tomorrow."

Buses and limousines awaited the arrival of the barge at the upper end of the canal. As the barge slowly approached the dock, a corpulent lobbyist who'd had too much to drink teetered on the edge, lost his balance, and fell into the water. There were whoops of laughter as everyone ran to peer down at him. Two crew members threw him a line and he was pulled to safety.

"Idiot," John Frolich commented to Marshall Jenkins, who'd joined Frolich and his wife near where they would exit to the dock.

"A buffoon," Jenkins said.

"I'll see you this weekend," Frolich said.

Jenkins said, "Call me."

Valerie Frolich and her dancing partner stood next to them, waiting for the barge to touch the dock. Her mother asked where she was going next. "Why not come back to the house?" she suggested. "I'll cook something and—"

"Can't, mom," Valerie said. "Another time." She kissed her mother on the cheek and she and the young man jumped to the dock, hand in hand, and ran off together, their laughter ringing behind.

Chapter Two

A trio of vagrants had witnessed the passage of the festive barge party up the C & O Canal the night before. They'd set up housekeeping beneath the bridge only a month ago, but they got along, each with his designated spot on the ground for a mattress of newspapers. Their personal belongings were carefully stored in shopping bags from Conran's, whose sign loomed large on the opposite side of the canal. A skinny yellow dog that had joined up with them a week ago had been named Blondie after a careful examination to determine its sex.

The weather had been kind to the partygoers. Now, at seven the morning after, a steady, gentle rain created thousands of dimples on the canal. Because the barge party had attracted so many people to the towpath, panhandling had been profitable, and one of the vagrants had gone into town in search of breakfast, returning with a bag of doughnuts and the morning paper, Blondie at his side. The men made coffee over an open fire and sat in dry contentment beneath the bridge.

"Don't give her the jelly," one of them said. "I like the jelly."

"I'll give her the cinnamon," another said, handing a doughnut to Blondie.

The third man leaned against the stone wall and started to read the paper, a steaming cup of coffee at his side. He'd finished the business pages and was about to turn to the sports section when Blondie started to bark.

"Shut up," the reader said.

"Hey, look," the vagrant closest to the canal said. The other two glanced up. "Over there." He pointed to a spot on the other side where a formation of concrete block jutted into the water. "What's that?"

The three men crossed the towpath and stood side by side on the canal's edge. "That's a body."

"Nah, it's only—"

"No, no, it is, damn it. Look—those are legs sticking out from the brown thing. See? Just under the water."

"Goddamn."

"It is, it is. It's a goddamn body. The cement caught it."

Two of them went in search of a policeman while the third remained on the towpath. Minutes later a Washington MPD patrol car pulled up on the narrow street fifteen feet above the vagrants' home, and two uniformed officers came down a set of stairs. "Where's this body?" one of them asked, his voice indicating his skepticism.

They pointed.

"That's not a body," said one of the officers.

"Yeah, I think it is," said his partner.

It was.

"We better get backup from headquarters," said one.

A half-hour later the body of a young woman wearing an Indian maiden's dress was pulled from the water. One moccasin was missing. Her face was swollen with large purple bruises.

"No I.D.?" one of them asked.

"No. What'a you figure, twenty, twenty-one?"

"Yeah, about."

A large detective wearing a cheap black raincoat and tan rainhat stood beside the three vagrants and their dog. "That's it?" he asked. "That's all you saw?"

"Yeah, that's right."

Blondie barked.

"That your dog?" the detective, whose name was Peter Languth, asked.

"Yeah."

"You got a license for it?"

The vagrants looked at each other.

"Get a license—614 H Street. You hear me?"

"Yeah, we hear you."

"And stay around. We'll want to talk to you again."

Chapter Three

The jarring ring cut through Joe Potamos like a machine gun. He groaned, twisted his pillow into a new shape, and forced his head into it. The ringing continued—louder each time, it seemed. He groaned again, then swore softly into the pillow. The clock at his bedside said noon. He'd gotten home at eight after covering a drug-related double murder.

He propped himself up against the headboard and angrily jerked the receiver from its cradle. "What?" he said loudly.

"Joe?"

"Yeah. Who is it?"

"Yvonne." Yvonne Masters was an editor at the *Washington Post*, where Potamos was a reporter assigned to the police beat.

"Come on, Yvonne, you know I was out all night. I just got to bed."

"Joe, I'm sorry, but this is a biggie. Senator Frolich's daughter has been murdered."

Potamos blinked and scratched his belly through a gap in his pajamas, shook his head, and said, "Yeah? Jesus, when did that happen?"

"Sometime last night. They pulled her out of

the C and O early this morning. We just got a positive I.D. on her."

"The senator's daughter. That's . . . yeah, that's a biggie all right. Who caught the case?"

"Let's see . . . Languth. Detective Peter Languth."

"Peter. They must be punishing him. He's got nineteen in. All right, I'll get to it."

"Joe, I am sorry but—"

"I know."

"Gil wants you to call him."

"Gardello? All right. A shower, I need a shower. See ya."

Potamos's dog, Jumper, had slept through the call at the foot of the bed. He'd inherited her six years ago at the scene of a rape/murder of an old woman in Foggy Bottom who lived alone, the dog her only companion. Whoever killed her had beaten the animal pretty badly. It had lost an eye in the process. Potamos had taken her to the vet and, after an expensive week there, brought her home. She was a mongrel through and through, but Potamos decided after watching a public-television special on African termites that she was descended from the rare African aardwolf. Aardwolves, according to the special, used their front paws to pound their way through the thick walls of termite mounds, then leaped high to flick the insects from the air with their tongues. Jumper possessed both traits: She could jump higher from a standstill than any animal Potamos had ever seen, and she woke him most mornings by pounding him with her paws.

"Get up," Potamos mumbled as he got out of

bed and went to the bedroom window. It was raining harder now, and a wind had kicked up, hurling raindrops against the panes.

He stumbled into the bathroom, tossed his pajamas into a corner, and turned on the shower, letting it run while he brushed his teeth. He stepped into the stall. The water was ice-cold. "No hot water. Great, just goddamn great." He put his head beneath the water, lathered his hair, and shivered as cold rivulets found his body. He rinsed, dried himself, used a blow dryer on his thick, black curly hair, and returned to the bedroom, where Jumper was now curled up contentedly on his pillow.

"Get up," Potamos said. "No pillows. How many times I have to tell you that?"

He put on the same blue button-down shirt he'd worn the night before, and the same gray slacks and tan tweed sport jacket. He chose a different tie—maroon instead of brown—and a scuffed pair of Docksiders, picked up his tan Burberry trench coat from where he'd dropped it on the living-room floor, put a leash on Jumper, and rode the elevator down six floors to the lobby, where the condominium manager was putting up a crude sign near the front door: BOILER SHUT OFF FOR REPAIRS UNTIL 6 TONITE.

"Why don't you warn people ahead?" Potamos said.

The manager shrugged and walked away.

After returning to the apartment and feeding the dog, Potamos called Gardello.

"Where the hell have you been?" Gardello said. "I've been calling. You were supposed to call me."

"I took a shower. There's no hot water. I walked the dog. I'm very tired. I was up all night."

"Yeah, well, call in when you're supposed to. Look, Joe, here's what we have. . . ."

Potamos took notes as Gardello, who was managing editor on the city side, outlined what they had on the Frolich murder.

"What's the father say?" asked Potamos.

"Nothing yet. We have that covered. Why don't you run down guests at that party on the barge, employees who worked it, anybody who might have picked up on something."

"You have a list?"

"Some." He read off a dozen names. "Joe, you might check out the booking agency that sent the band. They were there all night, maybe saw something, heard something. It's Elite Music, on Wisconsin." He gave Potamos the address. "Got it?"

"Yeah."

"Call in later. Every hour."

"I understand Pete Languth caught this one."

"Right. You know him pretty good, huh?"

"He's a psychopath."

Gardello laughed. "You two must get along then. Call me."

Elite Music was above a trendy furniture store.

"Joe Potamos, *Washington Post*. I'd like to talk to somebody who can tell me about the musicians who played the barge party last night," he said to the busty redheaded receptionist.

"I'm afraid Mr. Walters is the only one who can divulge that information."

" 'Divulge'? What do we have here, a national security problem?"

She drew a deep, haughty breath. "Mr. Walters is president of Elite Music. You'll have to speak with him."

"Fine."

"He's extremely busy right now."

"But he's here."

"Yes. He has a client with him."

"How long will he be?"

"I don't know."

"I'll wait."

"I prefer that you make an appointment. We work on appointments here."

Potamos looked around the room. The walls were covered with photographs of Elite Music musicians in the company of Washington's high and mighty. Framed letters of appreciation for having provided good music were mixed in with the photos. A large clock had been created from a drummer's cymbal. Coat hooks were in the form of quarter notes.

"Would you like to?" the redhead asked.

Potamos grinned. "Very much."

"An appointment." Ice in her voice. No sense of humor.

"I'll wait."

Another frustrated deep breath. "If you wish. Have a seat."

"Thanks."

He passed the next twenty minutes reading the current issue of the *Washingtonian*. Then the door to an inner office opened and a short, pudgy man in a blue and white striped shirt, red bow tie, and red suspenders came through, followed by two middle-aged women in fur coats.

" . . . and you needn't worry about a thing," the man told the women. "It'll be a lovely party. I'll send our best people."

The furs left and the man looked at Potamos, then at the redhead. "Mr. Walters, this is Mr. Potamos from the *Washington Post*. I told him he needed an appointment, but . . ."

A big plastic smile and an extended hand. "I'm William Walters," he said. "What can I do for you?"

"I'm covering the Valerie Frolich murder and want to know the names of the musicians who worked the barge party she was on."

"My God, yes, I heard. Incredible. But she wasn't killed at the party. Why are you interested in my musicians?"

"They might have seen something, heard something, that's all. How many did you have there?"

"Corrine?" Walters said to the redhead.

"Six. Dixieland."

"Oh, yes, six Dixieland jazz musicians. We have the best, all types of music."

"Yeah, I'm sure you do. How about their names and numbers? I'd like to talk to them."

"Oh, I'm not sure I'd like to do that. Don't misunderstand, Mr. Potamos. I'm always anxious to help the press. Publicity is very important in this business."

"Mr. Walters, we're talking about the murder of a U.S. senator's daughter. I don't want to spend any more time here. The names? Do I get 'em from you, or do I take another route?"

"I'd like to think about this."

"And so will I."

The door opened and a man and woman entered, both in fur coats.

"Jonathan, Melissa," Walters said, his smile bigger than ever.

"I'm still going to sue you for fraud," Potamos said.

Walters and his two clients stared at Potamos.

"You charged me for eight musicians, but two of them were ghosts, didn't play a note, just held their instruments up to their mouths and pretended."

"Really, I will not—"

"Names, then I go. No names, a good feature on using ghosts in bands."

Walters smiled at his visitors and whisked them into his office, turning to say to the redhead, "Give him what he wants."

Potamos's next stop was Martin's Tavern, his favorite Georgetown hangout. He ordered steak and eggs and called the numbers given him. He managed to reach four of the five male musicians, none of whom had anything to offer. His last call was to the pianist, Roseann Blackburn.

"Miss Blackburn, this is Joe Potamos from the *Post.* I'm working on the Valerie Frolich murder and wanted to talk to you about the party. Mr. Walters at Elite Music gave me your name. Did

you see anything last night that might have bear-
ing on the kid's death?"

"No. Well, I really didn't see anything except
that she did have an argument with her father. I
talked to her for a while during a break. She was
nice. I heard about what happened on the radio. I
can't believe it."

"Yeah, hard to believe. Look, maybe I could
come see you and we could talk. That possible?"

"I suppose so. I'm practicing right now and I'm
working tonight."

"Where?"

"The Four Seasons."

"Fancy. Walters books good places."

"This isn't through the agency. I play cocktail
piano in the lobby two nights a week."

"I see. What time do you play?"

"Five until eight."

"You take breaks?"

She laughed. "As many as I can get away with."

"I'll see you there. I figure I'll know who you
are unless there's a dozen piano players."

"There's just me. See you tonight."

The hot water was still off in his apartment.
When he called the manager, he was told it would
be off for at least another day. "How do I get
clean?" Potamos asked. "Use lots of deodorant"
was the reply.

He sat in a director's chair by the window and
drew from a can of beer. Jumper was asleep on
the hassock. "Dump," he mumbled. Until recently
he'd been living in a furnished room in a run-
down building on Carolina and taking his meals

in a nearby cafeteria. Then, about six months ago, his father had called from New York. Paul Potamos owned a diner in Queens. Joe had worked with him part-time during high school; his father had wanted him to come into the business full-time after graduation, but Joe wanted college, so his father sent him to New York University, where he majored in journalism.

The old man was proud when Joe graduated with honors, but then came marriage number one, to Patty Kelly, Irish Catholic with green eyes, freckles, and a distinct dislike for his family. The feeling was mutual. When Joe announced he planned to marry her, his father said, "If you marry someone who is not a Greek, you are no longer my son."

It had been a tough decision, but the freckles won out. That was the last time his father talked to him until that phone call. His mother had kept in touch but had to be secretive about it. His two sisters—one in Los Angeles (married to a Silicone Valley hustler), the other an inhalation therapist in Pittsburgh—sent him Christmas cards and birthday cards every other year. He almost lost his mother when he divorced Patty (she'd cried for days about losing her two grandchildren), and almost lost her for good when he remarried—this time choosing a nice Jewish girl named Linda, a secretary at the CIA. Four months after the wedding, she admitted she'd been cheating on him. Her lover turned out to be another secretary at the CIA, named Terri, which gave Potamos some comfort—at least he hadn't lost out to a man. The divorce was quick and simple.

His father's phone call six months ago had been to say that he was dying, cancer, three months to live unless he took chemotherapy, maybe six months if he did. Joe flew to New York and they had a brief, touching reconciliation climaxed by Paul Potamos handing his only son a check for $100,000. He wanted the satisfaction of personally giving out his estate while he was still alive.

Joe returned to Washington and bought the one-bedroom condo in Rosslyn, just over the Potomac via the Key Bridge. "A dump," he repeated. But it was better than the rooming house. Anything was better than that.

He tried to reach Peter Languth at MPD but was told Languth wouldn't be back until later that night. He called other contacts but came a cropper. Everyone knew only what they'd heard on radio or television.

"Gil, Joe."

Gardello asked what he'd come up with so far.

"Nothing, except I talked to five out of the six musicians. Not much there except maybe the one I'm interviewing tonight. She works at—"

"She?"

"Yeah. You never heard of a female piano player?"

"Interview? Joe, we don't have time for socializing. They're handling this like Watergate upstairs and we need information."

"That's why I'm seeing her. She says Valerie Frolich had an argument on the barge with her father. I figured—"

"Just figure fast. Call me."

"Of course."

Chapter Four

Potamos sat in a corner of the Four Season's large, luxurious lobby and watched Roseann Blackburn perform on a gleaming black Steinway in the center of the room. He hadn't anticipated she'd be beautiful.

Her hair was blue-black, and she wore it short, swept back at the sides and neatly trimmed to expose the back of her neck. She sat extremely erect on the piano bench, long, thin fingers gracefully arched over the keyboard, her beryl gown simple and floor-length, the bodice scooped low in front and even lower at the back. She was small-breasted, appropriate to her overall slenderness. Her makeup gave her cheeks and lips high color.

Potamos silently sang along with the melody. He looked around the room. A power place, lots of blue and gray suits, and furs, men and women huddled in small nests created by overstuffed couches and chairs and looking as though they belonged. Self-assured. At home. Some familiar political faces, a couple of high-rolling businessmen, most faces not known to him.

His waitress—dressed in a long black skirt and

frilly white blouse—asked if he wanted another beer.

"Not right now," he said. "In a minute."

Blackburn played Scott Joplin's "Maple Leaf Rag." Potamos smiled and tapped his foot. She ended with a flourish. He applauded, realized no one else had, and stopped. She turned and looked at him, smiled, got up and crossed the lobby to where he sat. He stood. She held out her hand. He shook it. "You knew it was me," he said.

"You don't look like a Four Seasons regular."

He looked down at his tie and old brown corduroy jacket. "I just got it back from the cleaners."

She smiled. "Mind if we go somewhere else? I'm not supposed to sit with customers."

"Yeah, sure. I'd better pay."

"Tell her you'll be back."

"Yeah, all right." He told the waitress, who looked at Blackburn, smiled knowingly, and said, "Okay."

Blackburn put a black shawl over her shoulders as they left the hotel and walked a block and a half up M Street to the Marbury House. "Want a drink here?" she asked. "A friend of mine plays in the tavern."

"Sure."

They settled into a booth. Potamos ordered a beer, Blackburn white wine. "Now," she said, "ask me questions. I don't have much time. They're pretty strict about my breaks."

"Okay. Let's see . . . By the way, you play terrific."

"Thank you."

"You do it for a living?"

"Yes." She laughed. "Occasionally it adds up to that. Anyway, I do play the piano for my daily bread."

Potamos nodded. "I like music. I don't play any instruments or anything like that, but I'm a good listener. I have a great stereo system and a big record collection."

"Really? What kind of music do you like?"

"Oh, I like all of it—jazz, rock, even some country-and-western."

"I'm classically trained, but there isn't much call for that, so I play anything."

"Classical. I like classical music. My father was an opera buff."

She smiled, almost purred. "I love opera. . . . Well, enough of this. By the way, Mr. Potamos, I told a friend of mine that I was meeting you tonight and he said you'd written one of the biggest stories of the decade, the one about that senator—what was his name?—Cables, that's right, Senator Cables, the one who—"

"Yeah, sure, Senator Richard Cables, loyal American who gets caught making millions by arranging illegal arms deals with Middle East potentates. He should've done time, but his money talked."

"You won a prize for uncovering that story."

"That's right. I tried to trade it for my back alimony bills, but my ex-wife turned the deal down."

"That's . . . that's funny."

"It wasn't to her. The barge party, Miss Blackburn. Tell me what you saw and heard."

"Call me Roseann?"

"Sure. Not Rosie?"

"Roseann."

"I'm Joe."

"Hello, Joe." They shook hands.

"The party." He took out a note pad and pen. "You said you heard the deceased arguing with her father, Senator Frolich."

"That's right. She hung around the bandstand. I liked her, full of life, very quick. She was a good-looking girl, very turned on, sexy. She did a lot of dancing with a young guy. They were both in Indian costumes."

"Why?"

"The party had a theme, something to do with a fur trader named Fleet. I never did get all of it."

"What'd Valerie argue with her father about?"

"I honestly don't know. I did hear him say something about wanting her at the house the next day—that'd be today—and she evidently didn't like the idea."

"Know why?"

"No."

"Anything else?" Never before had he seen such big, beautiful green eyes. His first wife had had green eyes, too, but there were no freckles on Roseann Blackburn, at least not on the portions of her that he could see.

"I don't think so. She talked a lot with George Bowen."

"Bowen?" Potamos's voice reflected his surprise.

"Yes. She called him 'professor.' "

"Yeah, that's right, she was a journalism student at Georgetown. How did you know it was
Bowen?"

"He isn't exactly an unknown face. TV, the
papers. Besides, he comes into the Four Seasons a
lot and requests songs."

"Yeah? What kind of songs?"

"He likes Gilbert and Sullivan."

"Did you hear what Frolich and Bowen discussed?"

"No, sorry. You must know him from the newspaper."

"Yeah, I know him."

"Wow, that bad, huh? You sound like I mentioned . . . I don't know, your ex-wife who wouldn't
accept your award for the alimony."

"Worse than that. She's the mother of my children. Bowen, he's . . . he's a mother of a different sort. He sold me down the river after I did the
Cables story. Cables was an old friend of his and
Bowen told me to lay off the investigation. I figured 'Screw you,' and I kept going. I got an award
and a permanent demotion to the cop beat."

"That's terrible."

"Yeah. I could've left and done something else,
especially after the story broke, but Bowen knows
everybody in the business. I could never prove it
but I know damn well he killed some nice offers I
had. . . . Well, that's *then.* I'm heavy into *now.* Anything else from the party?"

"I guess not. I did have one strong feeling,
though."

"What's that?"

"That Senator Frolich has something going on the side with Elsa Jenkins."

Potamos sat back and shook his head. "How do you know all those people? They request songs, too?"

"No, but I play a lot of posh parties. I've played a couple at the Jenkinses' house. House? *Mansion* is more like it."

"Frolich and Mrs. Jenkins? What makes you think they have it on?"

"Instinct, intuition. You sit on a bandstand all night and you watch the crowd, match people up, read their lives. It passes the time during the dull sets. I don't know, I just picked up on the way they looked at each other. This is silly. It has nothing to do with the kid's murder. I have to get back. I'm already late."

"I'll hang around a bit," he said. "I like to listen to you play. Hey, maybe when you're through we could get a bite to eat, coffee, whatever. You interested?"

She hesitated, which worried him. Then she grinned. "Okay, but don't stay until the end. I don't want people seeing me leave with anyone. Where are we going?"

"I don't know, the American Café?"

"Great. See you there at eight-thirty."

Chapter Five

"Pete, Joe Potamos."

"Yeah. What'a you want?"

"I called a couple of times. I left messages."

"Too busy. What'a you want?"

"The Frolich case. I'm on it."

Languth laughed. "You and every other media slob in town. You guys are crawling all over us."

"Not me, Pete. I'm doing color."

"Color? Jesus, you make it sound like 'Monday Night Football.' "

"Anything new?"

"No."

"The autopsy? When's it being released?"

"That's color, all right. Whenever."

"The funeral. You going?"

"Nah. It's in Jersey."

"I'm going."

"That's wonderful. I have to go, Joe. Thanks for calling."

"I figured I could buy you a beer and—"

"Forget it."

MPD detective Peter Languth hung up.

Potamos hung around the metro room at the *Post* until noon, when he went to the National

Press Club to meet an old friend, literary agent
Frank Belosic. Belosic had represented Potamos
after he broke the story on Senator Cables's under-
the-table arms deal with the Middle East. He had
gotten Joe a contract to do a book on the affair, but
Potamos never delivered a finished manuscript
and he'd had to return the advance. He and Belosic had remained friends despite the complica-
tion. Both belonged to the Press Club, and Belosic
developed many clients through it.

Potamos had the same reaction to entering the
club that he always had—the feeling that they'd
lost a lot in the $6-million renovation. Gone was
the crusty, smoky, smelly atmosphere, replaced by
a modern, state-of-the-art library complete with
cubicles in which out-of-town visitors could work,
and staffed by research assistants available to
members. The restaurant's food had always been
relatively edible. Now, a French chef named Ber-
nard served up gourmet meals that tasted better
but didn't stick to the ribs like in the old days. At
least not to Potamos's ribs—he'd grown up with
everything cooked in his father's diner in a special grease that pasted it to the rib cage like Krazy
Glue.

Potamos missed the all-night poker games
(hardly the atmosphere for them anymore), which
always gave him the feeling of belonging to a special and threatened species. He loved the stories
about when President Harding stayed all night at
the poker table, drink at his side, telling aides who
brought him important papers that he'd deal with
them in the morning—*after* the game.

Potamos was browsing in the library when Belosic came through the door. Tall and slender, with Slavic features and thinning blond hair combed straight back, Belosic crossed the room in a long, loping gait and shook Potamos's hand. "Hey, you look great. Must be in love," he said.

Potamos said, "As a matter of fact I am."

"No kidding. Who?"

"It doesn't matter. Where are we dining? I'd say eating, but having a French chef makes it 'dining.' "

Belosic laughed. "Where else? The dining room. Come on, it's on me."

"Selling?" Potamos asked as they went upstairs.

"Sort of."

"I'm not buying."

"For Christ's sake, Joe, at least let me do my spiel."

They filled the time over drinks with small talk. Finally, Belosic got to the point. "How about a book on the Frolich murder?"

Potamos shook his head and reached for a cigarette that hadn't been there since he quit four years ago. "There's no book there. Besides, I'm just chasing the fringe elements of the story. I've been banished, remember?"

"I sure do. George Alfred Bowen. Why in hell did you stay?"

"Insecurity."

"Crap."

"No, true, Frank. You know me, I'm not out to conquer worlds."

"A book could be a hell of a move for you, Joe.

I've had four major publishers call me looking for somebody to write one about Valerie Frolich. I suggested you every time and the reaction was positive."

"You didn't talk to . . . ?"

A laugh from the agent. "Of course I did. All is forgotten. Editors come and go. Yours went."

Potamos smiled and looked at the menu. They ordered. Belosic lighted his pipe and leaned forward. "What about Bowen and the murder, Joe? She was his student, and you know his reputation with young women."

Potamos shrugged. "One doesn't necessarily go with the other. You can sleep with kids, but murdering them is another ball game."

"Just a thought, Joe. Do you think Bowen slept with her?"

"I haven't the slightest idea."

After lunch they went out onto the new terrace where lunch and dinner would be served in better weather. Belosic walked to the edge and looked down. When Potamos came up beside him, Belosic said, "This is one of the biggest murder stories of our lifetime, Joe. Bright, beautiful college kid, daughter of one of the Senate's most powerful figures, gets her brains batted around by an unknown person. Her professor is America's leading muckraker, George Alfred Bowen. She and her father dislike each other intensely. She—"

"How do you know that?"

"What, that they didn't get along? Everybody knows that. The kid lives in a posh Georgetown apartment provided by her father's close friend, the multimillionaire real-estate developer Marshall Jenkins, whose wife is rumored to be having an affair with the senator. Shaping up juicy, Joe, the sort of thing best sellers are made of."

"Jenkins's wife and Frolich having an affair? Everybody knows that, too?"

"Rumor, D.C. style. Hey, what's happened to you, you fall out of the mainstream?"

Potamos smiled. "Yeah, I guess so."

Belosic turned and leaned on the railing, dead pipe in his hand. "What do you say, Joe? A book? It could turn your life around."

"No, absolutely not."

"Okay." Belosic fished an envelope from his pocket and handed it to Potamos.

"What's this?"

"A telegram of intent from one of New York's better publishing houses."

"I don't believe you."

"Hang on to it. If you don't want to, tear it up and I'll tell them. But don't make the decision here, now. Okay?"

"All right."

"Tell me about your new love."

"Who's that?"

"You said when I came in that—"

"Oh, she's a piano player. She was at the barge party the night Frolich got it."

"Good source?"

"No, knows nothing."

"But you'll cultivate it in the interest of journalistic investigation."

"Come on, let's go," Potamos said, crossing the

terrace. "I have to file what I have tonight, and I'm going to the funeral tomorrow."

"Take notes," said Belosic. "Could make a nice first chapter."

Rain poured on the crowd that ringed Valerie Frolich's New Jersey grave. The Episcopal bishop was an old man with a gray face. He clutched his black miter with one hand; his other hand held the Book of Common Prayer. He said in a barely audible voice, "Unto Almighty God we commend the soul of our sister departed, Valerie, and we commit her body to the ground. . . ."

Potamos stood apart from everyone and looked over the ring of people who'd gathered to pay their final respects. Several TV cameras recorded the proceedings, and a battery of still photographers and reporters stood behind ropes that had been strung to keep them in line.

The Frolich family—Senator John Frolich; his wife, Henrietta; and three of Valerie's grandparents—were clustered together at the foot of the grave. Next to them stood Marshall and Elsa Jenkins. Assorted friends formed distinct groups. Potamos figured that a group consisting of George Alfred Bowen and four young people was Bowen's seminar. A few feet behind them stood MPD sergeant Peter Languth. He wore a black single-breasted raincoat and gray fedora. *Typical cop*, Potamos thought. *Liar, too. He wasn't coming.*

He switched his attention to Senator Frolich, standing ramrod-straight, eyes focused on the gaping black hole that would be his daughter's final resting place. He wore a gray Chesterfield topcoat and was bareheaded. Others had turned up their collars against the rain that whipped across the open cemetery, but not the senator, looking as though he were defying God for what He'd done to Valerie.

Henrietta Frolich looked decades older than her husband, a dumpy, rumpled woman who seemed on the verge of collapse. Potamos found it strange that her husband wasn't touching her, had not even offered his arm for support.

The coffin containing Valerie Frolich's body was lowered slowly into the grave. The bishop sprinkled earth over it as it disappeared from view. "The Lord be with you," he said.

"And with thy spirit," a few people mumbled.

"Let us pray. Lord have mercy upon us."

"Christ have mercy upon us."

"Lord have mercy upon us."

Potamos hung around where the cars and limos were parked. Bowen passed with the students and ignored him. Languth lumbered toward him and Potamos said, "Must be your ghost."

"Huh?"

"You said you weren't coming."

"So?"

Potamos hadn't seen Languth in a while and had forgotten how big he was, and ugly. He stood six feet, four inches and weighed in at 250 pounds. Everything about him was big—hands, nose, ears, the whole face, big and red with watery blue eyes. Potamos noticed the wedding ring that dug deep into his left ring finger. "Still married. Amazing," he told himself. He considered Languth to be a cop off the deep end, warped, too filled with the grime and grim reality of his job to ever be fully human again. Still, there was a side to him that Potamos almost enjoyed—the side that matched Potamos's own cynical views from having covered too many fires and murders, distasteful scenes set in ghettos, seeing D.C. at night when a whole new world of pimps and hookers, knife artists and con men, perverts and dope hustlers emerged after the day people had fled the city to their warm, secure homes in the suburbs—after they'd raped and plundered in their own genteel, accepted white-collar way.

"Sad, huh?" Potamos said.

Languth shrugged, looked around at the last of the mourners getting into their vehicles, and turned back to Potamos. "You still buying beers?"

"Yeah, sure. You want one?"

"Yeah. Let's get outta here. You heading right back?"

"Uh-huh."

"We'll catch up back there."

"Good. Martin's?"

"You still go there?"

"Uh-huh."

"Yeah, Martin's. Five?"

"You got it."

Potamos arrived at the tavern early and called Roseann Blackburn but got her answering machine. He nursed a beer and wondered why Languth had decided to meet him. The answer

was obvious: He wanted something. So did Potamos. Whoever got the most out of it should pay,
but he knew it would be on him. He'd just have
to try to get enough for himself to make it worthwhile.

Languth came through the door a few minutes
after five and wedged himself into the booth opposite Potamos. He struggled with his raincoat,
then decided it wasn't worth the effort and left it
on. He ordered a vodka on the rocks and a chicken
salad sandwich. "You eating?" he asked.

"Later. What's new, Pete?"

"On Frolich? Not much. What are you chasing
on it?"

"I told you, color. Background."

"What about Bowen?"

"What about him?"

"He was the kid's teacher. He likes young girls.
How much did he like her?"

Potamos finished his beer and waved for another. "I don't know anything about Bowen and
Valerie Frolich. He and her father are tight. You
don't mess with your friend's daughter—do you?"

"Some do."

"Bowen? I doubt it. Why screw up a friendship
with a leading force in the Senate? Too much to
lose. Are you focusing on Bowen?"

"No, just keeping him in mind, that's all. I've
been talking to students who knew Frolich."

"And?"

"Nothing yet. Let's go back, Joe, to when Bowen
kicked your pins out from under you."

"Why?"

"Because I remember sitting with you one night in some joint on Mass. Ave. with you crying in your beer. You had lots to say about Bowen—nothing good, all bad. You knew a lot about him, only I forget most of what you said. Tell me again."

"About Bowen? You know as much as I do, Pete. He's a big man, America's leading columnist, a dandy, confidant to the rich and famous. What's to add?"

"The seminar. You ever hear him talk about it, about his students?"

Potamos laughed. "Pete, I haven't had ten words with Bowen since he cut off my legs."

"Who else at the paper would know what goes on in that seminar?"

"Lots of people. High-ups. Whoever he talks to, friends, I don't know." He narrowed his eyes. "Hey, be straight with me, Pete. You really *are* looking to Bowen on this thing, aren't you?"

Languth offered a patronizing smile and finished his sandwich. "Good chicken salad," he said, wiping his fleshy mouth with his napkin.

"Glad you liked it. What about the students you talked to? You get to everybody in the seminar?"

"Yeah, and a few others, too."

"And?"

"Nothin'. A bunch a spoiled kids. Bowen's God to them. They probably figure if they suck around him enough, he'll get them a job."

"Maybe he will."

"If they're especially nice to him. These college professors are scum, you know? They get these naïve kids—the girls I'm talkin' about—and they take advantage of them."

"Bowen's not a professor. He just does the seminar a couple of times a week and—"

"You know what I mean, Joe. It's the old casting-couch game, only this time it's on a campus. That'd be a good book title—*The Campus Casting Couch.* Maybe you ought'a write it. I get ten percent for the idea."

They left Martin's and stood on the sidewalk. "What about the autopsy?" Potamos asked.

"They're releasing it at a press conference in the morning. I'll give you a leg up. Multiple contusions of the head, fractured skull. Somebody beat her dead."

"Object?"

"Blunt, unknown. Thanks for the beer."

"And the sandwich."

"Yeah, that, too. See you around, Joe."

Chapter Six

Walking into a Georgetown University dorm brought a shock of recognition to Potamos, and a realization of how long ago he'd been a student. He admired two cute co-eds as they bustled past him and caught up with two young men who were also leaving the building. "That's right, a co-ed dorm," Potamos told himself as he started up the stairs to the second floor.

The door to Room 22 was open. Strains of a string quartet playing a Schumann piece came through it.

"Steve McCarty?" Potamos asked from the hall. A young man in jeans and T-shirt looked up from his desk. Potamos stepped into the room. "I'm Joe Potamos, *Washington Post*."

McCarty frowned. "Oh, the reporter." He stood and shook Potamos's hand, looked around the room, and laughed. "Find a place to sit if you can. Sorry it's such a mess."

"Looks neat to me," said Potamos. "Neatness was never my best subject when I was in school. Still isn't."

McCarty removed a pile of soiled clothing from a chair, tossed it onto the bed, and pushed the chair toward Potamos. "Thanks," Potamos said, perching on its edge. "Sorry to barge in. You studying?"

"Yes. I have a final this afternoon."

"Finals. I don't miss *that*."

"I don't either. I went through it all once, even law school."

"Law? I thought you were a journalism student."

"I am. The minute they handed me my diploma, I didn't want to be a lawyer. I decided on journalism. They took me into the master's program. I was lucky."

"Makes sense. Law training teaches you to ask questions and not believe most of the answers."

McCarty laughed.

They looked at each other in silence.

"The reason I'm here, Steve, is Valerie Frolich's murder."

"I figured that out already. I read the piece you did on the funeral. I was there."

"I saw you, with George Bowen."

"My seminar professor. You know him, right?"

"Yes."

"We still can't believe it. Incredible."

"You knew her pretty good?"

"Well, I guess so. We were in the seminar together. Sure, we knew each other."

"What'd you think of her?"

"Of Valerie?" A shrug. "I liked her. She was fun."

"Fun? How?"

Another shrug. "Nice to be with. A nice gal. She was a good student, too. Straight A's, I think."

"Yeah, evidently. Who else is in the seminar?"

"There were five of us, counting Valerie. Now . . . there's four."

"Cream of the crop."

"I wouldn't say that, although it was tough to get in. Bowen sets pretty high standards."

"Does he? Is he a good teacher?"

McCarty looked at him quizzically. "He's . . . well, you know what a name he is in the business."

Potamos smiled. "Sure, but sometimes those people don't make good teachers. What do they call it, the Peter Principle? Being promoted to your level of incompetence."

"Not the case with Mr. Bowen, Mr. Potamos. He's a great teacher."

"That's good to hear. What about the other students? They feel the same way?"

"I guess so. I mean, we all complain now and then, but I think he's pretty well liked by everyone."

"Valerie like him?"

"Sure. They had a . . ."

"Had a what?"

"A special relationship. Her father and he are close friends. I guess there was a lot of socializing."

"Between Bowen and Valerie?"

"No, between families. Why did you ask that?"

Potamos gave him his best noncommittal look. "Nothing intended, just a question. Let's get back to you. Ever date Valerie?"

The shift in McCarty's attitude was visible. He

leaned back and away from Potamos and for the first time gave the appearance of having something else to do.

"Hey, I'm just trying to get a handle on Valerie as a person. I'm supposed to generate a story a day on the case and figured I might as well start talking to the people who knew her best, her friends, especially students. You were first on the list."

"No need to explain, Mr. Potamos."

"I know that—and call me Joe. Ever date her?"

McCarty shook his head.

"Okay." Potamos stood and they shook hands. "Just one other thing, Steve, I have a list of the other students in the seminar. Can you tell me how to get ahold of them? It'd save me time." He handed McCarty a slip of paper. The young man scribbled a note next to each name and handed the paper back to Potamos.

"This is great. Thanks. Maybe we'll catch up again."

"Are you going to quote me?"

"No. This is just background. Take it easy, and good luck on your final."

Potamos called Roseann Blackburn from the dorm's lobby. She sounded sleepy. "I wake you?" he asked.

"No. I was half-awake."

"Late gig?"

"I went out after."

He resisted asking her whom she was with. "You busy tonight?"

"A job, but early. I'm doing a preheat at a catering house in Rockville."

"Preheat?"

"I warm them up before the band starts. Just two hours solo. I'll be done by seven, back by eight."

"Dinner?"

"Sure."

His next stop was a run-down rooming house on a small street off New Jersey Avenue, near the Capitol. He asked the landlady if Tony Fiamma, another seminar student, was home.

"He never is, especially on rent day," she said through a tiny, wrinkled mouth.

"Can I leave this for him?" He handed her his card.

She looked at it, then at him, and said, "If I see him."

"Can't ask for more than that," said Potamos. "Maybe I'll leave one on his door, too. Okay?"

"Number three, top of the stairs."

Potamos knocked on the door. No answer. He tried it; it opened. The room was small and sparsely furnished. The closet was a battered gray metal cabinet. Clothing hung from a row of hooks on one wall. What little Fiamma possessed was tossed everywhere. The only oasis of order was a desk in front of a window caked with dirt. The desk was made from a hollow door supported by two file cabinets. Everything on it was neat: paper stacked carefully, pens and pencils in coffee cups, a dictionary and thesaurus lined up beneath the window. The chair was of the old white kitchen variety. Next to it, on a gray metal typing table, was a new IBM Selectric typewriter, obviously a prized possession.

Potamos left his card on the desk and added a note: "Would like to talk to you as soon as possible."

Anne Lewis, the third seminar student on Potamos's list, lived at home. Potamos knew her father, Paul Lewis, one of Washington's most influential lobbyists. He called the house and was told by a woman he pegged as the housekeeper that Miss Lewis wasn't there. "When do you expect her?" Potamos asked.

"I do not know," the woman said, the Caribbean in her voice.

Number four on the list was Bob Fitzgerald. He lived off campus. His roommate answered, told Potamos that Bob would be back at five. "Tell him I'll be there then," Potamos said.

He spent the afternoon in his office writing that day's piece on the Frolich murder, at least what he could conjure up from the limited material on hand. Gil Gardello came into his office at four and handed him notes from the press conference that had been held on the autopsy. It had been covered by a young reporter whose story hadn't pleased Gardello. "Rewrite this thing, Joe."

Potamos would have balked—he'd gotten beyond the rewrite stage of his career a long time ago—but not having much of a story of his own tempered his response. "Yeah, okay."

He turned in the rewrite at 4:30 and left for Bob Fitzgerald's apartment, which was above a bar at the western end of M Street. Heavy rock music from the bar—and from the apartment's open window—competed for attention. Potamos opened the street door and looked up a long, narrow flight of stairs. He realized as he started up that the music from the apartment wasn't a recording. Someone was playing an electric guitar.

He reached the landing, saw that there were two doors, and knocked on the one containing the guitar. It took a succession of louder knocks before the whining glissandi ceased and the door opened.

"Bob Fitzgerald?"

"Yeah. You're Joe Potamos."

"Right. Mind if I come in?"

"No, come on. I was just jamming."

Potamos stepped inside. "You're a musician?" It wasn't exactly the word he wanted to apply to what he'd heard, but he couldn't come up with anything better.

"Yeah, I have a band."

"No kidding."

"Yeah, we've been rehearsing a month now. Just replaced the bass player with a dynamite new guy. I do all the writing."

Potamos nodded in appreciation.

"This is really something, having somebody from the *Post* here. I read you all the time."

"Good. You must know why I'm here. I wanted to talk about Valerie Frolich."

"Sure. Sit down."

Potamos sat in a yellow director's chair; Fitzgerald positioned a barstool with torn brown vinyl a few feet away. "You want to ask questions?"

"A couple. I'm just looking for some understanding of her, that's all. No story or anything, at least not now. I just want to learn more about Valerie from you and other students she knew."

Potamos watched Fitzgerald go into silent thought. He was a nice-looking young man, six feet tall, fine features capped by a mass of blow-dried black hair. What Potamos couldn't square was his dress—cutting-edge punk, faded blue T-shirt with the name of a band on it, black leather jacket covered with metal studs, a belt of machine-gun shell casings, black leather boots, and an earring (left ear, noted Potamos; presumably heterosexual). Somehow, he didn't fit the image of one of the university's top journalism students.

"Okay," Fitzgerald said, coming out of his trance, "Valerie Frolich was . . . she was one of the greatest girls I've ever known. She could write rings around everybody in her classes, and she had the best journalistic sense of anyone I've ever met. Besides, she was beautiful and good and kind."

Potamos cocked his head as though waiting for the next accolade.

"That's it, I guess," said Fitzgerald. His eyes had misted over and Potamos wondered if he might cry.

"You were close."

"Yeah, we were. Nothing romantic. We were good buddies, you could say."

"That's nice. Did you talk to her the day she was murdered?"

"That night you mean? Yeah, I did. I bumped into her after that party on the barge."

"*After* the party?"

"Yes. I was in a bar and she came in. We had some good laughs. She described the party to me. She hated—ah, I shouldn't say that. I don't think Valerie hated anybody. She thought all those people at the party—the society crowd, her father's friends—were silly, if you know what I mean. Lots of money but short on brains."

Potamos laughed. "Her father, too?"

"No, but . . . to be honest, she didn't get along so well with him."

"So I've heard. Any specific reasons?"

Fitzgerald shrugged. "A generation thing, I suppose."

"The night of her death, at the bar you mentioned, did she come in with anyone?"

"No."

"Who were you with?"

"A couple of musicians I know. Just hanging out, drinking beer and talking music."

"Bob, have you told this to anyone else?"

"Told what, about seeing her at the bar?"

"Yes."

"Sure. I told the police and—"

"Sergeant Languth?"

"Yeah, that's his name. Big heavy guy. Tough."

"Anyone else?"

"Friends. That's all anybody's talking about on campus and in town, Valerie being murdered. I think I was probably one of the last people she saw while she was alive and . . ." His eyes wetter this time, then a few controlled sobs.

"I'm sorry," Potamos said.

"She was such a good friend. Who the hell could do something like that to her?"

"I don't know. You have any ideas?"

He shook his head and reached for a Kleenex.

Potamos stood and went to a large, freestanding bookcase filled with record albums and cassette tapes. "You have a lot of records," he said. "Any Frank Sinatra?"

"Sinatra? No, I'm not into mood music."

Potamos said, "Thanks for your time, Bob. If you come up with anything else, I'd appreciate hearing from you."

"Sure. I've been thinking of doing my own investigation."

"For a story? Good idea."

"Everybody is—Steve, Anne Lewis, Tony. Well, maybe not Tony."

"The others from the seminar."

"Yeah. I think Steve and Anne are working on it together."

"Does Bowen know about it?"

"Gee, I don't know. I didn't mention it to him. Steve and Annie have an edge. He dated Valerie and—"

"Steve McCarty?"

"Uh-huh. He was pretty ticked off when she dumped him. I shouldn't say that. Valerie never dumped any guy, just . . . sort of said goodbye. Annie's father is a good friend of Senator Frolich's. I guess they figured they could combine the personal side from Steve's relationship with her, and Annie's inside info from her father."

Potamos puffed his cheeks and went to the door.

"I'll call you if I think of something," Fitzgerald said.

Back home, Potamos showered with hot water for a change, then made himself a drink and settled into a favorite recliner after turning on the local news. The Valerie Frolich story was the lead item, with various correspondents reporting on different aspects of the case. The final segment was a brief statement by an MPD spokeswoman: "We have no leads to date. The investigation is proceeding with every available resource committed to it. A special task force has been established, and any persons with information to offer should call this special number." She read a phone number as it appeared simultaneously at the bottom of the screen. The local anchor repeated the number, then led into a story about a congressional deadlock over a military-spending bill.

Potamos sipped his drink and thought of Bob Fitzgerald's comments about Steve McCarty having dated, and been jilted by, Valerie Frolich, and about having seen Valerie at the bar *after* the barge party. The name of the young man with her on the barge was David Field. He'd been questioned extensively by the police, and a *Post* staffer had interviewed him. Potamos had read the staffer's notes. According to Field, he and Valerie had left the barge and gone to a party at a friend's apartment, then split up. When asked why he hadn't stayed with his date for the evening, he'd replied, "We had different places to go, that's all." Field had dropped out of school and was, he said, looking for work as an actor. His means of support: "Daddy."

After showering and dressing, Potamos called Gil Gardello at the paper.

"Nice rewrite," Gardello said. "We'll go with it on page one."

"My big break. Any calls?"

"A couple." He reeled off some names and numbers, including Tony Fiamma. "Who's he?"

"One of the kids in Bowen's seminar. I left my card."

"Elegant."

"I'm a class act, Gil."

"Hey, Joe, I almost forgot. Bowen's doing a column for tomorrow on the Frolich kid. It's good, a real heart tugger."

"Why tell me?"

"I was sure you'd want to read it, being such a fan and all."

"The words are on the tip of the tongue, Gil, every one of them consisting of four letters."

"What're you giving us tomorrow?"

"I don't know. I've talked to two out of the four kids who were in the seminar with her. Maybe I'll do a human-interest thing."

"Maybe. Call me before you do. I might want you to do an in-depth on her."

"You already did her background."

"We need more. Call me."

"You want me to call you." He laughed. Gardello hung up after some four-letter words of his own.

Tony Fiamma answered on the first ring.

"I've been talking to other students in the seminar," Potamos said, "and I'd like to spend some time with you. I appreciate your calling back.

Hope you don't mind my going into your room and leaving my card, but—"

"What are you talking about?"

"I was at your rooming house today. I talked to your landlady and went to your room."

"I haven't been home."

"Oh, I . . . you're not returning my call?"

"No, I called *you*."

"Why?"

"I want to talk to you."

Potamos smiled. Fiamma was tough-talking, his voice raspy, like an impressionist doing a mob godfather. Potamos said, "Shoot. What do you want to talk to me about?"

"Valerie Frolich's murder."

"Funny, but that's what I wanted to talk to *you* about."

"We probably have different reasons."

"Probably. What's yours?"

"I want to work on the story with you."

When Potamos didn't reply, Fiamma said, "I can crack the whole case. I know a lot."

"Do you? Like what?"

"Meet me and we'll talk."

"Depends."

"You said you wanted to talk to me anyway. Maybe I can make your day."

"I doubt that, Mr. Fiamma, but sure, let's talk. Name it."

"Tonight, about eight?"

"Can't. I'm tied up."

"That's *your* problem."

Potamos laughed, said, "Not if you knew who's

tying me up. Look, Fiamma, let's knock off the tough-guy crap. I'll meet you tomorrow, your time, your place."

There was silence.

"Thanks for calling," Potamos said with finality in his voice.

"You tied up all night?"

"I hope so."

"I'll be at this number you called. If you get free, give me a call. I'll be here. If it's tomorrow, try me at my room about noon."

"What's your number there?"

"I don't have a phone, but I'll stay around." He hung up.

Potamos thought about the conversation all the way to Roseann's apartment. Fiamma didn't sound like any college student he'd ever known. The kid had rankled him, yet Potamos was intrigued with him, almost liked him, in a strange way. He heard a little of himself in the way Fiamma talked, and he realized he was looking forward to meeting him.

Roseann lived on the ground floor of a neatly kept row house on upper Wisconsin Avenue, near the Washington Cathedral. A white baby grand piano occupied the center of the small living room. The floor was covered with worn red Oriental rugs. One wall was taken up by a long white leather couch. In front of it was a black lacquered coffee table on which a variety of oversize art and music books were neatly displayed. The white walls were filled with art, most of it modern, a few large posters from concert halls mixed in. A cello stood on a stand in a corner of the room. In another corner was a stack of electronic keyboards.

"Nice," Potamos said after she'd greeted him at the door wearing a white fluffy robe.

"Thanks. I like it here. I'm comfortable. Excuse me, I have to finish dressing. I ran a little late."

She went into her bedroom. A fat white cat emerged, looked at Potamos, yawned, stretched, and curled up on a chair.

Potamos sat at the piano and picked out "Heart and Soul." Blackburn poked her head through the door and said, "Bravo."

Potamos laughed and said, "Then I wrote . . ."

Five minutes later she came to the piano, sat down beside him on the bench, and said, "I'm ready whenever your concert is over."

"You look great," Potamos said.

"Thank you, sir. Just simple black with pearls." She stood and adopted a model's pose to show off her gray skirt and black cotton sweater.

"I don't see any pearls."

"I know—they're in the vault along with the other heavy jewelry. Where are we going? I'm starved. I avoided the soggy canapés at the party in anticipation of this."

Later, after crepes at La Brasserie Breton (sausage and apple for him, caviar for her), and after satisfying what seemed like a desperate need to tell each other about themselves—she from an Ohio steelworker's family; three sisters; solid middle-American upbringing; love of music since childhood; secret passion for macadamia nuts, maple-walnut gelato ice cream, and lapis jewelry;

cat's name Snowball; favorite classical composer
Bach, jazz pianist Bill Evans, colors blue and
white—she asked him how the murder investigation was progressing.

"I don't know," he said. "The police know more
than they're admitting, but that's routine." He told
her about his conversations with the students.

"Fiamma sounds like a character," she said.

"Yeah, he does. I'll get to meet him tonight
if . . ." He looked into her green eyes. "If . . ."

"If you don't spend the night with me."

It was a sheepish grin. "That's right."

"What's your choice?"

"I have one?"

"There's always a choice, Joe. That doesn't mean
you will sleep with me, but let's say the option is
open. What'll it be, me or this Tony Fiamma?"

He grimaced and shook his head. "That's a
tough one."

"If it's that tough, your first option just dried
up."

"I've made my decision."

"And?"

"I've always been partial to fat white cats
named Snowball. Let's stop by my place first. I'll
introduce you to Jumper. She has to be walked
if . . ."

They walked Jumper together, returned to
Potamos's condo, and didn't leave until morning.

Chapter Seven

Marshall Jenkins stood by a window in the large study on the third floor of his Georgetown home. Outside, a battery of powerful lights illuminated formal Japanese gardens. A video camera scanned relentlessly, its pictures monitored in a small downstairs room.

He looked toward the door. Was someone in the hall? The room was dark except for a soft yellow light from the brass lamp on his desk, and ambient light through the windows.

There was the sound again, then a shadow beneath the door. His wife, Elsa, entered.

"What?" Jenkins said.

"I'll be leaving in a few minutes and wanted to see if you needed anything."

Jenkins leaned back against the windowsill, hands jammed into the pockets of a blue cashmere robe. "What do you think I could possibly need, Elsa, that you could provide me?"

She ignored the temptation to respond angrily. It was the sort of comment to which she'd become accustomed in recent years. Earlier in the marriage she would have flared, her retort prompting an all-out shouting match resulting in her being drained of everything except guilt.

She stood in the doorway and observed her husband of seven years. She'd celebrated her thirty-seventh birthday only two days ago; he was sixty-two. He no longer stood quite as erect as before; and his square face, tan until recently from sunlamps, had begun to sag and seemed to be graying, if that was possible with a face. He seemed . . . weary all the time. Yes, that was it, Elsa decided, her husband was weary. And so nasty. It was as though a sudden acceleration in the aging process were taking place, pages flying off the calendar as in an old movie, accompanied by a parallel irascibility that precluded all tenderness between them. Not that there had ever been an abundance of it. Marshall Jenkins was not a sentimental, sensitive man. Pragmatic was more like it, hard-nosed, steely eyed, touching the human dilemma by contributing heavily to favorite charities.

To say that she'd "celebrated" her birthday was wishful thinking. Since their only child, Jacqueline, had died two years earlier from a sudden and virulent blood cancer, celebrations were a thing of the past. Dinner perhaps, a cake, a few friends, but nothing festive. It was "inappropriate," Marshall had said, and that was that.

The child had been conceived shortly before they were married, at least according to Elsa's mathematics, but it wasn't a matter of his having to marry her because of her pregnancy. Hardly. They'd fallen in love three months earlier, and Jenkins had proposed the first night they made love, which was three days after they'd met. She hadn't accepted immediately, afraid that matching his impetuousness would somehow cause him to think less of her.

She'd found it interesting that this multimillionaire had acted like a schoolboy, gushing out his proposal so quickly and with such urgency. His first and only wife, a society woman from the Maryland shore, had died in an auto accident ten years before Elsa met him. She knew he'd been romantically linked with many women following his wife's death, and she took quiet pride in being the first one to excite him sufficiently to offer marriage. Obviously, Marshall Jenkins was not a man prone to reckless behavior. He did everything with meticulous precision. He'd built his empire that way, piece by piece, a step at a time, always looking ahead three or four moves like a master chess player. Breaking form with Elsa that night in a New York hotel delighted her, gave her the feeling that she possessed a feminine power greater than she'd ever realized. She had been born in Wiesbaden, Germany, but she and her mother had moved to Chicago after her father died, when she was four. She got her degree in economics from the University of Chicago, then went on to law school and a brief marriage to a sculptor. He committed suicide less than a year after they married. Why? That question had haunted her until one day she decided it would haunt her no longer. It hadn't from that day forward. She was good at dictating to herself what she could allow her mind to do and not do.

She'd met Jenkins in Munich. She was vacationing; he was visiting the manufacturer of heavy earthmoving equipment in which he had a considerable financial interest. It was Oktoberfest; he spotted her in a restaurant and, he told her later, was physically assaulted by her beauty: tall, slender, soft blond hair framing a serene oval face in which each feature was perfectly formed and positioned, eyes large and blue, mouth sensually full.

She had been having dinner that night with an aunt. Jenkins brazenly introduced himself and was invited to join their table. Elsa's aunt discreetly left them shortly after dinner. Two days later they traveled to New York on the same flight, had dinner, booked adjoining suites at the Plaza, and, an hour later, began their life together in her bed.

There had been passion and love at first. But after a couple of years both emotions evaporated and she found herself more a hostess and traveling companion than an object of sexual attention. She knew there were other women. She could sense it, feel it, smell it as surely as if there'd been lipstick on his collar and perfume on his clothing. She'd come to grips with that. The worst was knowing that he felt nothing toward her. Any feeling would have been welcome.

"Where are you going?" he asked in a tired voice.

"Kennedy Center. Rostropovitch is doing Bartok and Beethoven. I'll have dinner after the performance."

"I won't be here when you get back. I'm going

to Leesburg tonight." He owned a retreat just outside Leesburg, in northern Virginia's Loudoun County, where he went to hunt and fish with friends.

"How long will you be gone?" she asked.

"A day or two."

"I've been thinking of going to New York to do some shopping. I might as well do it while you're gone."

"Good." He turned from her and looked out the window.

"Goodnight, Marshall."

"Goodnight, Elsa."

Their driver, an older black man named Walker, opened a rear door of the pearl-gray Lincoln limousine he'd brought to the front of the house, and Elsa settled into the quiet, dark seclusion of the leather-and-wood passenger compartment. With her was her evening purse and an overnight bag she'd taken from the hall closet on her way out. Walker slid behind the wheel, electronically lowered the glass partition, and asked where she was going.

"The Kennedy Center, please," Elsa replied, pulling down a lighted mirror to check her hair and makeup.

Ten minutes later the limo pulled up the ramp in front of the Kennedy Center. Walker opened the door and helped Elsa out of the car. "Shall I return for you?" he asked.

"No, thank you, Walker, I'll be going on from here with friends. They'll drop me home."

"Yes, ma'am. Enjoy your evening."

As Walker pulled away from the curb, a new tan Toyota sat with its motor running a hundred feet away. Behind the wheel sat a handsome young man with black curly hair. He'd been parked on the Jenkinses' street and had waited until Elsa came out. He'd followed the limo, but now he wasn't sure what to do: Wait until she came from the concert, or go inside, buy a ticket and observe her? He ruled out the latter—there probably wasn't a ticket to be had—and decided to get something to eat and be back before the concert ended. He jotted down something in a notebook, took a last look at the entrance to the center, and drove off.

Elsa stepped into the grand foyer, 630 feet long and six stories high, ivory plaster walls alternating with floor-to-ceiling mirrored panels on one side, ten floor-to-ceiling windows overlooking the terrace and the Potomac on the other. She was early; few people had arrived. She looked up at one of eighteen Swedish Orrefors crystal chandeliers that jutted down from the lofty ceiling like glowing stalactites. Beneath her feet were miles of crimson carpet. It was wearing poorly; sections were threadbare, others had bunched up. "Disgraceful," she told herself as she walked to the base of the massive bronze head of John F. Kennedy sculptured by Robert Berks. It dominated the foyer, every cut of the chisel catching the thousands of lights hurled at it by the chandeliers.

She strolled to the windows and looked out to the terrace where, in summer, theatergoers would spill out during intermission and gaze at the Potomac River, the tranquil mood broken only by the screeching approach of jet aircraft into National Airport.

She checked her watch and crossed the lobby to where a young woman stood holding a supply of the evening's programs. Elsa smiled, took one, then went outside to the curb where she'd been dropped off. A taxi pulled up and deposited a couple. Elsa got in. "The Watergate Hotel," she told the driver.

Marshall Jenkins interrupted a telephone conversation to be told over the intercom by Walker that he'd returned after dropping Mrs. Jenkins at the Kennedy Center. "Bring the BMW around front," Jenkins told him. "I'll drive myself to Leesburg." He returned to his conversation with Senator John Frolich.

"You're going down tonight?" Frolich asked.

"Yes, almost immediately. Elsa is at a concert. What time can you be in Leesburg Friday?"

"I can be there by four, maybe five."

"Fine, we'll have dinner. Goodnight, John."

Jenkins dressed in wrinkled chino pants, a red and blue flannel shirt, and hiking boots. He turned off the lamp and came downstairs to the security office, just off the foyer. "I'll be in Leesburg through the weekend," he told the security man on duty. "I don't need anyone there."

"You're sure, Mr. Jenkins?"

"Yes, I'm sure." He grabbed his valise from where he'd left it earlier, went to the street, and replaced Walker behind the wheel of the silver BMW sedan.

The cab carrying Elsa Jenkins wove its way to the Watergate Hotel's private canopied entrance off Virginia Avenue. She tipped the driver generously, quickly entered the hotel, and went to the desk. She told the clerk she had a reservation.

"Name, ma'am?"

"Johnson, from Joel Associates." She slid a platinum American Express card across the desk. Printed on it was *Joel Associates.* The clerk handed her a key. "Luggage?" he asked.

"No, a business conference, of all things at this time of night," she said. "I'll need room service."

"Just dial, Ms. Johnson."

The suite was one of the hotel's most lavish. She flipped on the lights, picked up the phone, and ordered caviar, smoked salmon, and a bottle of champagne. Then she opened the drapes and looked down at the glittering lights of Foggy Bottom and the Kennedy Center. She closed the drapes and hummed the Allegretto from Beethoven's Symphony no. 7—which was on the program that night—as she pulled a sheer pink negligee from the large bag she'd brought with her and laid it on the king-size bed. She waited for room service to deliver, then hung her evening clothes in the closet, went into the spacious Italian marble bathroom, and drew water into the tub, emptying a package of the hotel's complimentary scented bath oils beneath the faucet.

Downstairs, in the Terrace Lounge, John Frolich quietly nursed his drink and checked his Rolex. He cocked his head to better hear the young pianist in a tuxedo play a familiar Ravel melody, then stood, left money on the table, and left the lounge. He was aware that people were talking about him, probably wondering why he'd be out drinking so soon after his daughter's murder. The hell with them, he told himself as he crossed the lobby to a bank of elevators that served the upper-floor suites.

Minutes later he knocked on a door, heard the latch being undone. The door opened and Elsa Jenkins, wearing the negligee, her face and body glowing from the bath, her blond hair cascading over her shoulders, the bottom fringes still damp, smiled and said, "Good evening, senator."

He stepped inside. She bolted the door behind them. The scent of her reached his nostrils. He breathed it in, smiled, sighed, and embraced her, feeling her intense softness and warmth against him. They kissed.

"You're right on time, senator," she said, taking his hand and leading him to the bed.

Chapter Eight

After driving Roseann home, Potamos headed over to Tony Fiamma's rooming house. He arrived precisely at noon. Fiamma was waiting for him. So was his landlady.

"Hi," Potamos said to her.

"You the one paying the rent?"

"Huh?" He looked at Fiamma, who'd come down the stairs.

"He said you had the money," the landlady said through her tiny mouth.

Fiamma said, "I told her I was selling you something. The rent's only sixty a week. I figured—"

"You figured wrong," Potamos said. "You've got big ones, kid."

"He's three weeks behind," said the little mouth.

"She's kicking me out," Fiamma said. "Big deal, you know, a lousy three weeks and—"

"What are you selling?" Potamos asked him.

"Information. Good information."

"Yeah?" Potamos dug into his pocket and pulled out a $50 bill, handed it to the landlady. "This is a downpayment," he said. "We'll go upstairs and talk and maybe—"

"It's only fifty dollars," she said.

"Patience," said Potamos, pushing Fiamma up the stairs in front of him.

Potamos slammed the door behind them and said, "You're a piece of work, Fiamma. What are you, some cheap hustler?"

"No, I'm . . . look, thanks for what you did downstairs. The old lady's crazy. She's making me crazy."

"She rents rooms. She gets paid rent. What's crazy about that?"

"It's all greed, man. The whole world runs on greed."

Potamos laughed. "And you're Mr. Philanthropy, huh? What do you have, information about Valerie Frolich's murder for sale? For sale! She's dead. You're a friend? You're a greedy son of a—"

"I'm a journalist."

"Not in my book."

"We read different books. Look, Mr. Potamos, I've been hustling since I was ten. I dropped out of school three, four times because I couldn't pay the tuition, or the rent, or eat. I graduate in a month and I want it all to be worth it, you know?" He curled his lip. "What the hell do you do, write for the *Post* for nothing? They pay you, don't they?"

"Yeah, because I work there."

"I wanna work there."

"Call personnel."

"Come on. I want a reporting job."

"You ever hear of paying dues?"

"I paid 'em, man, in spades." He shoved the

white kitchen chair at Potamos. "Sit down, huh? Let me tell you what I have and maybe you'll see it different than you do now." Potamos sat. Fiamma grabbed a manila file folder from the desk, sat on the edge of his unmade bed, and opened it. "You ready?" he asked.

Potamos couldn't help grinning. "Yeah, I'm ready. Just make sure it's worth fifty bucks."

"It's worth a lot more than that, man."

Fifteen minutes later Potamos decided that on the open market what Fiamma had gathered about Valerie Frolich's murder was indeed worth at least fifty dollars.

"Well?" Fiamma said.

"Yeah, it's interesting," Potamos said, "but I just realized something. Everything you've said has to be screened through your dislike of her. Maybe *hatred*'s more like it."

Fiamma shrugged. "What was to like? She was a spoiled brat. They all are in the seminar, precious little sons and daughters of rich people playing student, driving around in fancy cars daddy paid for, going to class every morning like it was a goddamn fashion show and . . . what really counts, Mr. Potamos, is that none of them can write their way out of a paper bag."

"That's a cliché," Potamos said.

"You know what I mean. Bowen says sometimes a cliché is okay, makes a point faster than coming up with a lot of big words. The point is, I'm a writer, a *real* writer, not like them. Valerie Frolich." The name came off his lips dripping with venom. "She played up to Bowen all the time and he fell for it, favored the hell out of her."

"They sleep together?"

"Yeah."

"Prove it?"

"Yeah."

"How?"

"That's later."

"After what, more money?"

"Yeah, and a job at the *Post*."

"Forget it. I'm just a working reporter, cop stuff, no clout at all. No sense promising something I can't deliver."

"You could let me work with you, share the by-line, make a name for myself. You have expenses, right? You could pay me for information. You do it all the time."

"Bowen teach you that brand of journalism?"

"Bowen's a pompous ass."

For the first time, Potamos liked Fiamma.

"Well?"

"You mentioned this student, the one you say dated Valerie and had a falling out with her in a bar after the barge party. What's his name?"

Fiamma grinned. "I'm not *that* dumb."

"Neither am I," said Potamos, standing and stretching. "You said this student had a fight with her, then arranged with a buddy to provide an alibi that they'd been studying together all night."

"Yup."

"The police know?"

"I don't know. Probably not."

"How do you know?"

"I get around. I listen. I'm a good reporter."

"Maybe. Sorry, Tony, but without substantiation your merchandise doesn't have much value.

Fifty bucks' worth of speculation. Keep it, my contribution to higher education. Nice meeting you."

Potamos opened the door to see the landlady lingering in the hall. "You want something?" Potamos asked.

"The rent. He's—"

Potamos closed the door and faced Fiamma. "Give me something more, Tony, and maybe we can make a deal."

"Like what?"

"Names of the two students."

"No . . . I—" His tone softened, and there was a hint of a plea in his voice. "Look, I've got to make it. I've worked my tail off and . . . Come on, give me a break, huh?"

Potamos fended off his temptation to soften, too. He said, "Give me the names and I'll do what I can. I'll pay Scrooge out there another hundred. That leaves you thirty bucks short on the rent. Do a shift at Burger King and you can come up with it. I'll also see what I can do about ringing you in on some stories, get you some credit, but I can't promise that."

"Okay." There was no hesitation. "She dated a clown named Walter Nebel, political-science type. His buddy is Sam Maruca, another political-science student."

"And you're sure what you said happened did happen, that Maruca provided an alibi for Nebel after he'd fought with Valerie?"

"It's what I hear."

"Cafeteria scuttlebutt?"

Fiamma laughed. "A little better than that."

"Okay, I'll go with it, look up Nebel and Maruca. I'll be in touch." He handed Fiamma another hundred.

"I appreciate it," Fiamma said, which surprised Potamos. Then, as Potamos was about to open the door again, Fiamma said, "I have her diary, too."

If it was intended to shock Potamos, it succeeded. He turned slowly and frowned at Fiamma. "Valerie Frolich's diary?"

"Yeah."

"How'd you get it?"

"Doesn't matter, but I have it."

"Maybe having it doesn't matter either. Anything in it that bears on her murder?"

"Plenty. We can talk about that next time. Thanks for the hundred."

"A hundred and fifty."

"Yeah, whatever. I'll call you."

"I hope so."

Chapter Nine

Marshall Jenkins spent early Saturday morning trout fishing in a private four-mile stream on his Leesburg retreat. He landed three trout, returned two to the water, and gave the third—a four-pounder—to the chef to prepare for lunch.

He was joined at lunch by one of his attorneys and a financial adviser, both of whom had been summoned by a midnight phone call to discuss the deterioration of South African gold stocks, which represented a sizable portion of Jenkins's portfolio.

After lunch—and after the others had been dismissed—Jenkins went to his skeet-shooting range, where he practiced until George Alfred Bowen arrived at three. Bowen watched patiently as Jenkins completed his final round of blasting a succession of silt-and-pitch targets around the semicircular range. When the last target had been destroyed, Bowen applauded politely and said, "Impressive."

"There are days," Jenkins said. "Come, John will be here at four. He couldn't get away last night."

Bowen waited in the study while Jenkins showered and changed into country-casual clothing. Bowen wore a pinched-waist charcoal-gray three-button suit, pale blue shirt with white collar, and gray tie that was almost black. When Jenkins returned, he said to Bowen, "You never do dress for the country, do you, George?"

"The 'country' is a state of mind, Marshall. I prefer consistency."

"One of these days I'll see you in a pair of waders in the trout stream."

"Not in this life. A drink? I'm thirsty."

"Help yourself. I ordered more Blanton's in your honor."

Bowen poured with precision from a bottle of Blanton's bourbon into a large snifter, then filled another glass with ice and seltzer. "Can I get you something?" he asked Jenkins.

"They'll bring me tea. You should try it instead of whiskey, George. It doesn't destroy the brain cells."

Bowen laughed and tasted his drink. "Some of us have excessive brain cells, Marshall. I can afford to lose a few." He waited for a retort, smiled when it wasn't forthcoming, and settled back into a blue leather club chair, legs carefully crossed, a glance down to ensure that his tie was straight.

Jenkins was busy arranging fishing flies in a series of divided cases. He focused intently on the project until Bowen asked, "How's Elsa?"

Jenkins looked up and narrowed his eyes. "Very well, George."

The intensity of the look wasn't lost on Bowen.

He sipped from the snifter and added, "She looked well the other night at the party."

Jenkins looked up again. "Elsa always looks well, George. She's in New York. We're going to Rome next week."

"Lovely."

"It should be pleasant. Have you talked to John about Valerie's unfortunate death?" He asked the question but seemed more interested in the flies.

"Of course. You?"

"Yes. He's handling it quite well."

"I'd agree. Henrietta's another matter, but then again, mothers generally take these things harder."

Jenkins look this time was more pointed. "How would you know?"

"Years of observation." Bowen knew Jenkins was thinking of the death of his own daughter but refused to soften for Bowen's benefit.

A member of the house staff brought Jenkins tea and biscuits. He put away the boxes of flies and went through the ritual of arranging the tray on his desk.

"I was surprised John agreed to come here this weekend," said Bowen.

"Why?"

A casual shrug. "Other things on his mind."

"He's practical. You don't become a U.S. senator by being otherwise, or president of the United States."

Bowen smiled and went to the bar for a refill, saying over his shoulder, "It's safe to assume that you have something important on your mind. I mean, after all, Marshall, I don't fish or hunt or shoot at little clay birds in the air, and John has a duty to comfort Henrietta in her moment of travail, as well as attending to affairs of state." He turned, freshened glass in his hand, leaned against the bar and asked, "Why *are* we here, Marshall?"

"The condo," Jenkins answered, not removing his eyes from the task of smearing raspberry jam on a biscuit.

"Ah, the condo." Bowen returned to his chair and resumed his previous pose. "More trouble?"

"The usual community groups clamoring for attention, the Russians delivering their daily protests, do-gooders deciding to march against it instead of against the last cause they marched against. We need editorial support."

Bowen said nothing, just looked down into the shimmering amber liquid in his snifter and reveled in Jenkins's asking for help that only he could deliver.

"They ought to be lined up and shot," Jenkins said, smacking his lips.

"The Russians?"

"All of them—the do-gooders, the activists, the misguided. Remarkable, George, how helpless people are." Bowen glanced up and cocked a salt-and-pepper eyebrow. "They're all pathetic, helpless sheep," Jenkins went on. "They don't understand that their very survival depends upon what people like me do for their benefit. It's very sad, and a burden."

"Responsibility. Never easy, like a string we

can see only the middle of. The ends are always out of sight."

"Exactly. As I said, we need more editorial support. The timing is crucial."

"I'm not sure I can do more. After all, there's—"

"I don't like that phrase, 'after all.' We do what we must."

Bowen sighed. He wasn't in the mood for a lecture on responsibility; he'd had enough of them from Jenkins in the past. He'd write another column supporting the construction of Jenkins's condominium on the upper reaches of Wisconsin Avenue, directly across from the newly constructed Russian Embassy. There was no trouble justifying it. It was a hot topic. The Georgetown Historical Preservation Society had been issuing statements about it ever since ground was broken, and splintered citizen groups had staged protest marches whenever the weather was fair enough to not cause them undue discomfort.

Jenkins had built numerous buildings in Georgetown and the Washington, D.C., area, but none had triggered such anger. The problem was that his plans called for a structure considerably taller than was allowed by existing zoning laws, a towering building that would dominate the skyline.

The Russian protest was expected. They'd built their new embassy on twelve and a half acres in the Mt. Alto area, in accordance with a deal struck in 1969 between the Soviet Union and the United States. Under its terms, each country was given a little over twelve acres on which to construct a new embassy. The Russians ended up with prime hilltop land in Georgetown that provided sweeping views of all Washington, while the Americans accepted a twelve-acre tract a block from the Moscow River, in a swamp, even lower than their existing Moscow Embassy.

Aesthetics aside, the major objections by critics centered on the strategic value of the Mt. Alto land. Because of its altitude, the Russians had been handed a prime location for electronic surveillance of radio transmissions from the White House, State Department, and virtually every other branch of government. New York's Senator Moynihan had said, "We just got snookered; it's inexplicable." Another critic, James E. Nolan, a former head of counterintelligence for the FBI and currently director of the State Department's Office of Foreign Missions, put it another way: "I'm sure if we knew everything then that we do now, we wouldn't have made the same selection. We wouldn't have picked nearly the highest site in the city."

In response to the growing criticism, a Soviet Embassy spokesman simply said, "We did not capture the site. We were given it." Which was true.

But then the Russians launched their own protest against the construction of Jenkins's high-rise condo across the street, claiming that it "violated the privacy and integrity of every Soviet Embassy employee and their families." Translated: "You'll be in a position to intercept our interception of your transmissions."

And so the fight continued, from the laying of the first Soviet Embassy brick to the first shovelful of earth removed for the condo. Another Washington flap. International. Them versus us. Everyone loved it, especially the press.

A long black limousine delivered Senator John Frolich to the retreat at four. After being greeted by Jenkins and Bowen, he was shown to his room, where he changed into more-casual attire—a tweed jacket with brown elbow patches, tan twill slacks, a champagne turtleneck, and loafers. He joined them in the study. "Scotch," he told Jenkins, who poured him a hefty glass of it. A housekeeper had placed a large tray of shrimp, caviar, smoked salmon, and toast on a table, and the three men tasted of it.

"I was talking to Marshall about the condo," Bowen said after they'd settled into leather chairs in a tight circle in front of a fireplace.

Frolich looked at Jenkins, who smiled, reached over, and patted the senator's arm. "I told George that we needed additional editorial support. Would you agree?"

"I suppose so, as long as it isn't blatant," Frolich replied, trying to keep a caper from rolling off his salmon-on-toast.

"I can do it," said Bowen. "I'd prefer having more breathing room since the last piece I did, but I'll do it. Any ideas on a slant?"

Frolich realized Bowen was asking it of him. He shook his head. "It's not *my* department."

"Of course," Bowen said, getting up and walking toward the bar. "Can I freshen anyone's drink?"

The others declined.

"I think we ought to pull back, Marshall, relax the pressure," Frolich said to Jenkins.

"I disagree," Jenkins said. "We've done too much of that already. I'm under pressure from my partners. Every day it sits there it costs money, my money—your money, John."

"I'd rather lose some now and be assured of future success. Doesn't that make sense?"

"You and your colleagues can afford to take that position, John. I can't. I want progress on it, and I want it now. Besides, it's no longer only money involved. There's the matter of—"

"We're all aware of that, Marshall," Bowen said in a voice that reflected his annoyance with the conversation, and also reflected the effects of the bourbon on his tongue.

"I'm pleased to hear that," Jenkins said. "I have a limited tolerance for losing sight of priorities."

"I never noticed," Bowen said, laughing to stress that he was joking.

Jenkins let the laughter fade away before asking Frolich, "How is Henrietta?"

"All right, thank you."

"Anything new on the . . . on Valerie's case?"

"No."

A heavy silence filled the room, which had sunk into darkness as night closed in.

It was Bowen who broke it. "Is there anything I can do, John?" he asked.

"No, nothing, thank you. Henrietta and I have finally come to grips with it. It was obviously the result of the people Valerie chose to associate with, the drug addicts and the freaks." He leaned back and spoke reflectively. "She had that need to associate with the down-and-out, the unsavory elements. You do that and you place yourself in their sickness, in their squalor. It's no comfort to realize that, but it does provide a certain . . . well, a certain understanding that's necessary if a parent is to survive it." He sat up straight and said in a louder, more convincing voice, "Enough of *that*. Let's get back to business."

"Let's not," Jenkins said, standing and coming around behind Frolich, his hands on Frolich's shoulders, fingers kneading the flesh. "Dinner is in order. We can talk later, over good brandy and fresh coffee. Come on, I've ordered something special for us."

Chapter Ten

Potamos's first reaction to the ringing phone was to wonder where he was. It wasn't his bed. He kicked against the covers and got a growl from Jumper in return.

He sat up against Roseann Blackburn's headboard. "Oh, yeah," he said as he fumbled in the darkened bedroom for the phone. His hand found it but didn't lift the receiver. Maybe he shouldn't answer her phone. Might be a boyfriend. Her mother. But he had to answer because he'd left the number with the paper. "Hello," he said, and was relieved to hear Yvonne Master's voice. "Joe?" she said.

"Yeah."

"What number is this?"

"What . . . what do you care?"

"It's not your number."

"That's right. It's the White House. I got a little drunk and the First Lady suggested I stay over."

"Joe."

"What the hell do you want at this hour? What time is it? Huh? Two?" He thought of Blackburn, who was out on a playing job. She'd said she'd be back by one. He hoped she was all right. He hoped she wasn't out with another guy.

"Joe, you had some phone calls tonight."

"They couldn't wait until morning?"

"One sounded urgent. The name is Fiamma, Anthony Fiamma."

"Anthony? What else?"

"An Anne Lewis called. She said you'd tried to reach her and she was returning your call. She said she'll be at home all day Sunday."

"Great. Anything else?"

"Gil left a note wanting to know what you planned to file tomorrow."

"Tomorrow's Sunday."

She ignored him. "He said he needs a feature on Valerie Frolich's friends, especially the students she was friendly with at school."

"Tell Gil I'll do everything I can. Tell Gil I'll write a Pulitzer piece after nine hours sleep. Tell Gil I'll call him."

"Okay. One other thing, Joe. George Bowen wants to talk to you."

"Now?"

"Monday, at ten, in his office."

"Why?"

"How would I know that?"

"That's right, Yvonne, how would you know that? Are we through?"

"Yes. . . . Joe?"

"What?"

"Is this a . . . a lover's apartment?"

"If it is, it's a cruel joke. Just me and the dog here."

"Oh. Well, goodnight."

"You, too, Yvonne."

"I'm working."

He hung up.

Blackburn arrived fifteen minutes later. "Sorry I'm late," she said, disrobing in seconds and tossing clothing in every direction. "Sorry I woke you," she said on her way to the bathroom.

"You didn't," he called after her. The cat jumped up on the bed, causing Jumper to snarl. "Hey, shut up," Potamos said, kicking the cat to the floor. "It's her house."

Blackburn came from the bathroom, its light silhouetting her slender nakedness. "Want something?"

"Like what?" He exaggerated the leer in his voice.

"A drink? Cognac? Warm milk?"

"Cognac."

They sat together in bed, brandy snifters in their hands, a bedside lamp casting a warm yellow glow over their upper bodies.

"How come you were late?" he asked.

"Overtime. I really didn't want it, but . . ."

"What's the matter?"

"I feel like I'm being interrogated."

"Ah, come on, I just wondered."

She turned to face him. "No, Joe, I mean it. I had funny feelings about having you go to sleep here while I was out working, but . . . well, it was appealing having you here when I got back. But I'm not used to accounting to anyone. I work nights. I'm a musician. Some nights I can't wait to get home and to bed. Other nights . . . well, other nights I feel like finding a place to jam until dawn, or feel like hanging out in a diner with other musicians, or . . . understand?"

"Yeah."

"Tonight it was overtime. Rich crowd tossing hundred-dollar bills at the band to stay around."

"I'm sorry."

"Why should you be? I just wanted to clear it up."

"You did."

"Good."

"Where'd you work?"

She snapped her fingers and faced him again. "I almost forgot. I worked a house party for Julia Amster."

Potamos turned to face her. "Bowen's girlfriend. Was he there?"

"No, but there was a lot of talk about him. Somebody said he was away fishing."

Potamos laughed. "His idea of fishing would be to have two kids hold rods and hand him fish when they reeled them in. Julia Amster. Funny, but she's the only woman I know of who's had a continuing relationship with Bowen. The others come and go, but she's a steady, always seems to be around when he needs a class broad on his arm. All the young ones are probably good in bed, but when it comes to social graces and dinner-table conversation, they don't make it."

Her silence was pointed.

"I say something?"

"Am I a young broad?"

"Younger than me. Younger than my two ex-wives."

"That's not what I mean. I mean . . ."

"I love the way you talk. I love the way you play the piano. You're smarter than I am. How's that?"

"I'll think about it." There was mirth in her voice.

"Tell me more about the party, about Julia Amster."

"Dull. Lots of talk about pre-Columbian art. Very precious crowd. I did learn that she's been getting obscene phone calls."

"Amster? Maybe Bowen's getting kinky."

"Maybe not obscene—annoying is more like it."

"Any idea who?"

"Not that I could hear." She placed her snifter on the night table and cuddled against him. "I never get obscene phone calls," she said.

"Want me to make a few?"

"Yeah."

"You got it. When should I start."

"Right now, and don't dial the wrong number."

He kicked Jumper from the bed and gently, surely, began placing his call.

Chapter Eleven

Potamos and Blackburn slept late Sunday morning, then took a leisurely walk, stopping for the newspaper and a breakfast of Danish and coffee. They passed the new Russian Embassy and stood across the street from it. He pointed to an eight-story white marble building and said, "That's the Chancellery. That building over there is the consulate, I think. There's a theater inside that seats four hundred people."

"I wish it weren't here in Georgetown," Blackburn said.

"You and a lot of people." He started to tell her of the strategic advantage the Soviets had achieved because of the site's elevation when she stopped him, grabbed his arm, and said, "I don't care about politics, Joe. I just don't like having an armed camp like this where I live—those walls and that black iron fence. I see some of the people from inside there in town, at parties I play, and they're so cold and unhappy-looking."

Potamos shrugged and kissed her lightly on the lips. "They're just people, that's all. The whole embassy game is like that. How do you think our people live in Moscow?"

"They have to because they're not allowed freedom. The Russians prefer it this way."

"Yeah, maybe."

They turned their attention to the condo going up on the other side of Wisconsin Avenue. Construction had stopped fifteen floors up. A massive crane on the roof stood silent against a blue sky dotted with fast-moving white puffs of cloud. A large piece of canvas flapped in the wind from the flat, open roof. The structure was surrounded by mounds of brown earth created by earthmovers. A white trailer stood in the middle of the mounds. A red sign painted on it said: *Jenkins Development*.

"And *that*," Blackburn said as they continued their walk. "Why don't they just pour concrete over all of us?"

Potamos laughed. "I think Jenkins intends to."

"Do you think he'll get the permit to keep going up with it?"

"Probably. His kind of money talks big, even when historical preservation societies are involved. He's stopped for now, but who knows what goes on behind the closed doors and under the tables?" Potamos shook his head. "Mr. Integrity, George Alfred Bowen, listens to the sound of Jenkins's dollar bills. He's been doing columns supporting the condo ever since the first permit was applied for. He and Jenkins are tight."

"Disgusting."

"Reality, that's all. Hey, you know, all the crap aside, Jenkins isn't *all* bad. He's put up a lot of good buildings in D.C. And that project of his to

buy up houses in Georgetown and rent them out
to deserving college students at low rates gives
him *some* redeeming qualities."

After they'd returned to her apartment and
read the paper, Blackburn asked what he planned
to do for the rest of the day.

"I have to make a couple of calls. In fact, let
me make 'em now." He called the only number
he had for Tony Fiamma but received no answer.
He tried the other seminar student, Anne Lewis,
and reached her at home. "I'd like to talk to you
about Valerie Frolich," he said. She seemed anxious to comply and they arranged to meet at seven
at Martin's Tavern.

His next call was to a number he'd found for
Walter Nebel, the political-science student who
Fiamma claimed had fought with Valerie the
night of her murder, and who'd arranged an alibi
with Sam Maruca. A young woman answered
and when Potamos asked for Nebel, her voice reflected anguish. "He left," she said.

"For where?"

"I don't know. He said he was dropping out of
school and going to Europe with friends."

"Why would he do that now? The semester's
almost over."

She cried, composed herself, and said, "I don't
know any more than I just told you, Mr. Potamos.
Maybe you can call his family. They live in Pennsylvania, outside of Pittsburgh." She gave him a
phone number.

"Have you talked to them?"

"No, I . . . they don't know me."

She obviously was romantically involved with Nebel. Potamos said, "Do you figure Walter's already left for Europe?"

"I really don't know."

"Did he talk to his parents about it, about the decision?"

"I don't know that either. Please, I just don't understand any of it and . . ."—her voice picked up strength and anger—"and, don't want to. Goodbye." The phone was returned to its cradle with considerable force.

"Mind if I make a long-distance call?" Potamos asked Blackburn, who was curled up on the couch reading the comics. "I'll charge it to my phone."

"Whatever."

He called the number in Pennsylvania. It rang eight times before a male voice answered gruffly, "Hello."

"Is this Walter Nebel's home?" Potamos asked.

There was a pause. "He's not here."

"My name is Joe Potamos. I'm with the *Washington Post* . . . and I teach journalism at Georgetown University." Blackburn glanced up, smiled, and returned to the funnies. "I just heard about Walter dropping out of school and thought he might have gone home."

"Home? This is where he grew up, but it ain't his home, not anymore."

"Yes, I can understand how you must feel. Any idea where he might be?"

"No. He called a couple of nights ago and told his mother he was dropping out, said he was taking off with friends to France or some other place. Who the hell knows? You were one of his teachers?"

Potamos coughed. "Yes, I was, and I was very upset when I heard what had happened. He was such a good student, doing so well and with a fine career ahead of him in . . . in foreign service."

Nebel's father said nothing, and Potamos could hear a woman in the background asking who was on the phone. Nebel's father yelled, "Some teacher at the school looking for Walter."

Potamos said, "Did he tell you why he left, Mr. Nebel? I assume you're his father."

"Yeah, I'm his father and I don't mind saying how disgusted I am. You sweat all your life to give your kids what you didn't have and they turn their backs on you, walk away, go off with their freaky goddamn friends who never had to worry about paying a mortgage or tuition. What the hell do they call it, getting their heads together? I got my head together by going to work in a mill at fifteen, like my father did."

"Yeah, I understand, I really do. He didn't say why he was leaving?"

"No. He talked to the missus here." Nebel's mother came on the line.

"Mrs. Nebel, I'm Joe Potamos of Georgetown University. I was just told that Walter left school and I'm trying to get in touch with him. Maybe we could have a talk and change his mind. Did he tell you where he was going?"

"No, just what my husband told you, that he and some friends were going to go away for a while, do some traveling, I guess, what the young people seem to like to do these days."

"Much to the chagrin of their parents," said Potamos. "You know, Mrs. Nebel, a very close friend of his, Valerie Frolich, was murdered recently. I wonder if—"

"Yes, we read about it here. The poor girl. My heart goes out to her family. Her father is a United States senator."

"Yes, I know. I was just wondering whether her death upset Walter to such an extent that he felt he had to get away."

"I never thought of that."

"He didn't mention her murder?"

"No."

"Mrs. Nebel, do you think he might still be in the Washington area, maybe hasn't left yet for Europe?"

"I don't know, Mr. . . ."

"Potamos. Joe Potamos."

"Mr. Potamos, I really don't. . . ." She'd been in control up until now. He heard her gasp against tears and then the sound of them filled his ear. She managed to say, "My husband and I are so upset. We had such plans for Walter. He was doing so well and . . . now *this*."

"I'm really sorry, Mrs. Nebel. If you hear from Walter, please call me and let me know how to reach him. I think I might be helpful in steering him back in the right direction. If he reinstates himself quickly, he won't suffer any penalty. Here's my number." He gave her his home number and Blackburn's number, looking over at her to see if she objected. She evidently didn't, or hadn't heard.

Mrs. Nebel said, "Thank you for caring about our son, Mr. . . ."

"Potamos. I liked Walter enough to take a personal interest in this matter. I'm sure everything will work out."

He hung up and discussed the conversation with Blackburn. "Why would he run away?" she asked.

"I hope the obvious answer isn't the right one," he said. "One more call, to Nebel's buddy, Sam Maruca."

"Want something to eat?" she asked. "I make a good bowl of canned soup."

"Love it."

Maruca answered on the first ring.

"Mr. Maruca?" Potamos said.

"Yeah. Who's this?"

Potamos introduced himself and said he'd like to meet with him to discuss Valerie Frolich.

"Why me?"

"Well, you or Walter Nebel. The problem is that Nebel seems to have flown the coop. Know where he is?"

"No. Look, Mr. Potamos, I've already talked to the police. I told them everything they wanted to know about what Walter was doing that night."

"What *was* he doing?"

"Studying with me for a final."

"I heard—"

"I don't care what you heard. Hey, who's been spreading rumors about me?"

"Doesn't matter, but it might make sense to straighten them out with me before they go any farther."

Maruca's laugh was more a snort. He said in a voice that matched it, "Talk to the press and have it all over the papers."

"I'm not writing about it—yet. I'm just trying to find out more about Valerie Frolich. That's it, I promise. I can get your view of things or I can go with what I have, including the fact that one of Valerie's boyfriends has a fight with her the night she's killed, cooks up an alibi with his buddy and the two of them lie to the police." Maruca started to say something, but Potamos kept going. "Now this boyfriend suddenly drops out of school a few weeks before the semester is over, disappears, claims he's going to Europe with friends. . . . Come on, Mr. Maruca, this isn't some classroom exercise in how to give an embassy party. This is murder we're talking about."

"I told you, I've already given the police my statement."

"And I should sit down with the police and give them the other side of the tale. They'd be interested, probably spend lots of time with you. Your choice. Spend a little off-the-record time with me, or lots of it in the rubber room."

"Huh?"

"Rubber room. Soundproof, a bright light, and some cheap garden hose."

"You don't scare me."

"I don't mean to." Potamos winked at Blackburn, who was standing in the doorway to the kitchen. "Look, Maruca, this is Sunday, my day off. I don't need to spend it on the phone trying to convince some goddamn college student it would be in his best interests to talk to me for a half-hour."

Maruca sighed and muttered a few epithets.

"Where do you live?" Potamos asked. "I'll come right over, won't take up more than twenty minutes of your time."

"I have to be somewhere in an hour."

"I'm on my way."

Maruca lived in a well-kept Georgetown Federal row house on a fashionable street a few blocks off Wisconsin Avenue. Potamos recognized the house. It had been the first property bought by Marshall Jenkins for use as low-cost housing for college students. At the press conference on its steps, Jenkins had explained that he felt giving students safe and pleasant housing would be of great value to their educational process, and to the future of the United States of America. Then he broke into a big smile and said, "Obviously, this does not represent true altruism. This house, and others I intend to buy, will increase in value. Because I do not need income from these properties right now, I'm able to allow deserving students to live in them at minimal rates. This is really why I'm doing it—it makes me feel good."

The press generally applauded Jenkins for his project. He obviously had good PR counsel; acknowledging in his remarks that the houses represented sound investment strategy took the wind out of the cynics' sails.

Potamos read three names above doorbells at the top of the steps. Maruca occupied the ground floor. Potamos rang the bell and heard it sound inside. The door was opened by a handsome young man wearing a maize chamois shirt, jeans cut off at the thigh, and leather sandals. He had an olive complexion, and his face had a sensual placidness to it highlighted by large, brooding brown eyes. His head was covered by a mass of tight black curls.

"Mr. Maruca?"

"Yes. You're Potamos?"

"That's right. I got here as quick as I could." He laughed, and looked toward the street. "They're right—a parking space in Georgetown is worth more than a whole house. I finally parked over there." He pointed to his red Datsun, which he'd managed to wedge between two cars in a space almost exactly the length of the Datsun. "I hope they can get out."

"It's all right," said Maruca. "The tan Toyota's mine. We'll be leaving together."

Maruca led Potamos down a short hall. The floor was highly polished oak. Large, expensively framed Kandinsky and Matisse prints dominated lemon-colored walls.

The living room was to the right. A phone rang as Potamos entered it. Maruca excused himself and disappeared to the rear of the apartment, leaving Potamos to take in his surroundings. Three couches formed a conversation pit in front of windows that faced the street. A rack that held custom stereo components, a twenty-five inch television monitor, and a VCR was at the opposite end of the large room. Tan wall-to-wall carpeting was velvet and thick. One wall contained original oils and watercolors; Potamos recognized some of them as being by Washington artist Yuriko Yama-guchi. A large Italian marble hand sculptured by Mortimer Haber stood on a pedestal in a corner, twin spotlights hitting it from two sides. All in all, it was an impressively furnished and decorated room, not the usual college student's apartment. Times have changed, he told himself as he closely examined the stereo equipment.

A few minutes later Maruca reappeared. "Sorry," he said.

"That's okay," Potamos said. "That wouldn't have been Walter Nebel, would it?"

"No. He's gone."

"Know where?"

"No."

"Know why?"

"No."

"The kid did a dumb thing, running like this."

Maruca's smile was crooked as he said, "What's the big deal? Who cares?"

Potamos said, "Valerie Frolich's family might care. The MPD might care. How's that for start-ers?"

"Look, Potamos, I didn't want you here in the first place and I'll be damned if I'll have you in my house and take this kind of crap."

"Call it what you want, Maruca, but I think

you'd better take another look at this whole thing because you, buddy, are in the middle of it."

Maruca glared at him. "Walter Nebel and I studied together the night Valerie was killed. That's that. I told the police, and so did Walter. End of story."

"What about the other version, the one where Nebel has a fight with her that night, drives around alone, then cooks up an alibi with you? That plays for me."

"It's not true."

"Maybe, maybe not, but I think Sergeant Languth at MPD would be more than happy to take another look, in another light, if I go to him with it."

"Go ahead."

"The way I see it is this. Nebel fights with her and does what most jilted young guys do—go out, get drunk, take a long drive, come home and fall asleep. But now the story gets unusual. He wakes up, hears that his girlfriend has been found in the canal, her head bashed in. Panic. They'll think it was me, he figures, so he goes to his buddy, Sam Maruca, and says, 'Hey, Sam, here's what happened and I don't need this kind of trouble, not with a cushy career in foreign service ahead of me. We studied together all night. Right?' And his buddy, Maruca, says, 'Right.' How's that play for *you?*"

"It doesn't. In the first place, Walter Nebel and I weren't buddies, just students in the same school."

"But he did date Valerie Frolich. Right?"

"I guess so. He dated lots of girls."

"And he did fight with her that night after the barge party."

"Not that I know of."

Potamos bit his lip and went to the window, turned and said, "Did it ever occur to you that maybe Walter Nebel *did* kill Valerie Frolich? If you provide an alibi for him out of friendship, you might be shielding a murderer. If that's the way it eventually falls, Maruca, your future in a cushy diplomatic job is as promising as a gay black with a felony record making it to the White House. Thanks for your time."

Maruca followed Potamos to the front door. Potamos said, "You live good, Maruca. Marshall Jenkins furnish it for you, too?"

"Some."

"That's nice. What's it cost you?"

"That's my business."

"True, but I think I'll make it my business, too. I think I'll make you and Nebel a priority on my list." He opened the door and stepped out onto the steps. "You moving your car?"

"Later. Lots of luck getting out." He slammed the door behind Potamos.

A few minutes later Potamos struggled to inch his car from its cramped space. He saw Maruca watching through the living-room window and gave the bumper of the tan Toyota a hard shot, looked toward Maruca, winked, and drove away.

Chapter Twelve

"Hello, Joe," a waiter said as Potamos entered Martin's Tavern. He wiggled his fingers in front of his mouth as though holding a cigar and said, "They're getting younger all the time." He nodded toward a booth in which Anne Lewis sat. "She's looking for you."

Potamos said, "Strictly business."

"Yeah, it's a tough life."

Potamos introduced himself to Lewis and sat across from her. He liked her looks: pretty face with big eyes and a quick, genuine smile. Her hair was brown and short, neat like the rest of her. She had a nice figure, at least from the waist up, a full bosom pressing against the beige sweater.

"You feel like something to eat?" Potamos asked.

"Sure, that'd be nice." She ordered a mushroom omelet and white wine. He had Welsh rarebit and a beer. They chatted about general topics until she brought up Valerie Frolich. "I've been reading your articles," she said. "They're really good."

"Thanks. It gets tougher as the information dries up. I thought maybe you could give me a fresh angle."

She smiled, obviously flattered to be asked, and said, "Let's see . . . I suppose I could tell you about Valerie, but you've already covered that."

"Unless you have something brand-new to offer."

"I really don't. We were friends only because we're both journalism majors. Valerie was bright and popular. It's beyond my comprehension how anyone could do such a thing, unless it was someone who was very, very mad at her."

Potamos couldn't suppress the grin. "I'd say that's a given, wouldn't you?"

She was a little embarrassed. "What I mean is that there's two kinds of murder, premeditated and one coming out of passion. Know what I mean, Mr. Potamos? I read your piece on the autopsy, and when you said that the medical examiner characterized the blows to the head as being 'random' and 'multiple,' I started thinking about the difference."

Potamos sipped his beer and studied her across the table. There was no hesitation in her speech. She knew what she thought and wasn't reluctant to express it. "Go on," Potamos said. "You were talking about—"

"The difference between types of murders. When I read what the medical examiner said, I realized there's a good possibility that it wasn't murder."

"Really?"

"Yes. Let's assume that Valerie simply had a fight with someone who was capable of sufficient anger to strike out at her, take a swing."

"The blows were multiple, and involved a blunt object, like a rock."

"I know, but sometimes when you're angry, *really* angry, you deliver that first blow and then keep hitting. Haven't you ever experienced that?"

"No, but I understand what you mean. Okay, let's assume it was an accident, that somebody didn't want to hurt Valerie but, in a fit of anger, lashed out, too hard and too often. Who'd she know that could get that mad at her?"

Lewis sighed and ate some of her omelet. "Valerie had a funny side of her, Mr. Potamos. She was beautiful and popular, but she went through boyfriends like . . ." She looked down at her plate and smiled. "Like omelets. Guys would fall madly in love with her and then she'd dump them, cruelly sometimes."

Potamos nodded. "Okay, potentially a jilted boyfriend had it out with her and got physical. Any names?"

She shook her head. "As I said, she dated a lot. I suppose you could just go down a list. Of course, there were others, too, who had reason to be angry with her."

"Like?"

"Like . . . her father, that's for sure."

"Senator John Frolich? No. He was her father. Fathers don't go around beating up their daughters, at least not fathers like John Frolich."

Lewis's smile was cynical.

"You know something to change that view?"

"Senator Frolich is not a man without a temper."

"He doesn't come off that way in public," said

Potamos. "Bastion of reason, cool-headed, a real leader."

"And with a bad temper when it came to certain aspects of his life."

"Like his daughter?"

"Yes. I don't know whether you're aware that my father and Senator Frolich are very close friends."

"Sure, Paul Lewis. Your dad's an important lobbyist in town."

"That's right. His most important client is the South African gold consortium."

"I know."

"And you probably also know that Senator Frolich's voting record in the Senate on South Africa is pro right down the line."

Potamos laughed. "Your father must be effective."

"My father knows how to wield influence."

"Your father's friends with Marshall Jenkins, too?"

"Of course." There was scorn in her voice.

"George Bowen?"

"Uh-huh. They have a . . . well, I guess you could call it a cozy little club."

"Old-boy network?"

"Exactly."

Potamos ordered another drink, then asked, "What does all this have to do with Valerie Frolich's murder? Are you suggesting that her father and his friends had something to do with it?"

"No. All I'm saying is that it's possible that her father, in a fit of anger that night, hit his daughter."

"And killed her."

"Yes."

Potamos blew air through his lips and sat back. "That's quite an accusation, Miss Lewis."

"I'm not accusing him. I'm just raising the possibility."

"Things were that bad between them, Valerie and her father?"

"From my understanding, yes."

"Who provided you with that understanding, Valerie or her father?"

"A little of both. Valerie was—how can I say this?—Valerie was not fond of her father. In fact . . . yes, I can go as far as to say that she hated him, hated what he stood for."

"Really? Politically?"

"Yes, and personally. She told me more than once that she detested the way he treated her mother."

"Uh-huh. What did you get from his side?"

"Nothing directly, but living in the same house with one of his dearest friends provides certain opportunities. I hear a lot."

"From *your* father."

"Yes. He talks to my mother, and sometimes the subject is Valerie Frolich and her father."

It suddenly struck Potamos that the pretty and bright young woman across from him was a little too matter-of-fact for his taste, particularly because she seemed to have no reservations about bringing up unsavory aspects of her own family's life. He decided to mention it.

Lewis said flatly, "If I thought I was doing

something that would reflect unfavorably upon my own family, I wouldn't be sitting here talking to you. But, the fact is, Valerie Frolich is dead. Someone is going to discover why it happened, and who did it, and I'd just as soon be the one."

Now Potamos understood. She was a female Tony Fiamma, more genteel and certainly better-looking, but her motives were the same: Break the story, make a name, get the old career started with a bang. There was only one thing that didn't square with that: "Miss Lewis, if you're looking to investigate Valerie's murder so that you can break the story, why talk to me? We're in competition, and I might end up using everything you've told me for my own stories. What does that get you?"

Her smile was big and pleasant and sexy. "Mr. Potamos, there's a lot more that I know about Valerie Frolich and the circumstances of her life that might have led to her death. I thought you might be interested in having me work with you, sort of an assistant, a researcher."

"With a shared by-line."

"Sure. That would be only fair."

"And impossible."

"Why?"

"Because . . . look, I don't work with other people. Besides, you're a student *and*, I might add, a potential suspect in the case, certainly a valuable source of information for the police."

"Suspect? Why would I have beaten Valerie to death? Do you really think I'd be capable of that?"

"Physically? Sure. A rock is a rock is a rock, in

anyone's hands. I'm not suggesting it, but it does represent a certain reality."

"So does the fact that I might have information that would be useful to you. I don't want to come off as impertinent, Mr. Potamos, but I know that after you wrote that big series on Senator Cables selling illegal arms to the Arabs, things went downhill. I have a feeling that breaking the Valerie Frolich story would be good for you."

"And good for *you*—if you helped me and shared credit."

"Is there anything wrong with that?"

"Lots of things, Miss Lewis. Thanks for meeting me." He waved for a check.

"You seem offended," she said.

"Offended? Me? Hell, no. I lost that capacity a long time ago. It's just that here's a young woman with her head smashed in and her friends—yeah, okay, I'll use the word—her *friends* are all looking to profit from it by making a score in journalism. Somehow, where I come from, that's not nice."

"But practical. I didn't kill Valerie, but I did know her, knew a lot about the way she lived, the people she dated . . . and I happen to live in a house in which Valerie's family is not a foreign topic."

Potamos sighed and paid the bill. "Look, Miss Lewis, I don't blame you for wanting to succeed and using what's at your disposal. I probably would have done the same thing myself. It's just that . . ."

She reached across the table and placed a nicely

tapered set of fingers on top of his hand. Her
voice was soft. "Please let me work with you on
the story."

The fingers radiated a wonderful warmth up
his arm, around his chest and down. "Let me
think about it," he said.

"You won't be sorry. I really think I have the
key to it."

"We'll see," Potamos said. He started to get up,
sat, and said, "Did you ever date anyone who'd
dated Valerie?"

His question took her by surprise. She frowned,
looked at him as though she were trying to get
inside his head, then asked the obvious: "Why do
you ask?"

"Just wondered. Anyone else in the seminar
date Valerie?"

"Just . . . Steve."

"Steve McCarty."

"That's right. I know you talked to him."

"How? He tell you?"

"Yes."

"Why?"

"Why? Because . . . he just mentioned it. No
reason."

"You ever date him?"

She guffawed. "No, of course not."

He didn't believe her but didn't say so.

They shook hands outside Martin's. He said,
"Keep in touch, Miss Lewis."

"Anne, please. My friends call me Annie. I
hated it until recently."

"What changed?"

"Me. I grew up." She locked him in a seductive stare that didn't miss its intended mark.

He asked, "What about Professor Bowen and Valerie?"

"What about them?"

"Their relationship. Did it go beyond teacher-student?"

She smiled. "Good question. The answer is even better. Please, call me. And thanks for dinner."

Chapter Thirteen

It occurred to Potamos when he awoke Monday morning that he didn't know to which of George Bowen's offices he was supposed to go. Although Bowen wasn't on staff at the *Post*, the paper served as the flagship publication for his syndicated column and provided an office for him. The main office for Bowen's journalistic empire was located in an old, abandoned embassy building on Massachusetts Avenue that Marshall Jenkins had bought and converted into offices. Bowen had the top floor.

A phone call straightened it out: Potamos was to be at the Mass. Ave. office at ten.

He'd spent most of Sunday evening jotting down ideas about the Valerie Frolich case based upon his conversations with students from Bowen's seminar, and with Sam Maruca and Walter Nebel's parents. His primary interest in them was whether he could develop a story based upon what he'd learned. He decided he couldn't; whatever he wrote would smack of innuendo and speculation. The only tangible piece of information he considered going with was Walter Nebel's sudden disappearance, but to report it was potentially actionable. The kid had a right to drop out of school and take a trip. Maybe it had nothing to do with the murder. Potamos couldn't shake the belief that it did, but what he believed didn't matter, not without a solid reason to link Nebel's disappearance to Valerie Frolich and to the alibi he had with Sam Maruca.

The alibi. Potamos had doubts but, again, nothing to back them up. He didn't like Maruca. In fact he realized as he took a long walk with Jumper before going to bed that he really didn't like any of the students, with the possible exception of Bob Fitzgerald, who seemed to be the only one without an ax to grind, and who didn't seem to be looking for gain out of Valerie's murder.

And then there was Senator Frolich. Ridiculous to think he'd beat his own daughter to death, but . . . what Anne Lewis had told him kept coming back.

Now, looking across the large reception room at Bowen's secretary, a matronly woman with blue hair and with a desk as neat as her coiffure, he tried to imagine Bowen's reason for wanting to see him. He hadn't had to respond. He didn't work for Bowen, and Bowen didn't work for the *Post*. But the reality was that Bowen wielded considerable weight with the paper's higher-ups. He'd proved that last time around. What most intrigued Potamos, however, was the possibility that Bowen, in his roles as professor to Valerie Frolich and confidant to the Frolich family, might actually want to share something of importance with him. It was far-fetched, he knew, but more pleasant to contemplate than the alternatives.

A buzzer sounded on the secretary's intercom.

She held down a button and Bowen's voice said, "Send in Mr. Potamos."

The secretary held open a door and Potamos stepped into Bowen's office, all dark wood and brass, a forest-green carpet spongy beneath his feet. Sunshine streamed through large windows behind where Bowen sat at his desk, rendering him a silhouette against the light. Potamos stood just inside the door and squinted.

"Sit down, Joe."

Potamos took a leather chair facing Bowen and settled into it. He still had to squint. "That light is annoying," he said.

"The light? Oh, the sunlight. A night person."

His comment and tone rankled Potamos. He said, "I like the daylight as well as anybody, Mr. Bowen, but not when I'm blinded by it."

For a moment Potamos thought Bowen was going to get up and close the drapes. He didn't. Instead, he slowly rose from his chair and came around the desk, looked down at Potamos, then went to a brass cart with a glass top on which a coffeepot, cups and saucers, cream and a sugar bowl rested. Now Potamos could clearly see him. He wore wide yellow suspenders attached to a pair of dark blue slacks. His bow tie was blue with white spots. He was wearing half-glasses, which, combined with his long, lanky frame, gave him a distinct professorial look. "Coffee?" he asked.

"No, thanks. I had some."

Bowen carefully poured himself a cup, added cream, and tasted it. "It's outstanding coffee, Joe.

Mrs. Carlisle blends amaretto with Chock Full o' Nuts. You should try it. What do you usually drink, instant?"

"Yeah. It's quicker. Besides, I don't have a Mrs. Carlisle around my apartment."

Bowen managed a chuckle and sat down in a matching leather chair next to Potamos. He crossed his legs and tasted from his cup again, saying without taking his eyes from it, "I understand you're hot on the Frolich case."

"Hot? I wouldn't say that."

"I've been reading your pieces. You seem to be exclusively assigned to the case."

Potamos looked at him quizzically. "They put me on it," he said. "I work the cop beat, remember?"

Bowen sighed, placed the cup and saucer on a small satinwood Phyfe card table next to his chair, and slowly turned to face Potamos. He rested his elbow on the arm of the chair, placed his pointed chin on his hand, and said, "You know *why* you're just a working reporter covering grizzle and grime."

Potamos wasn't sure whether to acknowledge his awareness that Bowen had virtually blacklisted him. He decided there was nothing to be gained by feigning ignorance and said, "Because you made sure I wouldn't be anything else."

"Do you really believe that?" Bowen's voice was tired and bored.

"Yeah, I do, because of the Cables story."

"Preposterous, Joe. I may have achieved a certain preeminence in my profession—*our* profession—but I'm hardly in a position to thwart the career of a talented journalist."

"Maybe I could have fought it, but that wasn't my style at the time."

"Interesting admission," said Bowen. "You and I had a conflict over a story. When the conflict was over—and, I might add, you won by doing exactly what you wished to do with that story—you *chose* to turn your back on the spoils. You never did deliver that book, did you?"

"No."

"You never did leave Washington to escape this dreadful man named George Bowen and build your career elsewhere. I wonder why, Joe."

Potamos shrugged and shifted in his chair. "Didn't appeal to me."

"Yes, obviously. What does appeal to you these days?"

Potamos smiled. "My dog, and a woman I met."

Bowen smiled, too. "Dogs and women, man's best and worst friends. When in doubt, Joe, go with the dog."

"Sometimes I think that. But then . . ."

A laugh this time. "I understand." Bowen stood and stretched. "Let's get back to Valerie Frolich's murder, if you don't mind dropping the previous subject."

"I don't mind at all."

"You've been interviewing students who knew her."

"Yeah. Gil Gardello told me to dig up human interest and . . ."

"And?"

"I'm working on it."

"You've been talking to students in my seminar." He said it flatly; Potamos took it as a flat statement. Then Bowen added, "I wish you wouldn't."

"Wouldn't what, talk to your students?"

"Yes."

"Why?"

"Because I am talking to them."

Potamos screwed up his face and sat forward. "I don't understand," he said.

"It is quite enough for one member of the press to interrogate those students, Joe. That one person is me. I am close to them. They trust me, they open up to me. To put it simply, leave them alone."

"Give me a reason besides the one you just gave me."

"Is that necessary?"

"For me. What are you saying, that you want an exclusive on them?"

"It doesn't necessarily involve that, but—"

"Sounds to me like it does. Funny, but I never thought I'd be in competition with George Alfred Bowen."

Bowen's voice was ice. "You're not. Just stay away from them."

"I'm still waiting."

"For what?"

"A better reason."

"And you'll wait forever. If it's really necessary to explain why I am in a better position to gather what information is available through them than you are, you belong in . . . a diner."

"You're a nasty bastard."

"And you are a bumbling fool."

"That's it?" Potamos asked, rising.

"No, it is not." Bowen came around to where Potamos stood and placed his hand on his shoulder. "Oh, Joseph Potamos, the hard-nosed reporter, trench coat and all, the curled lip, the sneer, principles on his forehead, J-school impracticalities branded on his brain. I didn't want this sort of confrontation, Joe. I asked you here to make you an offer you can't refuse."

Potamos had to hand it to him. He knew how to shift your balance so that you wondered whether you'd topple over. Bastard, then nice guy; threats, then offers.

"Sit down," Bowen said. "Hear me out."

Potamos sat, said, "A diner's a nice place to work. It's honest. My father was an honest man who owned a diner."

"I know that. Pardon my indiscretion. I apologize."

George Bowen apologizing to Joe Potamos. Potamos said, "What's this offer?"

"A job here with me, chief of staff, managing editor. I'm doing a new book. The column has never been more accepted, or more profitable. I'm starting a television series. The radio series is now on twelve hundred stations, with a dozen signing up every week. I need help and I think you're the man."

It was all too bizarre, Bowen offering *him* a job. One of his first thoughts was that he wouldn't work for George Alfred Bowen under any circumstances and for any amount of money, which is why he surprised himself when he asked, "How much?"

"Double what you're making now."

"Double?"

"Double. Regular hours, your own office and staff. Interested, Joe?"

"Only in why you're doing it."

Bowen grinned and slapped him on the back. "Because I think you'd do a good job for me—*and*, Joe, I'd like to have you where I can see you."

It was Potamos's turn to laugh. "That's it, huh? What do you care what I do? Am I stepping on toes again in the Frolich case?"

"Yes, very sensitive toes. Whether you accept my offer or not, stay away from the students in my seminar. The little they might have to contribute will come through me."

Potamos shook his head and puffed his cheeks. "Why the hell would you want to deal with petty stuff like that? I'm supposed to generate stories about the murder, and talking to the deceased's friends is part of my job."

"Not anymore."

"Says who?"

" 'Says who?' Dime-novel dialogue. How distressing! As of this moment, Joe, you are forbidden to set foot on the campus of Georgetown University, or to contact any students of that institution. Check with Mr. Gardello if you need confirmation. Now, one last time, want to work for me?"

Potamos stood and walked to the door.

"Well?" said Bowen.

Potamos turned and said, "You're a crazy man,

and I'm dedicated these days to avoiding crazy men. Thanks for the offer. I'm not taking it."

"Goodbye, Joe."

"Goodbye, George."

" . . . and so one of her boyfriends has a fight with her the night she's killed, arranges an alibi with a buddy, then skips town. Her father dislikes her enough to bash her head in, according to a friend. This Tony Fiamma, who'd sell his sister for a big break in journalism, disliked her, claims to have her diary. Another one, McCarty, the former law student, denies he ever dated her but lies about it. Now America's most influential columnist and a buddy of her father's warns me off. You were with her on the barge the night she got it. What'd you do, hit her with a weighted baton?"

Roseann Blackburn placed her finger on Potamos's lips. "Hush. You're all worked up."

Potamos sat up in bed. "I shouldn't be worked up? Do you realize what happened today in Bowen's office? He as much as acknowledged that he has something to hide, either for himself or his buddy, the Honorable John Frolich, or maybe one of his students. I shouldn't be worked up? I wish I still smoked."

"And I'm glad you don't. Are you spending the night?"

"Can't. I have to walk Jumper."

"Go get her and bring her back."

"Come with me and we'll stay at my place."

"I'm too sleepy."

"Then I'll see you tomorrow. Right?"

She said nothing.

"Wrong."

"Call me. I have a busy day, and I have a gig at night."

"Where?"

"Blues Alley. The name group canceled out, so they're using locals. We don't start until late, though, and go till two."

"Great. Come by my place early and I'll make dinner, send you off with a full stomach."

"Okay, but don't hate me for eating and running."

He dressed, and she accompanied him to the door. He looked down at her nude body and almost decided to let Jumper use her favorite spot in the kitchen. Roseann wrapped her arms around him and planted a long, deep kiss on his mouth.

"I should'a got a cat," he said. "Sleep tight."

Chapter Fourteen

Julia Amster seldom rose before eleven, but this Tuesday morning found her entering the shower at eight. She was grumpy; she and George Bowen had attended an intimate dinner party the night before, hosted by the secretary of state, and Bowen hadn't dropped her home until a little after midnight. They'd argued after the party. He'd been displeased with the tenor of her conversation with the secretary's wife. "She's a bore," Julia told him.

"An important bore," he countered. "I expect appropriate behavior from you, Julia."

"Appropriate behavior indeed," she muttered as she rubbed an imported French soap into her skin. "You're a pompous, arrogant bastard, George," she said aloud, adjusting the dial on her Shower Massage to "pulsate" and directing it over the length of her. "Why I put up with you I'll never know." She stepped from the shower and reached for a large, fluffy pink towel. The fact was she *did* know why she put up with George Bowen, knew why she said harsh things to him only in the shower or while driving alone. She needed to bask in the reflection of his power, to dine and dance and converse with the power brokers with whom he was on such intimate terms. She reveled in it and wasn't ashamed to admit it—to herself.

"Appropriate behavior indeed." She chose a new lavender suit from a closet and held it in front of her nude body. She smiled at her reflection in the full-length mirror. The sight of herself often caused her to smile.

Julia Amster was tall, stood eye to eye with Bowen. Her hair was remarkably thick, the color of copper, and her figure—although having gotten thicker through the hips—would have been a proud possession of a woman ten years younger. Amster was forty-two—a good age, she often told herself.

She'd met Bowen almost ten years ago, right after the breakup of her marriage of four years to a concert impresario named Maurice, who precipitated the separation and divorce by leaving Washington for an artistic director's job with a Houston opera company. Julia wasn't sorry to see him go. She'd grown quickly to dislike him, although she did enjoy the circle of friends to which she was introduced through his professional activities, including George Alfred Bowen.

At the time of the breakup, Amster had been teaching a course in pre-Columbian art at American University. She had a doctorate in the subject and knew there were few people, at least in Washington, who were as well grounded and informed about it. Shortly after accepting the position at American, she was invited to join the board of scholars at Dumbarton Oaks, whose pre-Columbian collection, along with its collections of early Christian and Byzantine art and its world-famous library devoted to the subject of formal gardens, had established the famed mansion as a major cultural and scholarly center in the nation's capital. She was naturally pleased by the professional recognition, but found her colleagues dull and stodgy. She much preferred the company of those at the political center, especially that of George Bowen. It didn't matter that their intimate moments together were few and far between, or that he openly slept with a succession of young women. Just as long as he turned to her when social grace, natural beauty, and brains were what counted. When he needed class on his arm.

The reason she was up earlier than usual this morning was a meeting at nine at her gallery of pre-Columbian art on P Street, in the heart of Georgetown. She'd been financed by Bowen's friend Marshall Jenkins, and the gallery had grown in worth and prestige since its opening three years ago. The meeting was with a dealer who had offered her a collection he'd garnered in London. It was a matter of price. She'd received a commitment from Jenkins for a certain amount and was determined to bring in the collection within budget.

Dressed and made up, she spent a few minutes at her desk going over notes on the market value of the pieces of art under consideration. Confident of her judgment, she placed her notes in a thin leather Gucci briefcase and was about to leave when the phone rang. She debated answering; she was running late. She picked up the phone and

heard the same raspy, slurred voice she'd heard
before. The person—male or female, she couldn't
be sure—had been annoying her with calls for
more than a week.

"Who is this?"

"He won't get away with it. Neither will you."

"If you don't stop this, I'll—" The line went
dead.

She replaced the receiver and clenched her fists,
said through tight lips, "Sick bastard."

The meeting at Amster's gallery went nicely—she
managed to buy the pieces below even what Jenkins had budgeted for. The seller, a cherubic little
bald man named Waldrup in a rumpled gray suit,
suggested they celebrate by having a drink at the
nearest bar. Amster thanked him but said it was
too early, realizing that it probably was never too
early for him.

He was about to leave when the phone rang.
"Excuse me," she said, wishing he would take it
as a cue to leave. He didn't. She answered, heard
the same voice she'd heard at home. She quickly
hung up.

"Something wrong?" her visitor asked.

She forced a smile, said, "No, of course not, just
a wrong number. The phone service gets worse
every day."

He suggested lunch, then dinner. Finally she
managed to get him out the door with the promise
of getting together sometime in the near future.

Once he was gone, she locked the door, sat at

her desk, and dialed the number for the police department.

Sergeant Peter Languth had just entered his office after conducting the daily meeting of the Valerie Frolich task force. The meeting had been as disappointing as it had been each day since the murder. There had been no progress in the case. Every possible suspect had been interviewed and reinterviewed, some as many as six times, but nothing concrete had resulted. Two detectives assigned exclusively to the Frolich family reported that the family seemed almost to have put the event behind them, especially Senator Frolich, who, according to one of the detectives, was unfailingly cordial to them, going out of his way to accommodate their every need. "But he's not there much," said the other detective. "He's a busy guy."

Languth suggested to everyone on the task force that they rethink the case and have fresh directions to suggest the following day. He didn't expect anything to come of that, but in his frustrated state it was the best he could do.

There were phone messages for him in his office. One was from the deputy chief medical examiner acknowledging Languth's request for a meeting to again go over the details of Valerie Frolich's autopsy. He returned that call and they set the meeting for five o'clock at the city morgue at D.C. General.

"Pete," a desk sergeant said through Languth's open door, "you wanted to catch all calls on the Frolich case, huh?"

"Yeah."

"We got one a few minutes ago from Julia Amster. Owns an art gallery in Georgetown."

"So?"

"She got perturbed that I handled it as routine and started throwing around George Bowen's name."

"Yeah. Amster. One of his girlfriends. What'd she call about?"

"She claims she's been getting crank calls."

"Yeah? Dirty ones?" He laughed.

"I guess so."

"Where is she now?"

"At her gallery on P Street."

"I'll take it. Thanks."

Amster answered on the first ring. "Ms. Amster, Sergeant Peter Languth, detective, MPD. You say you're getting obscene calls?"

"Not obscene. Crank calls, nasty calls."

He asked the usual questions: How many calls? Any pattern to their timing? How long were the calls? Did she recognize the voice? ("If I did, I wouldn't need you.")

"Tell you what," Languth said. "I'll come over. You'll be there for the next half-hour?"

"Yes."

"Relax, Ms. Amster. These things usually just stop."

When he got there, she unlocked the gallery door for him. He stepped inside, glanced around, and let out a whistle of appreciation. "Beautiful," he said.

"Thank you."

"It looks . . . Indian."

"Pre-Columbian."

"Oh, yeah? Hmmmm."

They sat at her desk and she reiterated the history of the calls. He said, "And the caller says something like 'You won't get away with it'?"

"Yes, '*You* won't get away with it.' "

"What does he mean by that, do you figure?"

"I haven't the slightest idea, and I told you, I'm not even sure it's a man."

"Sex undetermined." He scribbled it on a note pad. "Tell you what," he said. "Next time a call comes in, keep talking. I'll set up a trace back at the department. It doesn't always work, but it's worth a try."

"Thank you. I appreciate it," Amster said.

Languth put the pad in his pocket and surveyed the gallery again from where he sat. "You teach this stuff at American, don't you?"

Amster paused. "How do you know that?"

Languth shrugged and laughed. He said casually, "I heard about you through Mr. Bowen."

"George?"

"Yeah. I know you mentioned him when you called."

"That's right, but . . ."

"That's some mess he's involved in, huh, having his student killed."

"Yes, it was terrible, although I wouldn't say he's in any sort of a mess because of it."

"I didn't mean it literally. It's just that when you get that close to somebody and she gets her head bashed in, it must be tough on you."

Amster stared at him, said nothing.

"They *were* pretty close, weren't they?"

"It just occurs to me, Sergeant Languth, that you haven't come here because of the crank calls I've been receiving."

"What do you mean?"

"You're in charge of the Valerie Frolich investigation, aren't you?"

He started to say something, but she cut him off. "I remember seeing you on television at press conferences about the case."

"Well, I wouldn't say I'm in charge. We have lots of people on the case. When the daughter of a U.S. senator gets killed, we pay attention."

"That's beside the point. You're here because you want to talk to me about George Bowen."

"Ms. Amster, I responded to your complaint about annoying phone calls, but while I'm here I figured—"

"You figured wrong, sergeant. Please leave."

He narrowed his eyes and glared at her across the small desk. "Why so uptight, Ms. Amster? All I did was mention that Mr. Bowen was pretty close with the kid."

"Meaning what?"

Another shrug, a boyish grin. "I think you know what I mean."

"I resent very much the inference in what you've said, and I'm sure Mr. Bowen will, too."

"That's your problem—and his."

Amster stood and walked to the door, turned and said to Languth, who was still sitting, "Leave my gallery immediately."

"Okay," he said, standing and stretching. He

paused on his way to the door to admire a small
Chibcha carving on a pedestal. "What's this
worth?" he asked. She didn't answer. He came to
where she stood and looked into her eyes, pulled
his card from the breast pocket of his suit jacket,
and handed it to her. "Call me anytime, Ms.
Amster, about more crank calls or . . . or anything
else that's on your mind. Have a good day."

Languth spent the rest of the day going over
reports on the Frolich case. Up until that day
he'd handled press inquiries himself, but they'd
become too burdensome and a spokeswoman
from Public Affairs was handed the job. He had
trouble concentrating. His head hurt, and acid in-
digestion caused him to wince periodically. He'd
stayed out late the night before, hitting a succession of his favorite bars until fatigue, and alcohol,
sent him stumbling home to bed.

He checked his watch. Time to leave for the
morgue. The spokeswoman from Public Affairs
called. "Pete, I just got a call from a reporter at
WRC. He wanted to know what we had on the
disappearance of Walter Nebel?" The name obviously meant nothing to her.

"Disappearance?"

"Yes. He said this Nebel had dropped out of
Georgetown University and was nowhere to be
found. He wants to know whether we know anything about it."

"Tell him we know nothing."

She sighed. "Who is Walter Nebel?"

"Some student we questioned who knew Frolich. He's not a suspect."

"We know nothing."

"Right, nothing."

Languth hung up and found a transcript of the interview one of his detectives had done with Nebel, in which Nebel admitted having dated Valerie Frolich, and having had an argument with her between the time she was at the barge party and the time she was found in the canal. He claimed he'd left her after the argument and had gone to a friend's apartment where he studied until almost dawn. The friend—Sam Maruca—had verified the story. The interviewing detective's comments indicated he believed Nebel and saw little reason to pursue him as a suspect.

"So much for intuition," Languth said angrily as he stuffed the transcript into his raincoat pocket. On his way to D.C. General, he stopped at a drugstore, bought a large bottle of multiflavored Tums, popped two in his mouth, and put the bottle in his raincoat. He decided as he drove to his meeting that he'd have an early, light dinner and be in bed by eight.

John Finnerty, the deputy chief medical examiner, was waiting for him in a small office off the main autopsy room. Finnerty was a tall, rotund man who seemed perpetually to be laughing and humming Broadway show tunes.

"Hello, Peter, my boy," Finnerty said in a loud, friendly voice. "Sit down, sit down."

Languth sat heavily in a straight wooden chair and belched.

"You look like some of the guests in there," Finnerty said, indicating the morgue with a nod of his head. "I almost feel I should start cutting." He laughed heartily.

Languth grinned. "It's my stomach, John. Damn heartburn."

"Could be ulcers."

"Yeah, maybe. I'm hung over. Was out late last night."

"You're getting too old for that, Peter. Carousing is a young man's game."

"Yeah, I suppose. Look, John, let's go over Valerie Frolich again. I keep rereading your report and thinking that there's got to be something the autopsy revealed that would help us. I can't find anything specific, but I figured it was worth taking another shot."

Finnerty grunted and opened a thick file folder on the small, battered desk. "Let's see," he said, placing half-glasses on his bulbous nose and squinting at what he read.

"You say it was a blunt, rounded instrument that killed her. Can't get more specific than that?" Languth asked.

"Afraid not."

"A rock? We've never found the weapon."

"Undoubtedly at the bottom of the C and O," said Finnerty, "along with a million other rocks."

"So you do think it was a rock."

"It wasn't a hammer or any other instrument with a small, defined shape. The wounds to her skull were star-shaped, typical of what a blunt object creates. Blows from sharper instruments generally create a crescent in the skull."

"Her skull was fractured," Languth said flatly.

"Yes, multiple fractures—some simply cracks in the bone structure, some of them depressed and comminuted." Finnerty flipped through pages. "The attack came from the front initially, I'd say, although she probably received additional blows after she was on the ground. The first blow to the front of her head killed her, but whoever did it wasn't looking to simply strike her once. She was struck at least twice more after she fell."

"Sure about that?"

"Yes. The secondary radiating fissures would indicate it."

"What else?" Sometimes words on paper took on a different meaning when they came from the mouth.

Finnerty sighed, leaned back, and softly hummed "Memories" from *Cats* as he continued to peruse the pages in the folder. He said without looking up, "She obviously tried to ward off her attacker. Her arms and hands sustained numerous defensive wounds. She fought hard."

Languth thought for a moment. "She obviously knew her attacker."

Finnerty looked up and frowned. "Not necessarily."

"She was attacked from the front," said Languth. "It wasn't anybody coming up from behind and hitting her. She had time to try and fight him off—"

"Or *her*."

"I don't think so."

"Why not? It's the weight of the rock—if it *was* a rock—that would do the damage, not the strength of the arm."

"But what about height?" Languth said.

"Valerie Frolich was a short girl," said Finnerty.

"Exactly where was the initial blow, the one you said probably killed her."

"Just as I indicated in the sketch." He turned the folder around so that Languth could see it. The frontal view showed the wound to be in the middle of the forehead and to the top, at the hairline.

Languth slid the folder back to Finnerty and shook his head. "It's a dead end, John," he said, resignation in his voice. "We have nothing, just a bunch of people who knew her." He remembered Walter Nebel, which caused a momentary twinge of optimism, quickly wiped away by another attack of heartburn. He pulled the bottle of Tums from his raincoat and took two.

"Why don't you come in for an exam, Pete?" Finnerty asked.

"Yeah, maybe I will, as soon as this case is over."

Finnerty laughed. "From the way you've been talking, that'll be long after you're dead from bleeding ulcers."

Languth stood, put on his coat, and said, "That's what I like about you, John, you're a real fun guy."

Finnerty's laugh was loud and long as they left the office. They crossed the autopsy room, where two young doctors were cutting up the naked body of a young female who'd been raped and killed in the National Zoological Park the night before, and went into the hall.

"Thanks, John," Languth said. "See you around."

"I'm sure you will. Take care of yourself, Pete. No sense getting sick just when you're about to retire."

Languth walked away from the doctor, heard

him start humming "Hello Dolly" as he returned to the autopsy room.

He picked up frozen dinners on his way home, put one in the toaster oven in his pullman kitchen, poured himself a full glass of scotch, and slumped into an overstuffed chair that spouted its stuffing through numerous holes in its sides and back. The small room was dark. A sofa bed occupied one wall. Old newspapers were scattered on the floor, bare except for two large and stained powder-blue bathroom rugs.

Languth slowly drained his glass and closed his eyes, drifted into a light sleep until he was awakened by the sound of the couple next door fighting. He pulled his large frame up from the chair, poured more scotch into his glass, and walked unsteadily to the kitchen, where he removed the foil-covered dinner and dumped its contents on a plate.

He returned to the combination living room/ bedroom and pushed magazines and newspapers from a small table to make room for the plate. He stood by the chair, as though unable to decide whether to sit or continue standing. He looked toward a makeshift bookcase beneath a window. On it was an eight-by-ten color photograph of a young woman, perhaps eighteen years old. She had freckles and was smiling. Languth stared at the picture, then closed his eyes as tears stung them. He drew a deep breath, swallowed hard, and dropped back into the chair, the force of his weight popping a puff of stuffing through one of the holes.

Chapter Fifteen

On Tuesday morning Gil Gardello not only confirmed to Potamos that he was to stay away from the university and its students, but told him he was off the Frolich story altogether.

"Why? Just because that phony stuffed shirt Bowen has a thing for me?"

"I don't know what you're talking about, Joe," Gardello said. "I got the word from upstairs that I have too many people on the Frolich story. They think we've gone thin on other crimes and they want you back on the beat."

" 'They.' Translated: George Alfred Bowen."

"I don't know about that, Joe. Look, I have a meeting and I'm late. Get over to State and talk to Johnson in Embassy Security. Somebody's been defacing Arab embassies."

"And?"

"Do a story."

"I already have the lead," Potamos said disgustedly. "Jewish graffiti artist ravages city."

"Not bad," said Gardello, laughing. "Call me."

Potamos wrote the graffiti story, as well as covering the mugging of an elderly woman within shouting distance of the White House, and an

MPD raid on a house in which drugs, cash, and weapons were confiscated. He knew the cops had been led there by a disgruntled member of the drug ring, but he went with the MPD version: " . . . diligent and painstaking police work over many months . . ."

By Tuesday night he was seriously considering looking for a job as a short-order cook. The appeal was obvious—keep track of the orders, don't overcook the eggs, and slap the butter on the toast before it gets cold.

"You'd really like to do that?" Roseann asked as they sat at his kitchen table after an early dinner.

"Nah," he said, grinning, "but it did cross my mind. Something else did, too."

"What's that?"

"I think I'd better make my deal with Tony Fiamma before he figures out that I'm not on the Frolich case anymore."

"What deal?"

"Ring him in, promise him credit, get ahold of whatever it is he has, including Valerie Frolich's diary."

"Do you really think he has it?"

Potamos shrugged and poured more wine into their glasses. "Worth a shot."

Her face turned pensive. He asked why.

"You'd be lying to him."

"What'a you mean? What lying?"

"You'd let him think you could do something for him when you can't. You'd ask him to share with you what he knows without . . ."

Potamos reached across the table and clutched

her hand. "Hey, Fiamma's a hustler. I used to be. It's time I suited up again."

"Joe . . ."

"What? What's the big deal?"

"You aren't even on the story anymore. What do you care?"

Potamos sat back and slung his arm over the back of his chair. He licked his lips and shook his head. "What do I care?" he said slowly and deliberately.

"That's what I said," said Roseann.

He waved his hand. "I know, I know, and maybe that's what's wrong with us, with this relationship."

"What?"

"You don't understand me at all. You can ask why I care about the Frolich story with a straight face. You can *really* wonder why I won't let go of it no matter what Bowen and Gardello and the rest of them say."

"Joe . . ."

"What?"

"Don't lay this on me, and don't blow it up into some major squabble between us. You make it sound like we're married."

"No, I don't."

"The way you said 'relationship' made it sound that way."

"It's not a relationship?"

"Of course it is, but—"

"Yeah, there is a big *but,* isn't there?"

Blackburn got up and scrubbed the pan in which he'd cooked breaded veal. She glanced back at Potamos, who was still slouched in the chair, head drooping forward, fingers rolling over the tabletop. She started on the broccoli pot and said quietly, "Joe, I don't want to marry you."

"Huh? What did you say?"

"I said I don't want to get married."

"Jesus." He came to her at the sink. "I didn't think I proposed."

"You will," she said, looking up at him.

"I will?"

"Yes, I can feel it."

He put his arms over her shoulder and said good-naturedly, "Not me, Roseann. I'm a two-time loser."

"And you'd happily take a shot at three."

"You're crazy."

She started to say it, decided not to.

"Hey, Blackie, I have to make a call. I'll finish the cleanup."

"Thanks. Who are you calling?"

"Tony Fiamma."

"Oh. I wish you wouldn't."

"Trust me." He kissed her cheek, and his hand found a breast through the thin fabric of her blouse. "Don't run away," he said.

He tried the number he'd originally been given by Fiamma, his girlfriend's apartment. She answered; Fiamma was there.

"Let's get together," Potamos said.

"Yeah? Why?"

"I think we can work together."

Fiamma's silence said a lot. Potamos knew he was pleased but had to play the hustler's game. "We'll do it the way I want?"

"Yeah, Tony, we'll do it the way you want."

More silence, the faint sound of a contented sigh. "How do you want to start?"

"A meeting."

"Now?"

Potamos glanced over at Roseann seated at the table, long, slender legs crossed, a wisp of hair hanging over her forehead. "Ah, not now, Tony. How about eight? You ever go to Martin's?"

"Martin's? Oh, yeah, the bar. Yeah, I've been there."

"Good, and bring that diary."

"Let's talk first," Fiamma said.

Street-wise, Potamos thought. He said, "Look, all kinds of things are about to pop with the Frolich case. I don't have time to play games, Tony."

Fiamma reluctantly agreed, then said, "I haven't seen any stories by you lately."

Potamos hoped his casual laugh would help dispel what thoughts Fiamma might have. He said through it, "They put me on a couple of rush things, but we now have a special unit for Valerie. We want to break the case, Tony, before the MPD does. Nice if you were part of it."

The silence was back to positive. "I'll see you at Martin's."

"Yup. Listen, one other thing. Don't mention any of this to Bowen. Okay?"

"Yeah, I wouldn't anyway."

"Good."

Minutes later, as Potamos and Blackburn hurriedly undressed, she again expressed her objections to the way he was playing Fiamma along. He responded, "Do I tell you how to play a song?"

She giggled. "Of course not. You don't know how."

"So, since when do you know how to deal with murder?"

"A song is different. Murder is . . . well, it's *people*."

"That's right, and I know people. You know music."

She sighed. "All right, Joe, but I still don't think it's nice to lie to a college student. Besides, if you keep pursuing this after your boss told you not to, you're going to end up in big trouble."

"Bigger than that, my dear. Probably fired."

"And then what do you do?"

"Write a book. But first . . ." He kissed her belly and ran his hand down, and up, and down, and up her leg.

"You know what?" she said as she turned to face him.

"What?"

"That's what's wonderful about sex. Once you're started, the rest of the world goes away."

"That's right," he said, nuzzling her neck. "It's like an oasis, an hour of freedom."

She laughed. "Joe . . ."

"What?"

"An *hour*? I'm due on stage in half an hour."

Chapter Sixteen

Potamos wedged himself between other customers at the bar in Blues Alley and ordered a beer. Served, he turned, leaned back, and listened to Roseann and three black musicians weave their way through an up-tempo version of "All the Things You Are."

She seemed so small and delicate in the midst of the three big men sharing the bandstand with her, but her playing certainly wasn't frail. Potamos listened and watched with keen interest and appreciation. He didn't understand how the four of them could blend together without having rehearsed, each improvising against the underlying chord structure of the song, the bassist nimbly providing a smooth, walking bass line beneath the vigorous, flowing lines of the tenor saxophonist, the drummer creating a sheet of sound on multiple cymbals, the drumstick in his left hand and the bass-drum pedal beneath his right foot injecting unexpected punctuations, Roseann feeding a series of complex chords to everyone, her head bowed over the keyboard, long fingers probing the rich musical colors available to her. When it was time for her solo, she wove a series of choruses, each building in intensity until she'd exhausted her ideas of the moment. The customers applauded her enthusiastically, which made Potamos feel good. The quartet extended the tune's ending until it just faded away, the overtones of their instruments drifting into space along with the cigarette smoke.

"You came," Blackburn said once she'd navigated customers who wanted to compliment her and reached Potamos at the bar.

"Yeah. You were great, really great."

"Thank you. I become very inspired playing with musicians like them."

"I can understand that. They're good, too."

She smiled. "Feel like a walk?" she asked. "The smoke gets to me."

"Sure."

She told the bartender they'd be back and they left the club, went down the narrow alley from which the club drew its name, and down Wisconsin toward the C & O Canal. The night was balmy and humid, a precursor of the long, sticky Washington summer that wasn't far away. They held hands, said nothing to each other until crossing the canal and standing alone on the far side.

"I met Fiamma. He gave me a portion of Valerie Frolich's diary," Potamos said.

"Then he *did* have it."

"Yeah, he has it. How and why, I don't know, but he has it. He'd only give me selected pages. He's shrewd and tough, Roseann. He wants his name on a story before he'll share the rest with me."

She sighed and looked toward the Potomac. "You can't blame him, Joe."

"Of course not. Roseann, some of what he gave me is dynamite."

She faced him. He put his hands on her arms and felt a tremble in her body. "Cold?" he said.

"No. Concerned."

"About the diary? Why?"

"Not just the diary, Joe, about all of it. It involves murder."

"I know, but why should that scare you?"

"Because I'm . . . because I'm involved with you."

He grunted and looked down at the ground. "Are you saying you don't want to be involved with me anymore?"

"Oh, Joe, I don't know what I mean. I've spent my life with music. That's all I know. It's a beautiful way to live, making music, maybe not profitable, but satisfying, and simple—I play, I get paid. The people I spend my time with are happy because of the music. They laugh and dance. When I play in places like the Four Seasons, I see them touched by a song. Maybe they remember something pleasant from the past, or a song starts them thinking a new way. The right music sets a romantic mood for couples, or picks up the spirits of somebody who's blue about something. When I work with musicians like tonight, we share a wonderful bond that few people can understand. Like I said, Joe, it's beautiful and simple."

"And I complicate it."

"Not you, Joe, but what you do for a living, this whole Valerie Frolich thing. I don't understand why you want her diary. Give it to the police. They're the ones responsible for it, not you."

"Not true, Roseann. My job is a lot like theirs. I'm supposed to dig until I find something interesting for a story. That's my training and that's my job. Having the diary means I'll be able to scoop everybody, be first, maybe even be the one responsible for solving the murder. That's important to me."

"I know, and it isn't to me. I wish it were."

"You do? Why?"

"Then maybe we could . . . I should get back. I like to talk over a set ahead of time."

"Okay, but can't we see each other?"

"I'll be very late, Joe. I'll probably go out with the band after, get something to eat, rehash the night. We don't get many chances to play top places like Blues Alley."

Potamos had another beer and stayed through the next set. He told Roseann at intermission that he was going home, and asked her to call him the minute she got in. He knew the moment he said it that it set up, for her, that feeling of having to account, so he added, "Only if you feel like it. If you don't, we can talk tomorrow."

"I'll call," she said, kissing him gently on the lips. "And I do want to hear about the diary. I'm sorry. I can be very selfish sometimes."

He grinned and kissed her again. "You play great. I envy you."

His envy multiplied as the night progressed, especially when he thought about the idea of a simple life. He'd contemplated that often, thought about how much he wanted one, but always ended up asking himself why, if he wanted it so bad, he didn't go after it. He came to the reluctant conclusion that something inside him craved chaos and living on the brink. If not, why two divorces? Why the turmoil in his career? Why was he in an awkward, frustrating position with George Bowen again? You're a professional screw-up, he told himself. Some errant gene or unresolved argument with his father. Maybe a shrink would help . . . Nah—probably make things worse and charge handsomely for the privilege.

His phone rang at one o'clock. He hoped it was Roseann calling from the club. It wasn't. Tony Fiamma said, "What'd you think?"

"I'm . . . I haven't finished," Potamos lied. He'd read the selected pages of Valerie Frolich's diary three times, and was on the fourth.

"Remember, no copies," Fiamma said, reading Potamos's mind. He intended to photocopy the pages first thing in the morning, maybe even look for an all-night drugstore with a copying machine.

"Don't worry about it," Potamos said. "Look, call me tomorrow," he added, thinking of Gil Gardello.

"Let's just meet," said Fiamma.

"I have a crazy day, Tony. Call me here tomorrow night."

"Hey, you're not playing games with me, are you?"

"You feel that way, hook up with somebody

else." Potamos said it with as hard an edge as he could muster.

"I didn't mean anything by it, but that diary . . ."

"Yeah, yeah, I know, it's your ticket to stardom. I'll tell you this, Tony, for me to make a decision, I'm going to have to see more."

"More? Why?"

"So far I really haven't seen much I can use."

"You're nuts. What about the Bowen stuff?"

Potamos didn't want to let on that he'd read everything, so he said, "I didn't get to that yet."

"You read slow."

"And you've got a big mouth. Tomorrow, call me tomorrow."

A dejected Fiamma agreed and hung up.

Potamos dozed off in a chair at three. He was convinced he wouldn't hear from Roseann, but the jarring ring of the phone at 3:30 proved him wrong. "Where are you?" he asked sleepily.

"Home."

"You want to come over?"

She hesitated.

"I can come there," he said.

"If you wouldn't mind," she said. "I'm beat."

He arrived a little after four. She'd made coffee and had heated a tray of frozen Danish pastries. They sat in her kitchen. Roseann could see that he was excited. "The diary?" she guessed.

He smirked and handed her the pages Fiamma had given him. She held them like a teenage boy holds an infant, tentatively and with trepidation. "Go ahead," he said, "read."

She went to the living room and settled on the

couch beneath the single light of a floor lamp. Potamos stayed in the kitchen for a half-hour sipping his coffee and staring out a small window.

"Joe," she called.

He went to the living room and sat beside her.

"She mentions George Bowen," she said.

"Yeah."

"The others—do you know any of them?"

"Yeah. Steve McCarty's one of the seminar students. Walter Nebel. The other names don't register with me."

She handed him the pages and his eyes focused on a section describing a weekend spent in an inn in Leesburg with McCarty. Most of Valerie's entries were poetic responses to what she'd seen and done that weekend. There was a long discourse on how she felt about McCarty, some of it positive, much of it cruelly negative. She alluded to their lovemaking in a circumspect way, nothing graphic, an indication of gratification one night, disappointment another.

The section devoted to Walter Nebel was based upon a weekend at the same Leesburg inn. It was less personal than the McCarty pages, dwelling more on vast philosophic and intellectual differences between her and Nebel. He obviously was an ambitious young man, a climber impressed with wealth and position, at least from Valerie's perspective. There was a strong hint in her writing that she felt Nebel's interest in her had more to do with her father's position than with any attraction she exuded. She'd confronted him about it that weekend, and they'd fought. She'd written:

The hoop of power is dangled before the callous, ambitious young Walter and he leaps through it, again and again, always hoping to please his master, to be rewarded with cold water and biscuits and, if he jumps enough, happiness ever after as the bureaucratic dog seeking pats on the head and fur booties for his feet. No, just young and dumb and without spine. Unfortunate. He is handsome. A shame his coal-miner beginnings didn't stay with him. Would be an interesting package if they had.

Potamos flipped through more pages, saying as he did, "I keep thinking about Leesburg. Why Leesburg?"

"Because it's a beautiful place for a weekend with a lover," Blackburn said. "I know the inn. I've played it. It's lovely, very quaint and old-fashioned."

"Yeah, I know what you're saying, but that's where Marshall Jenkins has his retreat. So does LaRouche, another right-winger. He owns half the town."

"So? What does Marshall Jenkins have to do with this diary? You can go to an inn there and not have anything to do with Jenkins and La-Rouche or anyone else."

"You're right, but it keeps crossing my mind, that's all. Senator Frolich and Jenkins being so close, and Bowen and Frolich's kid sneaking off for trysts there. Silly, I guess." He found another page and handed it to her. "This is the Bowen stuff. You read it?"

"Yes."

"What do you think?"

She shrugged. "Looks like they had an affair. That's what I get from it."

"What else could you take from it?"

"Well, it could be the sexual fantasies of a young, impressionable woman."

"No way," Potamos said, again reading what Valerie had written:

> . . . the older man, the excitement of it, the stuff sexual clichés are made of—there she is, the young, sexually yearning student, wide-eyed herself but seeing a bigger, more interesting world through his eyes, through his wisdom, through his nurturing and mentoring, so skilled and gentle compared to the too-anxious young men trying to prove they are men—the older man, the professor (professor, no less!), sinfully handsome, body lean and without the folds expected in men his age—and the mind, bursting through in such a physical way and enhancing the sexuality—the professor and the student—Valerie Frolich, poor little rich girl, and the erudite, romantic professor, George Alfred Bowen—a soap opera—so what????—why limit one's sexual experiences only to peers?—so silly and confining and absolutely sophomoric—what's to be learned from it—and that's everything, isn't it, to learn, to keep learning?

"She doesn't say she was intimate with him," Roseann said. "It could be just a sexual daydream, sitting in class and writing a . . . a soap opera."

"Can't be," Potamos said.

"Okay," Roseann said, tucking her bare feet underneath her and adjusting her crimson robe over her breasts, "let's say they did have an affair. What does it mean? Can you write about that?"

"No," Potamos said, "and that's what's wrong with these pages. Fiamma gave me just enough to whet my appetite. There's nothing here except confirmation that she had affairs with Steve McCarty and Walter Nebel. McCarty denied it. Why?"

"Maybe because he's afraid it will involve him. I can understand that, Joe. He dated her, didn't kill her, and can do without becoming a suspect just because he took her away for a weekend."

"And Nebel takes off. Why'd he do that?"

"Same reason, I suppose."

"And Bowen slept with her."

"Maybe."

"Likely."

"Possible."

"Probable."

"Whatever."

Potamos crawled into bed while Roseann practiced a batch of new tunes in the living room. He closed his eyes and allowed the music to drift into his consciousness. There was something very special about being there as she created music. He considered it a privilege and wanted to tell her that, but at the same time didn't want to disturb her.

The phone jarred his reverie. Roseann answered and shook him totally awake. "It's Tony Fiamma."

Potamos slowly got up and stretched, yawned, and picked up the receiver by the bed.

"What's going on, man?" Fiamma said.

"Huh?"

"Somebody broke into my room, man. I just came back and the place is a mess."

Potamos was almost afraid to ask. "The diary?"

"No, I had it with me."

Potamos's sigh was audible across the room. "They take anything, Tony?"

"No, just turned everything upside down. I don't like it. No, sir, I sure don't like it. You know nothing about it, huh?"

"What are you getting at, Tony, that I'd break into your room to find the rest of the diary?"

"I don't know, but somebody sure as hell did. I have to see you."

"Yeah, that's probably a good idea. Bring the diary and we'll get it copied."

"And what, you take a copy?"

"Sure, why not? We're working together, aren't we?"

"I wonder."

"Well, just keep wondering, Tony. I'm your best shot. Of course, you can go to the police and be a good citizen."

Fiamma laughed. "What'll I get for that, lunch with some politician and a plaque?"

Potamos laughed, too. "There you go being greedy again. A *plaque?* Stick with me. Want breakfast?"

"Yeah. What time is it?"

"Six-thirty. Meet you at eight?"

"Where?"

"The Florida Avenue Grill. You know it?"

"Sure, that's the diner where the cabbies hang out."

"You got it. Eight."

Before leaving Roseann's apartment, Potamos handed her the diary pages and asked her to hide them somewhere.

"Joe, I'd—"

"I'll pick them up tonight. I just don't want them with me when I see Fiamma. Okay?"

"Okay." She placed them beneath sheet music in her piano bench.

"Thanks," he said.

"Take care, huh?"

"Sure. Get some sleep. Hey, what are we doing tonight?"

"I'm working. The Four Seasons."

"Maybe I'll stop in. After?"

"I think I need a couple of quiet nights alone, Joe. Okay?"

"Sure. Me too. I have to go out to see the kids this weekend, probably Saturday. Save me some time Sunday."

Chapter Seventeen

"Here's the APB that went out on Walter Nebel." The officer from Communications handed it to Languth. "And here's a background on Nebel."

Languth sat back and skimmed the pages, then picked up a similar background check on Samuel Maruca. Both Nebel and Maruca were from Pennsylvania—Nebel from Pittsburgh, Maruca from New Castle, about fifty miles north. Both fathers worked in the mines. Maruca had been a star high-school athlete, excelling in football and wrestling. Nebel had been more of a student, but had been a state all-star in track, and had played on the basketball team. Both students were on scholarships at Georgetown University. Neither had ever been in trouble with the law. Family means in both cases were meager.

He scanned a list of calls to be returned, picked up the phone, and dialed an extension within headquarters. "Detective lounge," a voice said.

"This is Languth. Morrissey there?"

"Yeah, hold on."

"Peter?"

"Yeah. How'd it go?"

"I got back a half-hour ago. He went to the

Florida Avenue Grill and met a male Caucasian, about twenty, dark complexion, medium height, dressed in jeans and a torn red sweater."

"And?"

"They sat in a booth and had breakfast. The guy he met gave him a large manila envelope. Potamos looked at its contents, replaced them in the envelope, and they went to the parking lot."

"Potamos keep the envelope?"

"Yeah. They got in separate cars and split."

"What about last night?"

"Yeah, let's see. Okay, I picked him up at his condo. He went to Blues Alley, had a beer at the bar, then left with the piano player, a Caucasian female named . . . ah, Roseann Blackburn. They took a walk down by the canal, talked for approximately ten minutes, then returned to the club. She played another set while Potamos split, returning directly to his apartment. He took an envelope from the trunk of his car before entering the building."

"A different envelope?"

"Sure, this was before he had breakfast at the Florida. He left his apartment at approximately three-thirty A.M. and drove to a small building on upper Wisconsin, near the cathedral, Glover Park, I guess. I checked the doorbells . . . there's an R. Blackburn living there. He left there at approximately seven-thirty and went to the Florida."

"Okay, Sean," Languth said. "I need somebody on him tonight, too."

"I'll catch it, I guess."

"Hey, Sean, what about the envelope?"

"Which one?"

"The one he took from his trunk last night. He have it with him when he went to Glover Park?"

"He carried something, but I'm not sure it was the same envelope."

"He come out of there with it this morning?"

"Not sure, Pete. I don't think he was carrying anything when he went into the diner."

"Tell whoever's on tonight to look out for envelopes. Okay?"

"Yup."

Languth had been making notes while Morrissey recounted Potamos's movements of the night before. One of them was "Met Anthony Fiamma at Florida Avenue Grill."

He dialed a number and allowed it to ring a long time. Finally, a male voice answered.

"This is Languth. You called?"

"Yeah. I wondered when I get paid."

"I'll stop by. You working tonight?"

"Yeah."

"Maybe tonight."

"Good. It was helpful?"

"Yeah. Take it easy."

He hung up on the young waiter from Martin's Tavern, who was one of many waiters around town on retainer to the MPD. All they had to do was report any unusual happenings, or the presence of people in their restaurants who might be of interest to the police. Their input, added to the information gathered from bugs on selected pay phones, considerably expanded the knowledge gained from direct police work.

Establishing the system hadn't been easy. There

had been considerable opposition within the MPD's hierarchy to this spying on random citizens who happened to frequent the wrong restaurant at the wrong time, or who used the wrong pay phone. Advocates of it had used the New York City experience—where entire banks of pay phones in such major terminals as Pennsylvania Station were hooked into a communications center deep in the terminal's sublevels—to help them make their case. Eventually, with support from the FBI and even the CIA, the system was put in place.

Little of importance had come out of it, mostly recordings of homosexual liaisons being arranged, conversations about politics that were incorporated into files on selected individuals, only occasionally a discussion of a crime to be committed that gave the police a leg up on the criminals. When a homosexual identified himself or herself during a call, and that person worked for the government, the information was shared with the FBI and the CIA. One day, it was reasoned, the network would uncover the makings of a major crime or terrorist plot, and that would justify everything. In the meantime, the huge reels of recording tape rolled on, and the waiters and waitresses kept their eyes open for someone from the most-wanted list, and their ears open for a dinner-table crime conference.

Languth's final call before lunch was to Detroit. The conversation was brief, ending with Languth saying "And that's what I pay you for, goddamn it. Just keep after it. I don't care if it takes twenty years."

Chapter Eighteen

John Frolich's Senate limousine glided along the Baltimore–Washington Parkway at eighty miles an hour until slowing down to take the Fort Meade exit. Frolich, who'd been studying papers in the rear, looked through tinted glass at the top of the nine-story concrete National Security Agency Building.

A team of security guards at the gate confirmed Frolich's identity, searched the trunk and interior of the limo, handed the driver a pass, and directed him to an entrance at the rear of the building where two young men in dark suits were waiting. "I'll be an hour," Frolich told his driver as he followed the men past more guards and into the building. Another guard, seated behind a console, pressed a button and what had appeared to be a stainless-steel wall slid open, exposing a long corridor with dark blue carpeting. The walls were white and bare.

There was no conversation as Frolich and the men walked the length of the hall and stopped in front of an elevator with blue doors. The doors opened and the men stepped aside for Frolich to enter. "They're upstairs, senator," one of them said.

There were no buttons to push and Frolich

waited until the elevator had completed its swift journey to the ninth floor. The doors opened and a tall, erect, craggy-faced air-force general extended his hand. "Senator, good to see you again," he said.

"Same here, general," Frolich said.

"Come on, they're inside."

They went into a large conference room. Beige drapes covered every wall. Behind the drapes were lights that gave the impression of sunshine, but Frolich knew there were no windows in the room. Its walls were thick and constructed of special materials designed to keep all sound within it, even if powerful microphones were directed at it from distant exterior points. The center of the room was taken up by a large, oval walnut table. Blank yellow legal pads, empty glasses, sharpened pencils, and a folder were neatly placed in front of each chair. A leather-covered carafe held chilled water. Recessed fixtures directed pools of light down to the table.

The moment Frolich followed the general into the room, two uniformed men appeared and closed the door behind them. Frolich looked across the room at the other two people in it and said, "Gentlemen."

One of the men crossed the room with his characteristic energy and shook Frolich's hand. Wade Poesser was the president's national-security adviser. He was short and stocky and fond of vested suits that displayed his Harvard Phi Beta Kappa key and chain. He'd never struck Frolich as being the Harvard type, not with his thick southern accent and tendency to slip into folksy metaphors. He'd quickly acquired a reputation for level-headed thinking, cordiality, and for being closer to the president than almost any other national-security adviser in recent memory.

"How you holdin' up, John?" Poesser asked.

"All right, Wade, considering."

The other man across the room hadn't made a move toward Frolich, so Frolich nodded and said, "Hello Geof."

Geof Krindler returned the greeting. He was much taller than Frolich, wire-thin and with bushy white hair that appeared to have been shaped into an Afro. A crisp tan bush jacket covered a brown silk turtleneck. A medal given him at an international dinner for intelligence experts lay against his chest on the end of a gold chain. Krindler, an acknowledged expert in intelligence gathering and counterintelligence, was an American but at home in countries around the world. He'd never been an employee of any U.S. intelligence agency but had been supplying advice on a contract basis during the past three administrations, including the one in power. He was smug, aloof, unabashedly egotistical, and openly scornful of elected officials. He especially disliked Senator John Frolich and didn't try to disguise it.

"Senator," Krindler said, allowing Frolich to come to him and offer his hand. "Sorry about the tragedy in your family." He had a trace of a British accent.

"Thank you, Geof. I'm afraid that old saying about life being what happens when you're making other plans is true."

"Would anyone like something before we begin?" the general asked. His name was Mike

Mulchinski, much decorated, a veteran of the NATO command in Europe, now air-force liaison to the National Security Agency.

"I wouldn't mind," Frolich said. "Scotch, water."

Poesser ordered bourbon. The others declined alcohol; Krindler asked for fresh-squeezed orange juice.

Mulchinski opened a small door on one wall, removed a telephone, and placed the order. It arrived within minutes from a kitchen down the hall.

"Good health," Poesser said as he took a seat at the table. The others joined him.

"Well," Krindler said, slowly moving his eyes from person to person, "does anyone have any brilliant ideas about how to proceed?" He came to rest on Frolich.

Mulchinski said in a raspy voice, "I don't see why all this delay is necessary. Hell, we're talking about the security of this country. Allowing a small group of private citizens to dictate security policy is asinine."

"It isn't that, Mike," Poesser said, "it's a question of keeping this project secret. The president considers this crucial. The Soviets must not learn of it."

Krindler, who'd folded himself back into his chair, said, "I agree with the general. The Russians have taken advantage of the land our Senate and House saw fit to give them and are using every conceivable electronic device to spy on us. That's no secret. The public is aware of it and doesn't like it and wants us to do something. As far as I'm concerned, we should move openly and quickly, finish construction and get our gear in place."

Poesser sighed and, with a lilting deliberation,

his southern heritage adding an aura of back-
woods wisdom to his words, said, "There are
far greater considerations here than pleasing the
public. Wouldn't you agree, senator?"

Frolich nodded. "Absolutely." He looked at
Krindler. "We're currently in the midst of extremely delicate negotiations with the Russians
on a variety of issues, including further talks on
arms reductions. The president is considering a
summit in the fall. No, the approach here can't be
to barge ahead. It has to be handled with delicacy
and restraint."

Mulchinski said, "And in the meantime they
train their microphones on every official building in Washington, including the White House
and the Pentagon. They keep right on raising hell
with our transmissions, and we sit like helpless
wimps in our own country, our own nation's capital. Sorry, senator, but this thing has gotten out of
hand."

"It's being worked on," Frolich said.

"The president will want specifics here," said
Poesser.

Frolich hesitated. "Certain steps are being taken
that should turn things around very soon. I'm
sorry, but I really can't be more specific than that.
I don't think the president would care to know the
details."

"A timetable?" Mulchinski asked.

A shrug from Frolich. "A month at the most,
two weeks at the least." He checked his watch.
"I don't think we'll have need to meet again," he
said. "Thank you. Each of you can report back to
your superiors that the situation is well in hand."

Frolich started to get up, but Krindler stopped him with, "Senator, one more thing."

"Yes?"

"You and Mr. Poesser claim we have to go slowly in order to keep the project secret, but there have already been serious threats to that secrecy."

"I don't think we have to get into that now," Poesser said, getting up and placing his hand on Frolich's shoulder.

"I think we do," Krindler said, his avian face cold and challenging.

"What's your point?" Frolich asked, meeting Krindler's eyes across the table.

"That unless we've taken care of every possible source of leaks, we should stop the charade and just do it!"

"Continue."

"You say we should tell our superiors that all is well. I can't do that."

"Why not?" Poesser asked.

"Because it isn't, and I think the senator knows what I mean."

Frolich laughed and shook his head. "No, Geof, the senator doesn't know what you mean, although he can guess, and what he comes up with makes the senator very angry."

Without another word, Frolich left the table and went to the hall, followed closely by Poesser, who again put a hand on his shoulder. "Don't let him get to you, John. You know those contract CIA types, little boys playing cops and robbers, right down to his bush jacket and medal." He laughed. "Damn, he must think he's back in Angola riling up the natives for revolt. Ignore him and do what you said you would, get this project back on track. I intend to tell the president that with John Frolich at the helm, there's not a damn thing to fret about. He believes in you, you know, John. He's damned pleased to have John Frolich watching over national security up on the Hill. Just ignore the great white hunter in there."

The elevator arrived as Frolich said, "I wish I could, but he's made that impossible. Well, it doesn't matter, Wade. My best to the president, and thanks for the vote of confidence."

"John?"

"Yes?"

"How's Marshall Jenkins?"

"Fine. He's taking care of his responsibilities in this quite nicely."

Frolich started to step into the elevator, but Poesser grabbed his arm. "John, can *he* be trusted?"

It was an incredulous laugh. "Of course. Do you think we would have involved him if he couldn't be?"

"I know, I know, but the president . . . well, you do know that Jenkins's wife is German."

Frolich stared at him.

"Not that that's of terrible import, but in something as sensitive as this, you consider every aspect. At least, a prudent man should."

"There's no problem with Marshall or his wife, Wade."

"That's good to hear. She's quite a woman, evidently. Gets around. Beautiful. He's a lucky man. *Any* man who gets close to her is lucky, I suppose."

"Goodbye, Wade. We'll be in touch."

Chapter Nineteen

The Press Club was building to its usual Friday peak when Potamos walked in for lunch. The card games were in progress, the serious drinkers (as opposed to the merely heavy drinkers) had staked out their spots at the bar. In general, TGIF looseness was in full swing and would continue late into the evening.

Potamos found room at the bar and ordered a double scotch with a splash of soda. His fatigue began to lift as he tuned in to conversations around him and enjoyed the taste of the scotch and the cool, pleasant sensation in his throat. His throat had been scratchy. His diagnosis: not enough sleep and too much talk. Gardello had him on a succession of stories, each of which demanded extensive interviewing. He missed Roseann, was tempted a hundred times to stop in where she was appearing, or to call her. "Admirable," he told himself each time he resisted the temptation. "Don't upset her, don't push." Even though pushing her was very much on his mind. He was crazy about her. She was right—he'd take the dive again anytime he thought there was a possibility of it with her.

A round little man with gray fringe over his ears, a drooping gray moustache, and half-glasses on the tip of his nose waved from the far end of the bar for Potamos to join him. Potamos returned the greeting and looked away. "Hey, Joe, come here," the man called.

Potamos took his glass and headed for where Marvin Goldson sat. Goldson was a regular at the club, especially on Friday, the day after his weekly newspaper, the *Georgetown Eye*, was published. The *Eye* had carved a niche in Washington journalism since Goldson took it over six years ago after having spent twenty years as a rewrite man in UPI's Washington bureau. Until that time it had been nothing more than a conduit for Georgetown social notes, weddings, parties, and press releases from area businesses. Goldson had gradually introduced real news to its pages, including investigative pieces. Owning a newspaper had been Goldson's lifelong dream, and he carried his title of owner and publisher with a certain flair. Owning *Time* magazine wouldn't have given him as much satisfaction.

"How're you, Marv?" Potamos asked, slipping onto a stool just vacated by a young TV reporter who'd recently joined the club.

"Splendid, Joseph," Goldson said, laughing and slapping Potamos on the back. "Couldn't be better. You?"

"I could be better, but all things considered, I could be worse. I got up this morning, took a breath, and everything worked. Can't ask for more than that."

"Indeed not," said Goldson. "Jose, fill up my friend here," he told the bartender. Potamos started to protest, then decided why not? It was Friday. It'd been a lousy week. He deserved it.

"So, Joseph, what's new in big-time journalism?"

Potamos joined his laughter. "Big-time? You're big-time, Marv. You *own* the thing."

Goldson didn't argue. He ordered another beer and devoured a shrimp. "Want one, Joe?" Potamos ate a shrimp. Goldson told him a couple of new ethnic jokes and asked how Potamos's buddy, George Bowen, was.

"He's terrific, tip-top. And don't say anything bad about my buddy. We're like family, blood brothers."

"Oh, of course, I forgot. He'll be best man at your next wedding. Speaking of that, Joseph, how goes it on the romantic front?"

"Good. I'm in love."

"Anyone I know? A reporter?"

"A plumber."

"A . . . ah, always the sense of humor. Well, I wish you and your bride every happiness."

"Thanks. You'll be invited."

"I'll send a photographer." Goldson turned serious. "What's new with the Frolich story, Joe?"

"You stop reading?"

"If the only thing new is in the house that Graham built, there's nothing new."

"You got it, Marv. I'm off it."

"So I heard. George Alfred did it again to you, huh?"

"Where the hell did you hear that?"

"Right here, at the communications center. Sorry. What did you do this time, hide his favorite bow tie?"

"Nothing that serious." Potamos told him a little bit about the confrontation with Bowen.

When he was through, Goldson ordered another beer, turned to Potamos, and said in hushed tones, "Joe, when the *Eye* comes out next week, the *Post* will consider getting into another business, like hot dogs or tourist souvenirs."

"Why?"

Goldson was even more conspiratorial now. He glanced around the room, leaned closer, and said, "I was given a story yesterday by a student from Georgetown U. that'll knock the socks off the Ben Bradlees and Katharine Grahams of this town."

"Yeah? What's it about?" The minute Potamos asked it, he had the sinking, nauseous feeling that he knew the answer. Before he had a chance to confirm it, Goldson did it for him by saying, "The only reason I'm telling you, Joe, is that this kid says he knows you, has been working with you."

"Tony."

"That's right," Goldson said. "Tony Fiamma. At first I wondered about the kid, with all his tough-guy talk, but when he showed me what he had, I damn near fell over. He's for real."

"Yeah?" His brain was filled with a Greek chorus of "Why? Why? Why? Why? Why?" that reverberated off every bone, every cell. Fiamma hadn't given him the complete diary at breakfast at the Florida Avenue Grill, just a few more selected pages. Potamos had gotten angry at the table but decided to play along. Fiamma had told him that he still wanted proof that Potamos intended to ring him in on any by-lines, and Potamos promised him that was in the works. When he again asked for the rest of the diary, Fiamma had said, "Hey, man, this is a one-way street. Let's make it two-way. I've got other things I can do with this thing."

Other things! The *Georgetown Eye.* Dummy!

Potamos motioned for Jose to refill his glass and to buy Goldson a beer. When he'd managed to shake off his initial shock, he asked, "What's the story about, Marv?"

"Scandal, Joseph, my boy, big scandal in Scandaltown."

"Scandal? The Frolich case?"

"No, but it does involve that bastion of moral decency, that warrior standing tall against the Communist threat, the Honorable John Frolich."

"It's . . . not about his daughter's murder?"

"I wish it were. No, forget that. From a purely investigative standpoint, this is bigger stuff, Joe— spies and foreign governments and James Bond space-age spooks and the rest."

"Marv," Potamos said.

"What?"

"Where would a college journalism student come up with that kind of material?"

Goldson laughed. "You should know, Joe. You taught him."

"I didn't teach him anything."

"He says you did, along with your close friend

George Alfred. Fiamma says you've been showing him the ropes of investigative journalism. In
fact, Joe, he said you were working together on the
Frolich murder."

"He did? He's a dumb kid with a big mouth."

"Hey, don't knock it, Joe. Come on, share with
Uncle Marv. I shared with you. What have you got
on it?"

"Nothing. Bowen pulled me from the story, remember?"

"Big deal. You have the book."

Potamos looked around the bar as though to
say to everyone, "Is nothing private here?" He
said to Goldson, "I'm not doing a book."

A slap on the back. "That's what I love about
you, Joe, your ingrained sense of modesty. A
Greek trait? They brought you up good."

"Jesus."

"How about lunch? You buy and I'll tell you
more about next week's blockbuster by your student."

"I got a better idea, Marv."

"Which is?"

"You buy and tell me about next week's blockbuster."

"Another Greek trait, bartering. Born traders."

"Big in diners, too. Come on, I'm hungry and
panting to hear what my protégé, Mr. Anthony
Fiamma, has come up with."

Chapter Twenty

"I thought Monet was the father of Impressionism," George Bowen said to Julia Amster as they stood before Edouard Manet's controversial masterpiece *Dejeuner sur l'Herbe,* whose nude young woman among a group of well-clad men had caused a scandal in nineteenth-century France.

"It depends on your interpretation," Amster said, stepping back to gain a better perspective. "Spiritual leader, perhaps. That's what the critics hung around his neck. Frankly, I think Manet was the father of the movement, although Pissarro, God knows, was the oldest and most outspoken. Or Degas. He dominated the round table at that café in the Grand Rue des Batignolles."

Bowen grunted and moved on to Monet's vision of Le Havre: *Impression—Sunset,* from which the term *impressionism* derived. Amster joined him. "It's lovely."

The French ambassador to the United States and his wife came to their side. "You like Monet, Mr. Bowen?" the ambassador asked.

"Yes, very much," Bowen replied. "Mrs. Ambassador," he said, taking the French woman's hand.

They strolled together through more of the exhibition. They'd had cocktails among the soaring marble pillars of the gallery's famed rotunda, and a selected number would move on to the newly completed French chancellery on Reservoir Road, where chefs were busy preparing a buffet of smoked French salmon, pâtés, quiches, lobster and crab in rich cream sauces, and multitiered displays of pastry that had arrived that afternoon from Paris on Air France.

Bowen and Amster drifted in opposite directions. It wasn't accidental; they'd driven to the National Gallery in Bowen's new Mercedes, and along with the rich smell of leather, the car had contained a distinct odor of tension. It had started that afternoon when Amster called him at home from her gallery to confirm their plans for the evening. She knew the moment he came on the line that she'd called at an inopportune time. That was confirmed by a youthful female giggle in the background and by the defensiveness in Bowen's voice. She'd hung up angrily.

Later, when she mentioned the call on their way to the exhibition, he responded with characteristic arrogance and nastiness. They hadn't said another word to each other until the paintings on the gallery walls prompted them.

Amster chatted amiably with friends from the art world, but she couldn't shake her feelings about what happened that afternoon. Usually such incidents didn't matter—*truly* didn't matter—to her. She was well aware of Bowen's love life outside of their relationship, but because it seldom was played out overtly, it seemed far removed from what was important in her life. But then there were those moments, like today, when the reality of his making love with pretty young women slashed through her defenses, leaving a gaping hole in the middle of her stomach that often took days to heal. The giggle. Walking in unannounced another time to find him in bed with a waitress who'd served them the night before. Those were the times it hurt, like this night, the feelings covered by a scab of proper behavior but festering deep beneath the skin.

She saw him across the room talking to a knot of people, one of whom was an attractive young woman with long red hair and a bright smile. She was flirting with Bowen, and he with her. Amster knew it as sure as if they'd hung signs on each other.

"Julia." Elsa Jenkins had come up beside her. "You look beautiful," Jenkins said.

"Thank you. You always do."

Jenkins didn't argue. She said, "You're going on to the embassy, I assume."

"Yes, we . . ." She saw Bowen crossing the room with the redhead. They paused to look at a painting, then disappeared behind a green marble column. "I'm not sure," Amster said. "It's been a busy week. I'm exhausted."

"Sorry," said Jenkins. "I'll be there. Marshall is in New York for the weekend on business. He'll be back Sunday morning. We leave for Rome Sunday night."

"How nice."

"Just six days. Well, good to see you."

"Yes, Elsa, good to see you."

Amster went to an area in which smoking was permitted and lit a cigarette. It was quiet there. She needed quiet, thought of a song she'd heard on the radio that had the line "Turn up the quiet." It suddenly occurred to her that if she didn't act quickly, she would cry, and that would be intolerable. She snubbed out the cigarette in a sand-filled urn, drew a series of deep breaths, and returned to the exhibition. Bowen was now talking with TV newsman Peter Jennings. Bowen saw her, quickly said goodbye to Jennings, and came to her. "Where have you been?" he asked.

"I had a cigarette."

"Bad for your health."

"Not necessarily."

"Ready to go? I'm hungry."

"You've had a strenuous day. Are we leaving together?"

He started to say something hard, smiled and said, "Can you ever remember a time when we didn't?"

He was right. With all his peccadilloes, he'd never failed to escort her home from an event or party they'd attended together. "I'm ready," she said.

The atmosphere at the French Embassy's party was considerably more festive, and Amster's hurt and anger were gradually replaced by good food and stimulating conversation with Washington's upper echelons of the arts, politics, and business. The redhead arrived and Bowen greeted her casually, but later Amster saw her hand him a slip of paper, which he put in his pocket.

They left the party at ten. "Coming in for a

nightcap, George?" Amster asked as they pulled into her driveway.

"I don't think so, Julia."

"As you wish."

"Maybe just for a few minutes."

Bowen settled himself in a large first-floor study that contained as many pre-Columbian artifacts as Amster's gallery. "Coffee?" she asked.

"No, maybe a drink, brandy?"

"Help yourself. I want to get comfortable."

Bowen poured his drink at a small bar in the study while Amster disappeared upstairs. He placed the glass on a white marble table next to a large blue leather wing chair, removed his jacket, and carefully placed it over a straight-backed chair behind a desk. He sat and ran his fingers over the blue leather arms, sighed, and sipped his brandy. Moments later Amster reappeared wearing a pale pink silk dressing gown loosely sashed. Bowen knew she was naked underneath it and a warm, tingling response traveled his body.

"Make me something," she said, sitting down in a matching chair and crossing her legs, a bare foot dangling free, the robe falling open.

"Yes," he said, his eyes on her. "Brandy?"

"That'll be fine."

He handed her the drink, leaned over, and kissed her copper hair that picked up light from a lamp, causing it to shimmer like the amber liquid in her glass. "You're beautiful," he said.

She looked into his eyes and held up her glass. "To mature beauty, George. To its advantages."

He smiled, took the glass from her hand and

put it on a table, grasped her hands and said, "Come."

She said nothing, simply allowed him to pull her from the chair and lead her to her bedroom on the second floor, where he slowly disrobed, hanging each piece of clothing with great care on an oak valet she kept there for him. He joined her in bed and ran his knuckle over her cheek, her nose, down and around her chin. She was motionless as he continued stroking her, her body immobilized by two conflicting and offsetting emotions: the physical joy of his manipulations and an intense anger welling up in her again, more intense than earlier in the evening. Downstairs she'd wanted only the pleasure of making love. Now, fury threatened to override it, and she was powerless to will it away, to save it for later after the pleasure had been experienced.

"What's the matter?" he said into her ear.

"Nothing, I . . ."

"You wanted this."

"I . . . I'm not sure what I want—from you."

"Right now you are," he said, laughing.

She twisted from beneath him.

"Hey," he said.

"I detest you."

He sat up and leaned against the headboard.

"Can't you understand how I feel?" she said, joining him there. She knew she'd lost control. There was no backing off. She'd desperately wanted to avoid confronting him with her feelings. It was so demeaning to have to admit he'd hurt her, hurt her again. It was what he wanted. He enjoyed it, the hold he had on her because of what she needed, and what he could provide because of his position and influence.

"I assumed you felt an urge for sex," he said.

"I . . . I did, and I do, but sometimes you go too far. I've never minded it before. Oh, yes, of course I have, but I know I have no right to treat you as if you were mine." She leaned over him and said in a voice that was on the verge of cracking, "But, George, tonight I—"

He pushed her away and got up. "You're sick, Julia. You need help."

"Please don't say that. It isn't sick to not want to share someone you love on the *same day.*"

"Love? You haven't the capacity for it, Julia." He slipped into his shorts.

She started to cry. "I do have that capacity, George." The tears stopped and her voice suddenly became loud and strong. "You talk about being sick. You're the sick one, George. You're nasty and uncaring and cruel."

"Go to sleep, Julia. I think you're drunk, too."

She got up and came to where he was putting on his pants. "Not too drunk to see you and the redhead. Going to the country this weekend with Marshall Jenkins? He's in New York."

"It's none of your business."

"Yes it is. I put up with so much, but I'm human, George. You have no right to hurt me like this, like this afternoon, like you've done so many times."

He continued dressing, checking himself in a full-length mirror.

"What is it, George, the need to prove your fragile, aging manhood?"

He laughed.

"You need so many, two a day, three? Was I the third today? Maybe the fourth. And always so young, mindless, vapid—"

"And pretty, and firm," he said.

"You're disgusting," she said. "Even your students, for God's sake, even Valerie Frolich."

The name stopped everything in the room. It had been poised on her tongue ever since the visit from Languth, waiting to be hurled at him at a time like this.

"Do you realize what you've just said?" he snarled, leaning toward her so that his face was inches from hers.

It was something else she wished she hadn't succumbed to. It . . . everything should have been left unsaid, as it was most times. But it hadn't been. It was now there, in the room, surrounding them like a physical presence.

"I said you slept with Valerie Frolich, your student and your best friend's daughter."

"You are—"

"Was she young and firm and dumb like the others? Did she giggle a lot and make you feel young?"

There were tremors in his body and he'd raised his right hand as though to strike her. She looked at his hand defiantly, then at him, and said in a level voice, "Did you hit her, too, George, because she laughed at an old fool?"

His hand turned into a fist, poised close to her face, his breath coming hard. Then he lowered it, and the rigidity in his body seemed to melt away. He smiled, said, "Yes, Julia, she was young and firm and she giggled a lot. She was good in bed, Julia. She pleased me very much."

Nothing he might have said could have taken her so offguard. She reached for words, found none.

"Take the weekend and go away," he said. "You're very tense. You'll have a breakdown if you don't get away. Please don't bother coming downstairs. I've been through this door before."

He was gone. Watching through the curtains, she saw him get into his car, start the engine, back slowly and carefully into the street, and drive away.

She stood there for a very long time before going downstairs and drinking her brandy. Then she filled the snifter again, and once more, until the effects of alcohol and fatigue sent her into a deep and troubled sleep on the couch.

Chapter Twenty-one

"You've still got the best freckles in the business," Potamos said to his first wife, Patty, as they stood in the foyer of her home. Their two children had spent the day cruising around the area with their father, stopping to eat, then a matinee at the local movie theater, more to eat, the final stop before returning home an ice cream parlor where they all feasted on multiscoop sundaes.

"They miss you, Joe," she said.

"Yeah, I miss them."

"I miss you, too."

"You should'a married again."

She laughed. "You did and look what happened."

"Come on, Patty, she turned out to be an aberration."

She giggled. "Don't tell that to the lesbian organization." She stopped smiling. "Joe, can I ask you a serious, personal question?"

"Sure."

"Are you happy?"

He smacked his lips and looked at the ceiling. "A state of mind."

"No philosophical cop-outs, Joe. Are you happy?"

"Yeah, I am. I have my moments, but . . ."

"Are you going with someone?"

"Nah, just a casual thing."

"Casual? Sure?"

"Uh-huh."

"Could we have dinner some night, just the two of us?"

"Sure, why not? You have a problem?"

"No, but it's been a long time since we talked about something other than the kids' grades and health. We shared a lot, Joe, and it might be nice to talk it over. I'm not suggesting anything like getting back together. In fact, I've been going with someone for a while now. Just casual."

He squinted at her. "You sure?"

"As sure as you are. Go on, I know you're anxious to get back. Just think about it, and if you feel like it some night, call me."

"Call you. You sound like Gardello. I will, Patty. Take care."

The phone was ringing at his condo when he came through the door. Jumper leaped all over him as he headed across the living room and picked it up. "Joe, it's Roseann."

"Hi. I didn't figure I'd hear from you until tomorrow. I was with the kids. We pigged out on ice cream and popcorn in the movie."

"Sounds nice. Joe, Tony Fiamma has been calling every fifteen minutes. He says he has to talk to you. He sounds . . . well, desperate."

"He say what he wanted?"

"No, just that he must talk with you tonight. He gave me a number."

Potamos wrote it down. "Thanks, Roseann. We'll catch up tomorrow?"

"Yes. Don't call before noon, though. Okay?"

"Sure. Play good, sleep good, and we'll do something special tomorrow."

"Oh, sounds exciting. Like what?"

"I don't know—fancy dinner, maybe. You'd like that?"

"Sure. I'm not playing. I had a wedding date canceled, which doesn't cause me a twinge of regret. Have a good night."

He walked Jumper and made himself a drink before calling the number she'd given him. Fiamma answered the moment the first ring sounded. "Jesus, man, where've you been?"

Potamos started to recount his day, then realized Fiamma wasn't looking for that. "What's up, Tony?"

"I'm being spooked, man."

"What do you mean?"

"You remember they broke into my room and turned it upside down?"

"Yeah, sure."

"Again." His voice took on a hysterical tone. "Again, man. Not only that, I got a call from a newspaper publisher, the guy who puts out the *Eye*. You know him, Goldson?"

"Of course I know him. By the way, Tony, why the hell didn't you—"

"I did a story for him, a beauty. I was going to tell you after it came out, let you see how good I was."

"And?"

"They busted into his offices last night and took my story, the notes I left with him, the works."

"Who's 'they'?"

"How do I know? Maybe the cops."

"Why suspect them? Did they know about the diary or the story you did?"

"Somebody did. Look, they didn't get the rest of the diary. I still have it, but I think maybe you were right, that we both should have a copy."

"It's about time."

"I can give it to you tonight."

"All right, but why don't you get it copied first?"

"I don't have time. I figured I'd give it to you and you could get the copies."

"No problem. What time do you want to meet, and where?"

"Someplace private, man."

"I'll come to your room."

"Don't be stupid. How about your place?"

"Here?" Potamos realized he didn't want Fiamma knowing where he lived, but he didn't have a choice. "Okay," he said. "Eight o'clock." He gave him the address. "You allergic to dogs?"

"Huh?"

"I have one. See you at eight. And don't ever call me stupid again."

He settled in to read Edmund Wilson's *The Forties.* He'd read Wilson's books on the Thirties and Twenties and was anxious to share the author's perceptions of another decade. It was quality time. There hadn't been an opportunity recently to read a book and he missed it.

He went to the kitchen at eight and started his drip coffee maker in anticipation of Fiamma's arrival. He had beer in the refrigerator, and pretzels.

Half a packaged coffee cake was too stale even for the dog and he dumped it.

He tried to get back to his book, but too many things crowded his thoughts—the conversation with Patty, the day with the kids, seeing Roseann tomorrow, and, of course, seeing the rest of Valerie Frolich's diary. There wasn't much of interest in the new pages. Most dealt with feelings she had about her father, few of which were favorable. She alluded to his "womanizing," and to how destructive it was to her mother. Even more pronounced were her feelings about his political posture. She considered him a hypocrite and, worse, a public servant whose only motivations were the needs of his rich and powerful friends, and his own checkbook. It started Potamos wondering how his own kids viewed him.

Nine o'clock. It wouldn't have surprised him if Fiamma was one of those people who were chronically late, a symbol of arrogance directed toward all those who were left waiting. He hadn't been late before, however; he'd arrived at the Florida Avenue Grill right on time.

Ten. Ten-thirty. He called the number Roseann had given him. There was no answer. He called the number belonging to Fiamma's girlfriend. She answered, sounded as though she'd been sleeping.

"This is Joe Potamos from the *Washington Post.* I'm looking for Tony."

"Tony who?"

"Tony . . . hey, is he there? He was supposed to meet me two and a half hours ago."

"I don't know where he is and I couldn't care less."

"Oh. You broke up?"

"Something like that. Try the little blonde from F. Scott's. She's got a new car. That's what Tony dates—cars, newer and fancier models each time."

"Hey, look, I don't know about Tony's romantic life, but I do know he might be in trouble, serious trouble. Forget the blonde from F. Scott's and tell me where I might find him."

"Try the little blonde. She'll know. He was with her last night."

"What's her name?"

"Bimbo."

"Come on."

"Audrey."

"She works there?"

"Yes."

"Thanks."

"Tell Tony he's a creep."

"With conviction. Thanks again."

He wanted to go look for Fiamma but was afraid he'd miss him if Fiamma eventually showed up. Finally, a few minutes before midnight, he drove to Fiamma's rooming house. The front door was locked. Knock and wake up the landlady? Maybe later, if all else failed.

F. Scott's was doing a booming business. There was a long line of yuppies on Thirty-sixth Street waiting to get in. Music from inside kept everyone happy out on the sidewalk. Potamos parked in front of the nearest hydrant, flipped down his visor to display his press placard, and pushed

past everyone to get to the front door. A few
people in line shouted at him. He said to a young
man guarding the door, "I'm Joe Potamos from
the *Washington Post*. I have to get in to talk to one
of your employees. It's urgent."

The door watcher frowned and gave him a now-
I've-heard-it-all look. Potamos produced his press
credentials and said calmly, but with quiet conviction, "This has to do with murder, my friend.
I need ten minutes inside, no more. Deny me that
and I'll write about every roach who ever sticks
his head inside this place."

"We don't have roaches."

"You will, by the dozen."

"Look, mister, I'm not supposed to—"

"Thanks," Potamos said, moving in the direction of the music.

The inside of F. Scott's was like a movie set, and
everybody looked like they'd just finished shooting a high-gloss Hollywood film. He reached the
bar and caught the bartender's eye. "I'm looking
for a waitress named Audrey." He showed his
press card and briefly explained the urgency of
the situation. The bartender pointed to a petite
little blonde who was in the process of serving a
tray of fancy, jelly-bean-colored drinks.

"Audrey?" He startled her. "Sorry. My name's
Joe Potamos. I work for the *Washington Post*, and
I'm a friend of Tony's."

Her round little face burst into a smile. "Sure,
he told me all about it."

" 'It'?"

"About working with you on the murder story."

A long list of things he wanted to say to Fiamma raced through his mind, none of them complimentary. He said to Audrey, "Where is Tony?"

"I don't know."

"You were with him last night."

"Yeah, but that was last night. He said he was busy for the weekend."

"What? The music is loud."

"They turn it up later."

"I'll be sure to hang around."

She repeated what she'd said.

"No idea where I can find him? He was supposed to come by my place more than four hours ago. He never showed."

She shrugged and started toward the bar. He followed. "Let me ask you something else," Potamos said when they reached the bar. "Did he say anything about an envelope he was supposed to give me?"

"No."

"He didn't? Did he give anything to you?"

"No."

"Sometimes a guy will give something to his girlfriend for safekeeping because he trusts her. I know he trusts you. He told me."

"He did?"

"Yeah, more than once."

"Gee, he told me not to . . ."

"Not to tell anybody, right? But he meant *any-body*. I'm not anybody. We're working together, re-member, and that envelope and what's in it is our whole story, Tony's by-line in the *Washington Post*.

His whole career rides on it, and if I don't have it tonight, we may lose the story."

She obviously was grappling with a big dilemma. The bartender told her to get back on the floor. She was flustered, looked around, then said to Potamos, "If you can't find him, I guess you can have it."

"Good. When?"

"I get off at two."

"Great, I'll wait."

"No, try to find Tony. I'd feel better about it."

"All right, but I'll be back at two. Don't leave without me."

"I won't."

Nevertheless, he decided to just wait outside in his car in case Audrey decided to skip out early. A bird in hand . . .

He returned to the club precisely at two. This time the fellow at the door didn't question him, and he walked in. He didn't see Audrey and panicked, then saw her come from a back room. She'd changed into civilian clothing. She was cute, bubbly and bouncy, all round, no sharp edges. She saw him and came directly to him. "Did you find Tony?"

"No." Potamos laughed to keep concern out of his voice. "That's Tony, always disappearing on me at the wrong time. Where do you live?"

"A couple of blocks."

"My car's outside."

"We can walk."

"I'm at a hydrant."

They drove to a strip of stores, above which

were tiny apartments. One belonged to Audrey, whose last name was Jankovich, which she would change to Janko if she made it as a dancer, which she was studying very hard to be; it wasn't easy when you didn't have any money and had to work nights at F. Scott's. She was so proud of Tony's working with Potamos and just knew they'd make it big together—not that Potamos hadn't already, but Tony had told her there'd been some kind of trouble in Potamos's career and Tony felt what he had about the murder would help Potamos out of it.

All that in a few blocks, and not one four-letter word passed Potamos's lips as they drove them.

The apartment consisted of one room, with a pullman kitchen off to one side. The walls were plastered with huge posters of dancers, most of them male. A sofa bed had been left unmade.

"This is exciting," Audrey said, kicking off her shoes and doing a spin in the center of the room. "I really feel I'm part of it all."

"You are," Potamos said, sorry he had to fake it, and slightly uncomfortable with carnal thoughts that the rumpled bed and the rear view of her as she did toe-touches caused in him. "Audrey . . ." he said.

She looked at him upside down through her legs. "Hi."

"Hi." He wiggled his fingers.

She straightened up and faced him, hands on her hips. "I get carried away after working all night as a waitress. I just can't wait to get home and dance."

"Yeah, I know what you mean." It was his best understanding grin. "The envelope. I have to get it back to the paper. We're on a tight deadline." He made a point of looking at his watch. "Damn, we're already over deadline. Let me get out of here and get it done. Then you and Tony and me and my girlfriend can celebrate. How'd that be?"

"Terrific." She made a few more dancers' motions, then opened the refrigerator and pulled out a thick envelope, handed it to him. "Here it is."

"Great." He wanted to kiss her.

"Where will we celebrate?"

"You name it."

"I can't wait to see Tony."

"Neither can I. Take it easy, and good luck with the dancing." He bounded down the stairs and broke the speed limit getting home.

Chapter Twenty-two

The first call to Potamos Sunday morning was from Marvin Goldson, publisher of the *Georgetown Eye*. It was seven o'clock; Potamos had fallen asleep at six after spending what was left of the night reading Valerie Frolich's complete diary.

"Did you hear what happened to me?" Goldson barked into the phone.

Potamos held the receiver away from his ear and groaned.

"Joe, it's Marvin Goldson."

"I know it is."

"Joe, remember we were talking at the club about that protégé of yours, Tony Fiamma?"

"Yeah."

"And I told you he wrote quite a story for us about what's really behind the building of that condo near the new Russian Embassy?"

"Yeah."

"Somebody broke into my office and stole the goddamn thing."

"I know."

"He told you?"

"Yeah."

"Do you know where he is?"

"No."

"I need to find him. I want him to write it again. He'll remember what he wrote."

"I told you, Marv, I don't know where he is."

"Boy, would I love to know who broke in! Could have been anybody—the Russians, CIA, FBI, a competitor . . . Hey, you didn't tell anybody about the story, did you?" Before Potamos could answer, Goldson said, "I always trusted you, Joe. It's just a little weekly paper, you know? Did you tell anybody at the *Post?*"

"No." Jumper came from where she'd been sleeping at the foot of the bed and licked his face. He pushed her away and said to Goldson, "Marv, I just got to bed. I'm sorry about what happened, and if I hear from Tony, I'll have him call you right away. How's that?"

"Okay. You know, Joe, it could have been anybody. That rich fruitcake Marshall Jenkins is behind that condo, and his buddy Frolich is with him. The State Department? Maybe even the West Germans? Jenkins is married to a German, and Fiamma's article got into Jenkins's West German holdings, which, Joe, are bigger than the national debt of Uganda."

"Marv, I have to go. Fiamma will call you."

"Good, great, thanks, Joe. See you at the club."

Nothing Goldson had said was news to Potamos. Not that any of it could be proved. Valerie had jotted down all sorts of disjointed notes based upon overhearing her father discuss the condo project. According to her, the condo's genesis and purposes was to provide a site for counter-electronics against the Russians' sophisticated equipment within their new embassy. But nowhere did she indicate having possession of a single piece of paper to support her claims. Potamos could understand Fiamma going ahead with the zeal and blind faith of a young person, but he was disappointed in Marv Goldson, who'd been around long enough to know better.

"Where are you, Tony Fiamma?" he asked as he turned over and welcomed sleep's return.

It was short-lived. The phone rang at eight. It was Gil Gardello. "Sorry to wake you, Joe, but I need you. They found a body in some woods just north of Georgetown U. I sent an intern up there to nail us down, but—"

"Male?"

"Yeah, about twenty, twenty-two."

"Give it to me," Potamos said, springing to a sitting position and pushing magazines and books from his night table in search of pencil and paper.

He was dressed in minutes, grabbed the envelope containing Valerie Frolich's diary, threw a leash on Jumper, and walked her in a grassy area near the garage. He didn't want to take the time to go back upstairs, so he put her in the car, tossed the envelope in the trunk, and headed for the location given him by Gardello.

The scene was swarming with police and media. Potamos locked Jumper in the car and made his way through the crowd, showed his pass to an officer in charge of the crime scene, and was allowed to join a group of press and police halfway down a steep, heavily wooded slope that ended at a narrow creek. He could see the body from where he was made to stop. Two detectives in civilian clothing were with two white-coated medical types and a couple of uniforms, all of them bent over the body, which had been placed in a black body bag.

"Hey, Joe, got an I.D.?" a reporter from another newspaper asked.

Potamos shook his head and kept his eyes trained on the scene.

"Maybe another student," the reporter said.

Potamos ignored him and tried to move a little closer. He was restrained by a cop. "Pete Languth here?" Potamos asked.

"Down there," the cop said.

Potamos handed him his card and asked him to give it to Languth.

"Can't do it," the cop said.

"Come on," Potamos said. "He's waiting to see me."

The cop yelled down the embankment, "Sergeant Languth, there's somebody here says you want to see him." Languth looked up the hill. Potamos waved. Languth looked down at the body bag, then labored up the hill, his feet slipping on wet leaves and mud, his face reflecting what was going on inside his overweight body.

"Who is it?" Potamos asked when Languth reached him. Other reporters crowded close to hear the reply.

"Come on," Languth said, bumping people out of his way as he led Potamos up to street level. He was breathing heavily. "Damn, I hate hills," he said, wiping sweat from his face with a well-used handkerchief.

"Age," Potamos said. "Happens to us all."

Languth looked at him and sneered. "I want to talk to you," he said.

"Go ahead, I'm here. Who got it down there, a student named Fiamma? Anthony Fiamma?"

"Yeah, and no big surprise that you know."

"What's that supposed to mean?"

"He's your buddy, a couple a' pains in the butt, only his pain's in his head." Languth looked pleased with his line.

Potamos took it differently. "He's still alive? The bag . . . I thought . . ."

"He's dead, very dead."

"Jesus, I—"

"I can take you downtown, or we can get coffee. Your choice, Potamos."

"Take me downtown? What kind of crap is that? Sure, let's have coffee, only you buy this time." It was a wasted threat. Cops never paid, especially when a reporter was involved. Languth had a conversation with the other detective who'd accompanied the body bag up the hill. Then he nodded at Potamos and walked toward his car. Potamos followed. "Where are we going?" Potamos asked, stopping at his car and putting the key in the lock.

"What the hell is that in there?" Languth asked. Jumper was beating against the window with her front paws and snarling at Languth.

"An African aardwolf."

"Looks like a dog to me. I hate dogs."

"I don't doubt it."

" . . . multiple head wounds, like the Frolich kid. What do you think of that, Joe?"

Potamos sat across from Languth in a booth in a greasy spoon on Wisconsin. Steaming coffee in chipped white mugs sat on the table. Languth had ordered a hamburger with onions, which hadn't been delivered yet.

"Two now," Potamos said, looking into his coffee. "Same M.O." He glanced up. "You figured it out yet?"

"No. You? You and the deceased were pretty tight."

"Meaning what?"

"You hung around together. What were you, some sort of guru for him?"

Potamos ignored the question and focused on his coffee mug.

Languth sat back as his hamburger was set in front of him. "Ketchup, huh, and some pickles. You got any slaw?" He turned to Potamos, "What were you and the kid up to, Joe?"

"Business."

"With a college student?" He guffawed. "Come on, the kid knew Valerie Frolich, was in the same classes with her. He must have known her pretty well. What'd he do, pass on info to you for a story?"

Potamos shook his head. "Pete, get off it. Fiamma came to me and wanted to work together on the Frolich story. He didn't have anything to offer, but he *did* have a drive. You know what I mean? He wanted a career in journalism and thought I could help."

"Did you?"

"Help him? Couldn't, but I liked him. He reminded me a little of myself when I was his age, all brass and no brains. Well, that's not true. He was smart, street-smart, like a cop."

"If I was smart I would have never been a cop," Languth said, sounding as though he meant it.

"It could be worse. Besides, looking back is a dumb exercise. Hey, what was that routine about taking me downtown?"

A shrug, then a bite of the burger that wiped out half of it and sent a trickle of ketchup down his chin. He wiped it off and said, "I consider you a suspect, Joe."

"Wonderful." Potamos extended his hands across the table. "Cuff me, Pete."

"I only do that with friends. Potamos I'm serious. You've been observed spending a lot of time with the deceased recently. You've been observed meeting with him and exchanging material."

Potamos smiled, then broke into laughter. "You've been following me?"

"I ordered surveillance."

"Following me."

"Whatever. What were you doing with him?"

"With who, Fiamma?"

"No, Jerry Falwell. Who the hell else would I be talking about?"

"Nothing. I told you, he came to me for help in getting started in the business."

"What'd he give you at the Florida Avenue Grill the other morning?"

"His résumé."

"Get off it."

"And clips, things he'd written."

"Like the story for the *Georgetown Eye?*"

Potamos widened his eyes and nodded. "You broke into Goldson's office, huh?"

"*Broke in?* Come on, Joe, I'm a cop, a protector of rights."

"I forgot. No, I never saw that story. How was it?"

"Interesting."

"So I heard. How come you didn't break into my place?"

"I don't have to." Languth pulled a search warrant from his pocket and handed it across the table.

"This is the dumbest thing I ever heard."

"I can execute it, or you can invite me over after coffee and let me look around, only put that goddamn dog someplace."

"The dog goes with the territory. Love me, love my dog." Languth wasn't amused, so Potamos said, "I'll put her in the bathroom. Of course, you'll want to check that room, too—toilet tank, top of the shower—so then I'll put her in the bedroom, *after*, of course, you've messed that up."

"I don't find you cute."

"I think you're adorable," Potamos said, grabbing the grease-stained green check and standing. "Come on, I'll open the castle for you."

It occurred to Potamos as he led Languth to his condo that the time spent having coffee had nothing to do with coffee or hamburgers or talk. Languth had wanted to detain him. Why? Had they broken into his apartment while he sat in the booth? Unlikely. If so, why bother with the warrant and going to his apartment now? Actually, he was glad they'd spent the time together parrying and thrusting. It had taken his mind off the tragedy of Fiamma's murder. *That* hit him when they were halfway to the condo, and he felt a rush of anger and fear and confusion and myriad other emotions. Until that moment in the car, Jumper sitting proudly next to him, her ears and eyes taking in every movement outside, Fiamma's death hadn't been real—a body in the woods, cops and medics at the scene, something he'd seen too many times before. But Fiamma's face now covered the windshield, and his brash voice rang in Potamos's ears. He slowed down to avoid running into the car in front of him, checked his rearview mirror, and saw Languth a few car lengths behind.

He came back to reality, which meant wondering what to do with the envelope in the trunk. All he wanted now was to get rid of Languth, hide the pages, and call Roseann. She still had those initial pages in the piano bench. He'd get them out of there that afternoon. It wasn't fair to lay that on her. Look at Audrey, Fiamma's girlfriend, who'd been used the same way he'd used Roseann. He'd square it as soon as Languth left.

Thinking of Roseann picked up his spirits. They'd do something special, as he'd promised, maybe take a long walk, make love, go to the best restaurant in Washington. His final thought as he pulled up in front of his building was that he'd marry her on the spot, maybe propose that afternoon, and if she accepted, they could drive down to North Carolina, where it was easy. Maryland wasn't hard, but it wouldn't work there overnight.

Languth parked behind him and came to Potamos's door. Jumper acted vicious, and Languth
stepped back a little as Potamos grabbed her leash
and stepped out. He realized he enjoyed seeing
the big, hulking cop afraid of something. If Languth knew all the dog wanted to do was jump all
over him and lick his face, he wouldn't be afraid,
so Potamos played it to the hilt, held the leash
short and spoke sternly to her, as though only he
could stave off the rabid mutilation of Sergeant
Peter Languth. He had an idea. If he left Jumper
in the car, it might discourage Languth from
searching it. He said, "Look, I'll leave her here if
you're afraid. She's used to it. I leave her all the
time when I'm on assignment." He didn't wait for
a response, put Jumper back in the car, and locked
the door behind him.

He put the keys in his pocket and was about
to walk into the building when he spotted Blackburn's white Chevy station wagon turning the
corner. "Forgot something," he said, quickly
going to his car and shaking his head at her, hopefully enough to wave her off, hopefully not overt
enough for Languth to see it. She slowed down;
he gave her a jerk of his thumb, his body shielding the motion from Languth. Her expression was
one of puzzlement. Then she speeded up and continued down the street.

Potamos turned, smiled, and started toward
Languth.

"What'd you forget?" Languth asked.

"Ah . . . I didn't forget anything. I remembered
I didn't forget anything." He laughed. "Too early
for me, Pete. Come on, look around, and don't

forget the cookie jar, or the Tupperware containers with Chinese from six weeks ago. Just don't
breathe deep."

"You're not funny, Joe."

"*This* isn't funny, Pete."

Languth spent an hour searching the apartment, and Potamos had to give it to him for thor-
oughness. He didn't miss a thing, including the
containers with old food in the refrigerator.

"So?" Potamos said when Languth appeared to
be getting ready to leave.

"So nothing. You going to level with me?"

"About what?"

"About Fiamma. Did he have something on the
Frolich case?"

"Nope. All he had was some theories about the
Russian Embassy and the condo going up near it.
But you know that. You read his story."

"I'm going to break this case, Joe. Count on it.
When I do, whoever's involved is going down the
tube, with me pushing all the way."

"I hope so. Two kids murdered in their prime.
It stinks."

"That's right. How come they sent you to cover
the thing this morning?"

"What do you mean? Why shouldn't I cover it?
I'm a crime reporter."

"You're off the Frolich story."

"You know that."

"Yeah. What'd they bounce you for?"

"I flunked a loyalty test. They give it once a
month."

"Bowen."

"Right."

"Like before."

"Right again. How'd you hear?"

"We get the results of the monthly loyalty tests."

Potamos smiled. "Good line, Pete."

"Don't screw me, Joe. That tube's open to everybody."

"We're on the same side, Pete. Believe it."

Potamos wondered if he should accompany Languth downstairs. He decided against it. It would make it easier for Languth to ask for the key to the car trunk. He said, "Take it easy, Pete."

"You, too." He opened the door, then turned and said, "You know what I think, Joe?"

"What?"

"I still think Bowen's the one."

"That what, killed Frolich and Fiamma?"

"Yeah."

"No, Pete, as much as I hate the guy, it doesn't add up." He was touched by Languth's statement of personal opinion—it created an instant, momentary bond between them, colleagues exchanging information. But Potamos held his reaction in check. He wasn't about to exchange anything with Languth.

Languth started through the door, and stopped again. "What about the dog? You going to leave it down there?"

"Oh, I'll come down later. I like her in the car. Better than any security system. She's a killer."

"Yeah? She comes at me, she's dead." He patted his revolver beneath his coat and closed the door behind him.

"Psychopath," Potamos muttered. He went to

the window and looked down at the street, saw Languth walking to his car, saw Blackburn parked at the end of the block. He waited until Languth drove away, then bolted down the emergency exit stairs. Outside, he waved to Roseann. She didn't see him. He ran up the block and knocked on her window. She looked up, smiled, and unlocked the door.

"Hey, what are you doing here?" he asked.

She got out of her car and threw her arms around him. "I'm so sorry," she said.

"About what?"

"They came to my place. They had a warrant. They pulled everything apart, and they found the pages you gave me to keep." She started to cry.

He held her tight and said over and over, "It's okay, it's okay, don't worry about it."

"They were the police, Joe. The *police!* In my apartment!"

"I know, I know. I'm sorry, damn it, I'm sorry."

She pulled back. "He was a cop, wasn't he?"

"Yeah. He searched my place, found nothing."

She suddenly stiffened, turned from him, and placed her hands on the top of her car. "I don't want it, Joe," she said.

"Huh?"

"I don't want this." She faced him again. "This isn't me, cops in my apartment. Please understand, I'm a musician, a piano player."

"Simplicity."

"Yes."

"I'm sorry. They followed me, must have seen me going into your place."

"I . . ."

"Yeah?"

"I love you, Joe."

"I love you, too."

"I never want to see you again."

"Will you marry me?"

She stared at him as though he had three heads and had stepped from an alien spaceship.

"Tonight. We can drive to North Carolina. It's easy there, and we can come back Mr. and Mrs. Joe Potamos."

She started to laugh, pressed her fist against her mouth, laughed louder, and said, "Joe, please, don't think I'm laughing at you. It's just that you're . . . you're crazy."

"I'm in love."

"Joe . . . no!"

"You won't marry me?"

"That's right, no, absolutely not."

"I don't blame you."

"I'm glad."

"Yeah, because I'm a loser, a jerk, a banana. My father knew that years ago. Okay, go, take off. I have to get Jumper."

"Joe?"

"What?"

"Will you call me, after all this is over?"

"You want me to?"

"Yes, I do."

He beamed. "You bet."

Chapter Twenty-three

Things had happened in such rapid sequence that it wasn't until later Sunday afternoon that the full impact of Fiamma's murder hit Potamos. He sank into a deep depression, compounded by losing Blackburn. Sure, she'd invited him to call when everything was over, and that had pleased him initially. But now, in the quiet of his living room, with Jumper curled up against his feet, a different reality set in: that he'd never see her again; that she'd find it easy, even pleasant, to be away from him; that she'd find another guy, probably a bass player or a drummer, and that would be that—end of story.

He realized he missed Tony Fiamma. Tony's brashness and arrogance had been invigorating. He went to the paper at five and wrote a brief news story about Fiamma's murder. There was so much he wanted to include from his personal experiences and thoughts, but knew he couldn't. The headline writers would probably say: SECOND STUDENT MURDERED. As simple as that.

He left the paper at seven and, instead of returning home, drove to National Airport and caught the eight o'clock shuttle to New York.

There, he parked his rented car in front of his mother's house. Lights were on in the living room and kitchen. He rang the bell, heard a commotion inside, then a voice, "Who is it?"

"It's me, ma, Joe."

"Joe?" The door opened a crack and there she stood, smaller and older, face wrinkled, black eyes looking for something inside him, waiting for him to say something.

"Hi, ma," he said. He stepped inside and hugged her. She was stiff at first, then returned his embrace with warmth and strength.

She'd been cooking a variety of *mezethes*, fried Greek appetizers, for a party the next night at a neighbor's house. He followed her into the kitchen, where her efforts were laid out on paper towels over every available surface. There were sautéed lamb meatballs, black-eyed peas in olive oil and lemon, fried feta-cheese cubes, and other dishes he remembered as a child. *"Keftedes?"* he asked, pointing to the meatballs.

She smiled and nodded. "Very good. You're still a Greek. How's Patty and the children?"

"Good. I was with them yesterday. She said they'd be coming up to see you soon. How come you never go down there?"

She shrugged and busied herself with the next batch of food.

"You're welcome there anytime, ma. You know that. You could visit your grandchildren and see me, too."

"You!" She laughed to soften the way she'd said it. "You're a stranger. Married twice. My, my, what a way to live!"

"A couple of mistakes, that's all. I learned my lesson and—"

"You're seeing someone?"

"Nah, I'm too busy with the job."

She turned from the stove and gave him the same look she used to when he was obviously fibbing as a child. He said sheepishly, "Well, I've been going out with a pretty nice girl. She's a piano player. I mean, she's a pianist, classical and all that."

"She's Greek?"

"No."

His mother finished putting the next tray of food into the deep-fry unit that used to be in the diner when his father was alive. Then she wiped her hands on a black apron with a red and green rooster on it and said, "Come, Joe, let's sit and talk. It's been a long time."

He looked around the living room. Not a thing out of place. On the false mantle above the false fireplace stood a series of framed photos of him and his sisters. The sofa and chairs were covered with plastic. Greek Orthodox religious artifacts were everywhere. His mother sat on the couch. He chose a chair. "You want some Metaxa?" she asked.

"Yeah, that'd be nice. You still have the seven-star?"

"No," she said as she went to where a bottle stood on a small table. "The five-star is good enough in this house now that your father is gone." She carefully measured two tiny portions into etched stemmed glasses and gave him one.

"You're having one?" he said.

"On special occasions, like having my only son home."

He swallowed hard and held up his glass. "Good to see you, ma."

"And I am glad to see you, Joey. So, tell me all about yourself, about this pianist who plays classical music and isn't Greek."

A half-hour later, after he'd capsulized his life for her, she asked why he was there.

He shrugged. "I don't know, ma. I just wanted to touch base again with home. I'm glad I did."

"You're staying?"

"Just overnight, if it's okay with you. I have to catch the first plane in the morning."

"I'm glad you're here. Your sisters ask about you all the time."

"I think about them a lot, too."

"Next month they'll both be here."

"Yeah? How come?"

"Because I asked them to come. I was going to ask you, too, Joey, to be here."

"Something wrong? You okay?"

"I'm fine, but I would like to see my family together again." She gave him the date, a weekend. "You'll be here?"

"Count on me, ma. I'll be here."

"If you want to bring this Roseann with you, that will be fine."

"Okay, I appreciate that."

"You look tired."

"I am—exhausted."

"Go to bed. Go to your room."

"*My room.* Sounds good."

"I'll fix you a big breakfast in the morning."

"Ma, you don't have to bother."

"No bother, Joey. I want to."

He kissed her goodnight and went to the room in which he'd grown up. He stripped down to his shorts, brushed his teeth with his finger, and pulled down the covers. Sitting on top of the pile of his clothes was the envelope containing Valerie Frolich's diary. He opened the closet door and placed the envelope on a shelf, beneath a pile of his old sweaters and athletic uniforms, climbed into bed and pulled the covers up under his chin.

Roseann Blackburn had agreed to fill in for the week at the Terrace Lounge of the Watergate Hotel. The management had prepared a sign announcing her appearance, complete with an eight-by-ten glossy of her.

Now, at eleven o'clock Sunday night, as couples playing the mating game and important men in dark suits huddled in corners of the room, she spun out a succession of songs appropriate to the hour and situation: ballads with a bluesy feel, familiar themes from her classical repertoire. She was bored; too many men who'd had too much to drink had requested too many stupid songs. She was anxious to finish. That would be at one o'clock.

Her mind wandered as her fingers automatically found the right combination of notes. It had been an upsetting morning. The police had been so brusque, so uncaring, as they pulled the apartment apart. She'd stood to one side, a copy of the search warrant in her hands, trying not to cry, wanting to scream at them to get out, desperate to call Joe but knowing she couldn't yet. When they opened the piano bench and started tossing sheet music onto the floor, her heart felt as though it would burst through her chest. Then one of them had held up the diary pages, looked at her with a crooked smile that said so many things, none of them flattering, and they'd left without even so much as a goodbye.

The anger of the morning flared up and she hit a loud, dissonant chord that caused heads to lift. She smiled and returned to her previous musical mood.

It was a little after midnight when she saw the big man come into the lounge and take a seat at the bar. He looked familiar, but she couldn't place him for a few minutes. Then, after a furtive glance over her shoulder, it hit her. He was the one on the curb with Joe that morning, the cop. She'd seen him on the news, too. What was his name? No matter—she didn't like the fact that he was there. It had to be because of what had happened.

She concluded her set with "Here's That Rainy Day," sat back on the bench, took a deep breath, got up, and walked toward the bar. If he was there to see her, she'd give him the chance. Nothing to be gained by trying to avoid him.

His first move heartened her. He nodded and applauded, the way many drunken men did as a way of establishing contact. "Thank you," she said, passing him by.

"Excuse me," he said. "Miss Blackburn?"

"Yes?"

"Got a minute? Buy you a drink?"

"No, thank you."

"Just a couple of minutes of talk, that's all. I'm not on the make. I'm a . . . I'm a music lover, and a cop." He started to reach for his wallet, but she waved him off and sat down on the stool next to him.

"A cop? Why would you want to talk to me?"

He laughed. "Like I said, I'm a music lover, too. It's possible to be a cop and still love music. Right?"

"Right, but I'm not in the mood to talk music, if it's all the same to you."

"Okay, whatever you say. In the mood to talk about murder?"

"Pardon?"

"Murder, a specialty of mine. And diaries of young women who *get* murdered."

Blackburn looked to the bartender, who'd deliberately distanced himself from them. A couple hung on each other at the far end. The bartender had flipped a switch; Muzak drifted out of speakers. She turned to the cop and said, "Go ahead, talk about murder."

"Drink?" he asked.

"Sure."

Languth motioned for the bartender, told him to refill his glass of scotch, looked at Blackburn. "White wine," she said.

"A lady's drink," Languth said.

"Men drink wine, too," she said.

"Of course. I like Guinea red with spaghetti, lasagna."

"You were discussing murder—and diaries."

"Just trying to establish a friendly atmosphere, that's all," he said. "Those were interesting pages we found in your apartment this morning."

"I wouldn't know. I don't even know what your people took from me."

He smirked. "I think you do, Miss Blackburn. Those were pages from Valerie Frolich's diary that your boyfriend, Joe Potamos, gave you for safe-keeping."

"He's not—"

"Not a boyfriend? Oh, right, this is a new age. Lover, huh? Relationship? What'a you call them these days?"

"I don't know about any diary pages, Officer . . ."

"Languth, Peter Languth, Homicide."

"I don't know about those pages. Joe must have left them accidentally."

"Yeah, no doubt. Where's the rest of the pages?"

Blackburn tasted her wine and looked away from Languth. He said, "We'll find them, you know, but it would be in your best interest if you helped us. If you don't . . ."

She turned and looked him in the eye. "That sounds like a threat."

"I never threaten anybody, Miss Blackburn. I just point out facts, reality, that's all. I used to make threats when I was young, but no more.

What was it Al Capone said, 'Kindness and a gun will get you further than kindness alone'? He's dead. I prefer the kind route—unless people don't leave me options."

"And my option is to tell you where a diary is that I don't even know exists? Some option."

"Could be worse. Those pages are vital evidence in a murder investigation. I could bring you in for withholding them from authorities."

"Go ahead."

"I'd rather not. Maybe I'll haul in your lover, Potamos."

"On what grounds? You found the pages in my apartment, not his."

Languth started to laugh.

"I say something funny?"

"No, but it reminded me of a joke. There's this old Jewish couple goes to a lawyer. The wife wants a divorce. The lawyer asks them if they have grounds. The wife says, 'About an acre and a half.' The lawyer asks if the wife has a grudge. She says, 'We got a carport.' The lawyer asks her if her husband beats her up. She says, 'I'm up an hour earlier than him every morning.' Finally the lawyer asks, 'Why do you want a divorce?' The wife says, 'We have trouble communicating.' "
Languth laughed loudly.

Blackburn smiled. "And you're telling me I'm not communicating."

"No, Miss Blackburn, I'm telling you that two college students have been murdered, and I'm telling you that I'm through being nice and playing games. That diary might hold the key to solving both murders and I intend to have it in my hands very soon. You help, I'm nice to you. Your boyfriend helps, I'm nice to him. The two of you don't help, I start the Al Capone philosophy of life."

"Thanks for the wine, Officer Languth. I have to get back."

"Sure, anytime. By the way, where is Potamos?"

"I haven't the slightest idea."

"Break up over this? Must be a lot of tension."

She walked away, leaving the wine on the bar, sat down at the piano, and began playing "Smoke Gets in Your Eyes." She was almost through the bridge when Languth came to the piano, placed her glass on it, and stuffed a dollar bill into a tips glass. "Next time play 'Misty' for me, Miss Blackburn. I like that song."

Chapter Twenty-four

Jumper was hiding under the bed when Potamos arrived at his condo at nine Monday morning. "It's okay," he said without having to check the kitchen. "I'll clean it up. Stop pouting."

An hour later he walked into the city room of the *Post*, where Gil Gardello was in animated conversation with two reporters. Gardello spotted Potamos across the vast room and almost ran to him. "Where the hell have you been?"

"Around. I saw you yesterday."

"And I called you all night. You're supposed to call in."

"I know. What's the matter? Bowen die?"

"You should be so lucky. Come on." He led Potamos to his office, closed the door, and said, "Joe, you really did it this time."

"What'd I do?"

"I don't know."

Potamos's expression said it all. Complete confusion.

"You're fired."

"Huh?"

"You're fired, Joe. That's all I know. They told me to fire you the minute I saw you."

"For what?"

"I don't know, but it must have been a beauty."

Potamos sat down in a chair and started laughing. "This is idiotic. You on something, Gil?"

"Don't play wise guy with me, Joe. I'm serious. I hate this. I like you, you're good, but I guess you ruffled too many big feathers upstairs."

"But how did I do that, Gil?"

Gardello shook his head, sat down behind his desk, and rubbed his eyes. "I've been dreading this ever since they told me. I figured the best way was to just hit you with it."

"You did that, Gil. I'll protest. I'm going upstairs."

"I don't blame you, but . . ."

"But you'd rather I didn't?"

"I just don't think it'll do any good." Gardello's voice and face gave testimony to the genuineness of his feelings.

"Okay, Gil," Potamos said, rising and going to the door. "I'll let you know how it falls."

"Yeah, Joe, do that. You know what I feel about you, huh?"

"Sure. Call me."

Potamos grinned. Gardello shook his head and laughed. "I say that a lot, huh?"

"Yeah."

He went to George Bowen's office and was told Mr. Bowen was in his Mass. Ave. office. Potamos drove directly there, told the secretary, Mrs. Carlisle, that he wanted to see Bowen on an urgent matter. She told him Mr. Bowen was in conference. Potamos persisted. The secretary, with as deep and long a sigh as Potamos had ever heard, called Bowen on the intercom. Bowen's words were a shock to both of them: "Oh, yes, please ask Mr. Potamos to wait a few minutes, and apologize for making him wait. I'll see him shortly."

"I heard," Potamos said as she started to give him the message. He cocked his head and smiled at her. "Apology?"

She looked away and pretended to read something on a clean yellow legal pad.

Five minutes later Bowen came through his office door with two other men. They shook hands and the two others left. Bowen looked at Potamos and said pleasantly, "Hello, Joe, come in, come in. I've been expecting you."

Potamos came right to the point after Bowen had closed the door behind them. "You got me fired," he said, "and I won't sit still for it."

"Sit down, Joe. Relax. I think once I have a chance to explain it to you, you'll feel differently."

"I doubt it."

"Let me try?"

A shrug and a desperate urge for a cigarette. Bowen lit up and sat on the edge of his desk. The smoke drifted in Potamos's direction and stung his nose. It was a pleasant sensation.

"Joe," Bowen said, "somebody's looking out for you."

"Yeah? How do you figure that?"

"You've been given a marvelous opportunity to make the best use of your abilities."

Potamos blinked. "I don't believe this garbage," he said.

Bowen smiled. "Joe, you're too good to be covering a regular cop beat for *any* newspaper. That's why you've been asked to leave."

" 'Asked to leave?' I wasn't asked to leave, I was canned, and it's because of you."

"Exactly." Bowen stood and walked to the coffee service. "Coffee, Joe?"

"No."

He poured himself a cup and went to the window. This time the blinds were drawn. He cocked his head and looked to the ceiling as though in deep thought, then said, "Joe, you've been working very hard on the Frolich story, and now we have the murder of this young man named Tony Fiamma. I'm afraid there are certain connecting links between them that are going to have to be—how shall I say it, Joe?—links that will have to be managed very carefully."

"Wait a minute, that term *managed* is a bad one. Since when do you or anybody else in the press advocate managed news? That's for politicians and the corporate flacks."

"I didn't suggest managing the news, Joe. I said these murders, because of their extremely sensitive nature, particularly Valerie Frolich's, must be—I'll phrase it more palatably for you—must be looked at with sensitivity and mature judgment."

Potamos was becoming increasingly edgy. Bowen was playing with him, treating him like some oafish schoolboy who needed lessons in manners. He said, "What the hell do manners have to do with murder?"

"Manners? Oh, that's the way you're translating what I've said. All right, let it be manners. The fact is, Joe, that your manners have not been accept-able."

"*You* don't like them."

"No, I don't, but I've already told you that. I told you to stay away from the university and its stu-dents, but you didn't listen to me."

"You bet I didn't. Those murders came out of the university, and as far as I'm concerned, man-ners be damned, that's where the action is in this investigation."

"*Was*, Joe. There is no more action for you."

"Is this you talking, Bowen, or does it represent management at the paper, too?"

"It's me, Joe, although my instincts on it are re-spected."

"But why fire me? They took me off the Frolich story. Isn't that enough?"

Bowen chuckled. "It should have been, would have been with most people, but not with Joe Potamos. No, indeed, Joe Potamos kept right on poking his nose where he shouldn't, carrying his spear and his press card and looking for a scoop, looking for justice as he defines it."

"Joe Potamos sounds pretty good to me," Pota-mos said.

"Only to you, Joe, only to you."

"It doesn't matter," Potamos said. "I'm going to make a stink about this, Bowen."

"Yes, I'm sure you would. Maybe this will change your mind." He picked up an envelope, the only item on his desk, and held it out to Pota-mos, who kept his hands in his lap. "Go on, Joe, take it. I think you'll find it interesting."

Potamos reluctantly accepted the envelope and

opened it. Inside was a check made out to him for $100,000. "What's this for?" he asked.

"It's your severance pay."

"Yeah? How come you're paying me severance pay. I don't work for you."

"You could have."

"But I don't."

"What does it matter, Joe? You can take that money, move to a warm climate, and—"

The laugh exploded from Potamos. "Is that what this is all about? Pay me off to get me out of town?"

"Just a suggestion."

"Forget it." He tossed the check and envelope onto Bowen's desk.

Bowen's pleasant manner changed. He said sternly, "You'd better take it, Joe, and you'd better accept the conditions attached to it. You've been fired for insubordination. You'll never work again in Washington. Take my word for it."

Potamos reached over and looked at the check again. In the bottom left-hand corner was the word *Retainer.* "In what way can this be viewed as a retainer?"

"I'm retaining you as a consultant. There'll be more, paid quarterly, as long as you do as you're told. You'll leave Washington, forget about the Frolich and Fiamma murders, and, of course, hand over to me any materials you might have in your possession that bear upon these cases, including Miss Frolich's diary."

Potamos shrugged and again returned the check to the desk. "Sorry, Bowen, but these negotiations can't go forward. I don't have what you're buying."

"The diary?"

"Exactly."

"My sources tell me differently."

"You should develop better sources."

Bowen ran his fingertips over his thin gray moustache as Potamos got up and said, "You're crazier than even I figured, Bowen. I want my job back."

"Your job is gone. Take the money and enjoy your life. If you don't, your life will be anything but enjoyable."

"That's a real threat."

"Yes, *very* real."

Potamos looked at the check on the desk, at Bowen, then at the check again. He picked it up and said, "What if I cash this and don't accept the conditions?"

"More trouble for you, that's all."

"I don't have any diary."

"If you cash the check, Joe, I expect to see the diary on my desk by tomorrow morning."

"Don't hang around waiting for it."

Bowen smiled. "You do have your reasonable side, don't you, Joe? I knew it was there."

Potamos jammed the check into his pocket and went to the door. Bowen said, "Remember, Joe, as of this moment you've lost interest in murder cases in the nation's capital."

Potamos said nothing.

"And tomorrow morning at this time you'll be here with a diary in hand."

Potamos opened the door. His hand went to his pocket and for a moment he considered dropping the check on the floor. He didn't.

"Have a nice day, Joe," Bowen said.

Potamos closed the door, walked past Mrs. Carlisle, and left the building.

Chapter Twenty-five

"Joe, Roseann."

"Hi. I was going to call you, but . . . you told me not to until this was over."

"I know, but it's not over for me, either." She told him of Languth's visit to the Watergate.

"Son of a . . . He has no business hounding you. I'll call him."

"All right, but I do want to talk to you."

"Sure. I want to talk to you, too. This whole thing is getting weirder all the time."

They agreed to meet for lunch at Martin's at noon.

Potamos had come directly home from Bowen's office and had been sitting at the kitchen table when she called, the check in front of him. The thing he was having trouble dealing with was that a portion of his brain was telling him to cash it, turn over the diary, and move to California, or Mexico, maybe even Greece. Living was cheap in Greece. His mother would be happy. He wondered what the quarantine laws were for dogs coming into the country. He also wondered whether he could sweeten the deal. Bowen had said there would be more money coming. Maybe he could get it in a lump sum, turn the key on the condo, and take off, forget Washington and murders and the rest of it, except Blackburn. Maybe if he accepted Bowen's terms and started living a simpler life, she'd marry him. She'd said that was what she wanted. Maybe. He wouldn't push, just let it unravel naturally.

She was late to lunch, which was okay by him. He'd finished his first drink and been served his second when she came through the door, spotted him in the booth, and joined him. He'd forgotten how beautiful she was; he felt warm enough to melt away. She kissed him lightly on the lips, slipped out of her raincoat, and sat across from him.

"Good to see you," he said.

She gave him what he perceived as an it's-inevitable look. He liked it. It made him feel secure.

"Roseann, I'm really sorry about what's happened. Languth is a clod. I'll make sure he doesn't bother you again."

"How can you do that?"

"I don't know, but I'll do *something*. Did he hurt you?"

"No, just a lot of upsetting talk. He said he wants the diary."

Potamos shook his head. "Everybody wants the diary."

"Maybe he's the one who should have it, Joe."

"No, he's the last one I'd give it to."

"He said he could arrest me for withholding evidence, even those few pages you left with me."

"He's browbeating you, Roseann. Forget what he said."

"I can't." She grabbed his hands on the table. "Joe, I just don't understand why you insist upon keeping it. Are you writing a story based on it?"

Potamos said, "Not anymore. I've been fired." He told of his meeting with Bowen and the check in his pocket. He put the check on the table between them. Her eyes widened. "A hundred thousand dollars? God, Joe, you're rich!"

"I figured I'd leave my options open."

"Your options? You mean you're really considering cashing it and giving Bowen the diary?"

"It crossed my mind."

"You can't."

"Huh? I thought you'd be all for it. Look, Roseann, I've been thinking a lot about us, about what we've said to each other." She started to say something, but he hushed her with a finger to her lips. "Hear me out. I've been thinking about that simple life you say you love, just playing music and not getting bogged down in the sort of nonsense I'm always drowning in. I asked myself, 'Joe, could you stand a simple life, *really* stand it?' I wasn't so sure at first, but this check from Bowen put things in perspective. What do I need Washington and journalism and all the rest of it for? The fact is, I don't. Maybe with this money, and with you, I could get used to simplicity. You understand what I'm saying? I could get used to anything as long as I had you."

She sat back and bit her lip. Her brow was wrinkled and there was a cast to her eyes that Potamos couldn't read, except to assume it stemmed from anger. "Roseann, let me go a little farther. When I met you I—"

"No, Joe, stop talking. I don't like what you're saying."

"What am I saying, that I love you? Is that so bad?"

"No, it's not bad at all, but one of the things I love about you is that you have a complicated life because you're willing to take chances, to live by some sort of code. That's rare."

"You just threw me a big curve, Roseann, and I'm a fast-ball hitter. I thought—"

"So did I, but you've helped me see things differently, too. I don't want to play lounges anymore with drunks asking for 'Melancholy Baby' and trying to shove dollar bills down my dress. That's like taking Bowen's check, selling out, not being true to yourself. I love jazz, Joe. That's what I want to play, because it pleases me, satisfies my soul. Understand what I'm saying? You never sell out and I always seem to."

Potamos got her point. "So you think I should tear up the check and keep on after the story."

"Yes."

"I'm fired. I don't have a forum anymore."

"Write the book that agent offered you."

He held Bowen's check and rubbed his thumb and index finger over it. Then a smile came to his craggy face, made craggier by fatigue. "How's this play for you?" he asked. "Maybe I cash the check, *then* do the story."

"That wouldn't be ethical."

"Roseann, none of the players in this game is ethical."

"That doesn't mean you have to be like them."

"Sometimes it helps, like cops who do a good job because they're basically wise guys anyway. Yeah, I think I'll do that—cash this sucker and go after everybody anyway."

"You do that, Joe, and you'll end up in the canal."

"Everything's a risk, huh? I'll think about it. In the meantime, let's talk about us. Will you marry me?"

"And be the wife of a hunted man?"

"We'll assume false identities and go to Greece."

"Greece? They don't have jazz in Greece."

"Sure, they must. Somewhere in Greece, maybe on one of the islands, there's got to be a dynamite band playing Dixieland."

She made a face. "I don't like Dixieland."

"Whatever. I'll import a band, a hundred pieces. I'll book 'em through Elite Music."

The giggle turned into a laugh. He joined her. When the spasm had subsided, he said, "I love you, Blackburn, and you will become Mrs. Joseph Potamos one day. By the way, my mother's having a family reunion and you're invited."

"Big deal."

"Huh?"

"I'm just invited so they'll have a piano player."

"No, that's not . . ." More laughter. "What are you doing tonight?"

"Playing at the Watergate."

"I'll be by."

"Maybe you shouldn't."

"Why not?"

"I don't know . . . maybe we shouldn't see each other until this is over."

"That's what you said yesterday, and here we are. No, no more of that. Let's go at it together. You play jazz and I'll play my game. Deal?"

She hesitated, then grabbed his outstretched hand and shook it. "It's a deal, crazy man."

He went immediately from Martin's to his bank and deposited Bowen's check in his checking account. "How long to clear?" he asked the teller.

"It's a local bank. A day."

"Great."

He went home and called Pete Languth at MPD. "Pete, Joe Potamos. Lay off Roseann."

"Who?"

"Roseann Blackburn. You searched her apartment and hassled her last night at the Watergate. Lay off."

"Who the hell do you think you are, Potamos? You're nothing but a former reporter who couldn't sell two lines of copy to any rag in Washington and you're throwing orders at me? I ought to run you in right now."

"Do it, baby. I'm home enjoying my retirement."

"Don't push me, Joe," said Languth. He hung up.

Potamos's next call was to Liza Dawson, who wrote a popular twice-weekly gossip column in an area magazine. They'd been friendly for years and had done each other favors from time to time. "Liza," he said, "I have a scoop for you."

"Delicious," she said.

He told her of his book deal, ending by saying, "It'll be an exposé of what's really behind the murder of Valerie Frolich and Tony Fiamma."

"What *is* behind it, Joe?"

"Read my book, sweetie, and don't fail me with this. I need the publicity."

"Thanks, Joe. Got anything else?"

"Sure. The D.C. area's hottest piano attraction is Roseann Blackburn. Keep your eye on her. She's about to make major moves toward becoming one of the top jazz pianists in the world."

Dawson laughed. "In love again, Joe?"

"You bet, with the hottest piano attraction—"

"I know, I know. Thanks, Joe. Let's have a drink soon."

"Sure, my treat. I'm about to be rich."

As Potamos hung up on Dawson, Peter Languth, still fuming from Potamos's call, left MPD headquarters and went to a pay phone a few blocks away. He placed a handkerchief over the mouthpiece and dialed a number. Julia Amster answered in her studio.

"We know what you and your boyfriend, Bowen, did, and you'll pay." His voice was distorted and raspy. He hung up, put the handkerchief in his pocket, and returned to his office.

Fifteen minutes later he received a call from Julia Amster. "Sergeant Languth, I think we ought to talk," she said.

"Anytime at your convenience, Ms. Amster. Just name it."

Chapter Twenty-six

By the time Potamos walked into the Press Club for lunch on Tuesday, the news of his firing was no longer news. A few friends offered their condolences, which he dismissed with a laugh and the line "Best thing ever happened to me. Time I became a former newspaperman."

The bar was relatively empty. Marvin Goldson was at his customary spot at the end, a buddha with drink and shrimp cocktail set up before him like an offering. Usually he was gregarious in his greetings, but this day he only glanced at Potamos, nodded, and continued eating. Potamos went over with his drink and sat next to him. "Mind, Marv?"

"No, no, Joe, go ahead."

"You heard about Fiamma."

"Sure. Jesus, what kind of a nut is running around Georgetown?"

"You ever figure out who broke into your shop?" Potamos asked.

"Just guesses, Joe. It really doesn't matter anymore."

"It doesn't? How'd you come to that conclusion?"

"Just because it doesn't, Joe, that's all. Case closed." He carefully dipped a shrimp into the spicy red sauce and nibbled from its end. Potamos watched out of the corner of his eye and didn't break the silence. It was Goldson who finally said, "Sorry to hear they canned you, Joe."

"Not me. I've been ready to pack it in for a long time."

"Yeah, but—"

"No buts, Marv. It gives me time to pursue other things that have been hanging fire."

"Like what?"

"Free-lancing, maybe magazines, maybe a book. By the way, I have Tony's notes that he based the article for you on. Interested in an old pro doing his version of the story?"

"You?"

"Yeah. I know you don't pay top dollar, but I did hear you dropped the penny-a-word fee last year."

Goldson smiled for a second, then reassumed the glum expression that had been on his face since Potamos came in.

"Interested, Marv?"

"No."

"Why not? The kid was my protégé. It might be nice to do it as a tribute to him."

"Forget it, Joe. That story is past history. I want nothing to do with it."

Potamos hesitated before asking, "Somebody putting the pressure on you, Marv?"

Goldson stopped a shrimp halfway to his mouth, slowly put it back on the plate, and turned to face Potamos. "No offense, Marv," Potamos said, "but I just get the feeling the arm is being put on a lot of people around town and figured it might have reached you, too."

"You're wrong, Joe. Don't ever accuse me of selling out. You hear me?" His anger radiated from him like heat. Potamos was sorry he'd upset him, but at the same time hadn't a doubt in the world that he was right. Somebody had gotten to Goldson. Who? Bowen? The police? Senator Frolich? Marshall Jenkins? Who else was there? Probably hundreds of people he hadn't ever heard of.

"Sorry, Marv. I wasn't accusing you of anything, but you have to admit that—"

"Joe, drop it. I'm sorry for the kid and his family, and I'm sorry you got the ax, but I've reached a point in my life where I want to keep things simple."

Potamos laughed and motioned to the bartender for a refill. "The simple life," he said. "My girlfriend's always talking about the simple life."

"I never cared about it when I was young, Joe, but I do now. No more tilting at windmills for me, no more causes."

"Okay," Potamos said, "but will you do me a favor?"

"Like what?"

"If you come up with any ideas, fall into any information that bears on either murder, give me a call, huh? Strictly between us."

"Sure, Joe, sure."

He decided to skip lunch at the club, caught a hamburger and shake at a diner, and drove to Bob Fitzgerald's apartment above the bar on M Street. He knew Fitzgerald was there the minute he pulled up; the sounds of the guitar poured out of the upstairs window and echoed off surrounding buildings. Potamos climbed the stairs and knocked. The music stopped and Fitzgerald opened the door.

"Hi, Bob."

"Oh, hi, Mr. Potamos. Come in."

The room was as cluttered as it had been the last time. "Find a place to sit down," Fitzgerald said, "if you can." He managed a laugh and pushed sheet music off the end of his bed.

Potamos chose to stand, went to the window, and looked down over M Street. "Well, what do you think?" he asked, not looking back at Fitzgerald.

"I think . . . I think the whole world is sick."

Potamos turned and leaned against the window frame. "That's probably a fair assumption, Bob. What's the talk around campus?"

"Nobody can believe it. I guess Tony being murdered isn't as shocking as Valerie, but it sets people on edge, you know, like there's some kook looking to knock off everybody in Bowen's seminar."

Potamos watched Fitzgerald try to decide where to perch. He was obviously very upset. Potamos said, "I want you to work with me."

Fitzgerald, who was wiping his guitar with a cloth, looked sharply at Potamos. "What do you mean?" he asked.

"I've decided to do a book on these murders.

I have a contract with a leading New York publisher. I'm through with the *Post*—too many restrictions, too much politics. I need somebody inside, somebody who knows the players without a scorecard. You understand?"

"I don't know, I . . ."

"I need somebody who liked Valerie, and who knew Fiamma. Frankly, you're the one who fits both criteria. The others I've talked to from the seminar weren't fans of Valerie, and that's being kind. I don't know whether you're aware that I got pretty close to Tony."

A smirk crossed Fitzgerald's face. "How could I not know it? That's all he bragged about, how he was working with you and had a job lined up at the *Post* because of it."

"He told you that?"

"He told *everybody* that."

"Damn fool."

"He was proud. Tony had more pride than anybody I've ever met. I guess it's because he came out of such a poor background. He really wanted to make it. I mean, we *all* want to make it, but with Tony it was an obsession. There was nothing else in life. I understood where he was coming from. He was honest, you know? Wasn't walking around puffed up because his family had money and power, nothing like that. He was alone. Damn, was he alone! I liked him."

"You seem to like everyone."

Fitzgerald shook his head. "That's not true. There's lots of people I don't like. Maybe that's not the best way to put it. There's people I don't believe in, don't want to spend time with, but I don't put them down. They have their own problems and . . ." He started to cry. Potamos wanted to put his arm around him but didn't, just stood and watched the young man with the ponytail and deliberately shabby clothes sit on the edge of his bed and sob.

When he'd brought himself under control, Potamos asked again, "Want to work with me?"

"What do you mean?" Fitzgerald said, wiping his eyes and blowing his nose.

"On the book about Valerie's murder, and Tony's murder. Obviously they're linked. I need somebody who really knew them, somebody to give me a real inside feel for the university, Bowen's seminar, anything I don't have access to."

"Gee, I . . ." Fitzgerald got up and started pacing the small room, stepping over boxes and clothing on the floor, musical instruments and records. "I don't understand," he said. "You were working with Tony, and Anne Lewis told me she was doing something with you."

"She did? She's not."

"She said she had lunch or something with you."

"That's true, but we never agreed to work together. I thought she and Steve McCarty had hooked up."

"They did, but they had a falling out. At least that's what Annie told me."

"It doesn't matter, Bob. Now that Tony's dead, the only person I want to work with is you."

"How come?"

"Because you're the only one who seems to care that somebody killed Valerie. Not only that, but from what you said you even liked Tony, which wasn't easy. Look, Bob, I can't promise you a lot right now except some money and a credit in the book. I'll be as generous as I can with both. Game?"

"I guess so. I have classes, though. I mean, I may not have enough time for you."

"Whatever time you can give me is fine. The first thing I want to know is what Tony did the day he was killed—where he went, who he saw. He was supposed to meet me at my apartment Saturday night, but he never showed. Now I know why. The question is, what did he do right up until somebody hit him in the head?"

"I know where he was Saturday afternoon."

"You do? Where was he?"

"Here."

"You serious?"

"Yeah. He called me and said he wanted to talk to me. I thought it was about a seminar project, but when he got here he wanted to know about Walter Nebel."

"Nebel? He's still gone."

"I know. Walter and I knew each other pretty well. Not that we were close buddies, but we enjoyed the same kind of music, the same groups. He'd always wanted to play an instrument, but he said his family didn't have enough money. He used to hang around when my band was gigging or rehearsing."

"Do you know where he is?"

Fitzgerald shook his head. "I heard from somebody that he'd gone down to West Virginia, but that was just a rumor. I think he has relatives down there around Charleston. Anyway, Tony told me he was working on a big story and that if he could find Walter he'd have the missing piece he needed."

"Did he say what that piece was?"

"No."

"Nebel dated Valerie."

"I know. It didn't last long, although it got pretty hot and heavy for a while. They went away together on weekends."

"I know."

"How do you know that?"

"I read . . . It doesn't matter for now. Let's get back to Tony. How long did he stay here?"

"About an hour. We listened to some music and . . . and got high."

"Uh-huh. Where did he go after leaving here?"

"I'm not sure. He tried to call Sam Maruca from here, but there was no answer."

"Maruca. Because he and Nebel are friends?"

"I suppose so."

"Okay, Bob, how about checking further for me? Do you know Maruca?"

"Yup."

"I met him, didn't like him. What's your opinion?"

"I don't know, Sam's okay, I guess, but he . . ."

"Let's drop the I-never-met-a-man-I-didn't-like philosophy and get honest."

Fitzgerald smiled. "I don't like Sam. It always amazed me that he and Walter were such good friends." He snapped his fingers. "I was just thinking that it was more of a master/slave relationship between them. Whatever Sam said, Walter did. I remember seeing them at parties where Sam had Walter running all over the place for him. He'd say 'Jump!' and there was Walter asking 'How high?'"

Potamos thought for a moment, then asked, "Any idea why Walter skipped?"

"Only that he was afraid he'd be a suspect in Valerie's murder."

"You think he could have killed her?"

"No."

Another moment of thought. "What about Anne Lewis and Steve McCarty?"

"What about them?"

"McCarty dated Valerie and was unceremoniously dumped, at least according to what I've heard. Think he could have gotten mad enough to kill her?"

"No."

"What about Anne?"

Fitzgerald laughed. "Annie? She wouldn't kill anybody. How come you even ask?"

"I learned a long time ago, Bob, that it's the questions you *don't* ask that have the best answers."

"No, she wouldn't kill anybody."

"But what if she hated Valerie as much as McCarty obviously did? Do you think McCarty might have done it at her behest?"

"Mr. Potamos, these people are my friends. We've been in the same classes, gone to parties together, are shooting for the same careers."

"Which is an interesting point—and please call

me Joe. There seems to be an incredible competi-
tiveness within Bowen's seminar."

"We're all scared, Joe."

"Of what?"

"Of failing. There aren't many jobs out there for
J-school grads. I guess it was different when you
came into the field."

Potamos nodded. "Yeah, maybe it was, but
I don't think things have changed *that* much.
Anyway, can you do some more checking on
where Tony was the rest of Saturday?"

"I'll try."

"It looked to me like he was killed where they
found him Sunday morning. Maybe he went there
to meet somebody—Maruca, Nebel, whoever."

Fitzgerald promised to call Joe that night at his
apartment. Potamos's final warning was for him
to keep everything to himself and to share it only
with his new partner.

"Joe," Fitzgerald said as Potamos was on his
way out.

"Yeah?"

"I have to think about this a little more."

"About what, working with me? Why?"

"Because . . . because I'm not sure I want to get too
involved, considering what's happened to Valerie
and Tony. Bowen told us we were not to speak with
any members of the press except him. The police
told us we couldn't reveal anything we know except
to them. I just don't want to end up like Tony."

"Who would? You think about it, Bob, and call
me tonight. Either way it's okay. I like you."

"Thanks."

Chapter Twenty-seven

Potamos woke Wednesday morning to the rattling of his bedroom windows. A storm had raced into Washington in the early hours, heavy rain whipped around by strong winds. It occurred to him that there wasn't any compelling reason to get up. He was unemployed and had a hundred thousand dollars in the bank. Perfect day to roll over and sleep until noon.

But Jumper was standing at the bedroom door wagging her tail. She barked, telling him what *her* needs were. He got up, pulled on pants over his pajamas, slipped into a pair of sneakers, put on a raincoat and rainhat, and accommodated her.

Back inside, he got down to his pajamas again and made coffee. Then he decided to take a leisurely bath instead of his usual shower. He realized as he filled the tub with hot water that he hadn't taken a bath in a year, maybe two; the last time when he was in a posh hotel in New York. Maybe he'd have more time now that he was about to indulge himself in a simpler life-style. The thought was appealing: hot baths and good books to read; prolonged walks with Jumper, who never got more than a cursory walk that terminated when business was completed; maybe time to learn something about music (that would be necessary if he were married to Roseann); life off the fast lane, a *normal* life, whatever that represented.

He turned off the spigots and tentatively dabbed a toe into the water. He was halfway into the tub when the phone rang. He cursed, wiped the wet foot with a towel, then told himself that one of the perks of being "retired" was not having to answer the telephone. It kept ringing; he argued with himself over what to do. "Like Pavlov's dog," he mumbled as he crossed the living room naked and grabbed the phone. "Hello," he said in a nasty voice.

"Joey, it's mama."

"Mama? Hey, I didn't . . . It's good to hear from you." It dawned on him that she called only when something was wrong. "Are you okay?" he asked.

"Joey, what have you done?"

"What do you mean?"

"The police were here this morning. They came at six o'clock, three of them, from the Federal Bureau of Investigation."

"The FBI? Why were they there?" He knew, and a vision of the envelope on the shelf in his room now in the hands of authorities sent all the coffee he'd consumed flying around his stomach.

"They searched the house. They had a warranty."

"A warrant. Why did they do that?"

"They wouldn't say. They went everywhere, pulled things down and opened things. I kept asking why they came to my house and they wouldn't tell me, only one of them said . . . yes, he said exactly, 'Your son has something we need.' He called me ma'am, always called me ma'am. Joey, what have you done?"

"I didn't do anything, ma, honest."

"Did you bring something with you when you were here?"

"No, of course not. Did they find anything?"

"I don't know. I asked, but they wouldn't say. They made me sit in the kitchen with one of them while the other two searched the house."

He wanted desperately to ask her to check his closet for the envelope, but restrained himself. Instead he said, "I'll be up this afternoon, as fast as I can get there."

"Maybe you shouldn't, Joey."

"Why shouldn't I? You're my mother. They had no right."

"It sounds like you're in terrible trouble."

"Ma, what trouble could I be in? I'm a writer, that's all."

"I don't know, I—"

"You stay there, ma. I'll see you later. Don't worry, it's just a mistake."

One of the things he had planned to do that day was stop by the condo Marshall Jenkins was building near the Soviet Embassy. Anxious as he was to get to New York and see whether Valerie Frolich's diary was gone, he decided to get this out of the way first. Valerie had devoted a considerable number of pages to talking about the "scam" the condo represented. Unfortunately her writing was adolescent, everything wrapped in poetry, oblique sentences, foggy phrases that left him wondering what *really* was going on. That's the way it was with her entries about the condo—references to her father profiting from it, speculation that the money to build it was coming from foreign governments, especially West Germany, funneled through Marshall Jenkins, whom Valerie obviously hated. Her father's private life wasn't any more palatable to her than his public one. Although she never came out and accused him of having an affair with Elsa Jenkins, it was evident that it was very much on her mind.

The storm was at its strongest as Potamos drove toward the condo. Roads were flooded, and a couple of downed power lines forced him to take detours. Eventually, he reached the construction site, parked in the shallowest of the puddles, and walked through an open gate in the chain link fence that surrounded the property. He saw a light inside a large trailer and knocked on the door. It was opened by a broad-shouldered man in dark blue work pants and shirt.

"Mind if I come in?" Potamos asked, water dripping from the rim of his rainhat, his shoes soaked.

"What can I do for you?" the man in the trailer asked.

"I'm wet," Potamos said, grinning. "Just want to talk to you. I'm from the *Post*. George Bowen sent me."

"Mr. Bowen?" There was a moment of decision making before he stepped back and allowed Potamos in. The trailer contained file cabinets, a drafting table, a typewriter and calculator, and a half-dozen folding chairs.

"Whew," Potamos said, removing his hat. "Joe Potamos." He held out his hand.

The man took it and said, "Jim Blake, site foreman. Mr. Bowen sent you?"

"Yeah. I work with him. He wants to do another piece about the condo—you know, sort of see if he can help it along." Potamos shook his head. "I think he's reached the end of his string with all the goddamn dogooders who keep getting in the way here."

Blake nodded in agreement and said, "It don't make sense to me that a handful of people can keep a building from getting built."

"Me, either, Jim, especially with people like Mr. Jenkins and Senator Frolich and the others behind it."

"That's right," Blake said. "What's Mr. Bowen want you to do out here?"

"Just look around, get some angles for future columns he wants to write. I picked a hell of a day, huh?"

"No day to be taking a tour, that's for sure."

"I don't need a guided tour. No sense in you getting soaked. I'll just walk around for a half-hour. If I have questions, we can talk when I get back."

"Well now, I'm not sure I can let you do that."

Potamos was sorry he'd suggested it. He'd be lucky to gain access at all without wanting to be on his own. He was afraid Blake might decide to call someone to check him out, so he said, "If you don't mind getting wet I'd appreciate your coming along, maybe go up top, whatever *you* think is interesting. Besides, I don't need to fall into a hole or get hit in the head. You have an extra hard hat?"

"Sure." Blake grabbed one from a pile of them on a file cabinet and handed it to Potamos. "That's not much of a raincoat you're wearing," he said.

Potamos laughed. "I know. It strains the rain. I'm okay. I really appreciate this, and I know George does."

"George? Oh, Mr. Bowen. Sure thing." Blake put on a hard hat and a heavy yellow rubber slicker with a hood. He opened the door and they leaned forward against the wind and rain. Blake led them to the base of the condo and looked up. Large pieces of canvas flapped from the edges of the fifteenth floor, and the top of the crane was etched against the gray sky.

"You sure that crane's secure in this wind?" Potamos asked.

Blake laughed. "Don't worry. Take more than this to topple it. Come on."

The path he chose was through mud. Potamos's shoes sank deep into it; once, it came up to his right ankle and oozed down into his shoe. They entered the condo through a metal rear door. It was a relief to be out of the elements. Potamos kicked his shoes against a cement wall and shook the water from his hat. "Damn, that's wild out there."

Blake laughed and pushed a button for the large freight elevator that ran up through the gutted interior of the building. It creaked and groaned as it came down from the roof, arriving at ground level with a thud that sent dust and dirt flying. "You want to go up, right?" Blake asked.

"Yeah, right, Jim, sure do." They got on the elevator and Blake pushed a button that sent the rig skyward. "How many stories you planning to go?" Potamos asked.

"Plans call for twenty-five," Blake said.

"That's what they're fighting about, right?"

"Right. They wanted it stopped at twelve, but we snuck in a few floors before they got on to it." He laughed. "Now they want us to take off the top three, but Mr. Jenkins says he'll see hell freeze over before that happens."

"I don't blame him. We need a building like this."

"That's right, especially with the Russians sitting on their goddamn hill watching everything the whole city does."

Potamos feigned surprise. "I never thought about the Russians and the embassy. I meant we could use some nice places to live in the area."

"I guess most people feel like that," Blake said as the elevator lurched to a stop, then continued its slow, wrenching ascent. "Got the whole place almost sold already."

"No kidding? Must be expensive."

"People got money these days, though you can't prove it by me."

"How'd you sell 'em if you don't know how many floors there'll be?"

"Oh, there'll be the twenty-five, all right, Mr. Jenkins'll see to that."

They reached the top and Blake opened an accordion gate. Potamos put his hat on and stepped out onto the flat concrete slab that was the fifteenth floor. He waited for Blake to join him and they walked toward the far edge. When they reached it, Blake pointed down to the bleak, fortressed compound and said, "There they are, the Russians. Frankly, I'd just as soon not live so close to them, but lots a'people don't feel the same."

Potamos realized that if the condo were to have any intelligence value, it would need the final ten floors to give it an unencumbered view. Now, the interior of the compound could be seen only on a slant.

Potamos moved closer to the edge, turned, and said to Blake, "I guess the ones who get the top floors pay the most, huh?"

Blake shook his head. "The top two floors aren't for sale."

"How come?"

"I guess they're taken already."

"Yeah, I guess so," Potamos said, walking along the edge to get a different perspective of the embassy.

"You'd better get back here," Blake said. "I don't need a visitor falling off."

A sudden gust of wind blew Blake's words back into his face. Potamos looked around and said loudly, "What'd you say?" Another gust, this one even stronger, took Potamos's hat from his head and sent it into the air toward the embassy like a Frisbee. Potamos grabbed for it, started to lose his balance, and quickly stepped back from the edge of the roof. "Damn," he said. "Sorry about the hat."

"Better the hat than you," Blake said. "You seen enough?"

"Yeah, thanks, that's it."

Blake asked him for a card before Potamos left the site, and Potamos accommodated him. "Potamos," Blake said, squinting at the card. "You write about those murders, don't you?"

"That's right, but now I'm on Mr. Bowen's payroll."

"Give him my best, tell him to come around himself again. He's okay."

"That he is, Jim, a prince among men. Thanks again for getting wet."

Potamos drove straight to National Airport, where he was told all flights to New York were temporarily canceled due to fog in New York. He got a sandwich and a beer and called Roseann from a booth, woke her, told her he was going to New York on business but hoped to be back that night. "Maybe I'll stop at the Watergate," he said.

"Okay," she said. "Are you all right?"

"Yeah, hassled but hanging in. You?"

"I think so. At least the police haven't been around again. Joe, be careful."

"Sure. You, too. If I don't get back, I'll call you."

They resumed flights at three that afternoon and he was at his mother's house at five. She was clearly upset and he cursed himself for putting her through it. But, he reminded himself, it didn't matter whether he'd left the diary there or not.

As long as the police thought he might have, they would have visited her anyway.

He sat with her in the kitchen and calmed her down, got up and said he'd be down in a minute. The diary was gone from his closet. No surprise but disappointing anyway. He rejoined her in the kitchen and explained that the FBI had probably been there because of a very sensitive story he was working on for the paper. "Other reporters on the story had the same thing happen, ma. Nothing to be upset about. I'm sorry they ruined your day." He kissed her cheek.

She smiled and hugged him. "I just don't want anything to happen to you, Joey."

"What could happen to me?" he said, laughing.

"I don't know, but I worry sometimes. You haven't forgotten the party here?"

He had. "No, of course not. It's in big red letters on my calendar."

"Good. You're bringing that pianist?"

"Ah, probably. It depends on whether she has a concert or something."

He stayed another hour before announcing that he had to be back in Washington that night "for a meeting." His mother cried when he left and he promised to come back even before the party, which seemed to satisfy her. He *would* be back soon, he told himself as the cabdriver took him to LaGuardia.

Roseann was in the middle of a set when Potamos walked into the Terrace Lounge. She saw him, smiled, and continued with a medley of Cole Porter songs. When she finished, a man one

stool removed from Potamos applauded. Potamos looked at him. He'd learned since meeting
Roseann that few people applauded lounge piano
players, who, Roseann explained, were there to
provide background music unobtrusively. "If they
applaud," she told him, "you've done a bad job."
He didn't necessarily understand why, but who
was he to argue? The man continued applauding
and Potamos joined him, felt good doing so. Roseann nodded toward them and started another
tune.

Potamos ordered a double scotch with a splash
of soda. It had been a long day. I'll probably get
pneumonia, he told himself as he reflected back
on his visit to the condo. It made sense that the
condo represented more than a simple real-
estate investment; the location was perfect for
electronic surveillance and countersurveillance.
But West Germans behind it? Why? What was
Marshall Jenkins's stake in it except to get richer?
Potamos could understand why Senator Frolich might be involved. He was chairman of the
Senate Select Committee on Intelligence. Jenkins
could have agreed to cooperate with the government by installing electronic gear on the building's roof. The CIA, or FBI, or any one of a dozen
intelligence-gathering agencies could be dictating Frolich's moves. But so what? Was the project so sensitive that it was worth killing people?
Frolich's own daughter? Preposterous, Potamos
concluded.

Roseann finished the set and came to him. "Hi,
Joe," she said. He kissed her cheek and suggested

she sit between him and the man on his left. "Can't," she said. "How about the coffee shop?"

They had coffee and talked for a few minutes. Then she checked her watch and said she had to get back.

"I have to go, too. I left Jumper by herself."

"I would have walked her."

"I didn't want to inconvenience you. Besides, it's good training for her. Maybe I can get her up to twenty-four hours. Call me when you get home?"

"Sure. Drive carefully. You look beat."

"I am. I'll take it easy." He left her at the entrance to the lounge and drove cautiously home.

Blackburn had a number of requests during her next set, a few from the man who'd applauded her earlier. She responded favorably to him because his requests were for songs that she enjoyed, melodies rich in harmonic structure on which she could discreetly improvise. She also appreciated his attention to her playing. Most customers requested a tune and immediately went to a rest room. Not he. He sat there, a large brandy snifter in his hand, legs crossed, entirely focused on her playing.

They chatted briefly during her next intermission, which was a short one so that she would have sufficient time to play a longer final set. He never left the bar, barely seemed to move except for his foot, which kept time in the air during songs with a strong underlying rhythm. She finished the night with "Limehouse Blues," closed the piano's fallboard, and walked across the room toward a rear door leading to employee lockers.

The man at the bar said, "A wonderful evening, Ms. Blackburn. I haven't enjoyed music this much in a long time." He reached into the pocket of the tan bush jacket he wore over a dark blue turtle-neck and pulled out a roll of bills, some of which he laid on the bar.

"Thank you," she said.

"I was wondering if you'd be interested in a cup of coffee. I'll try not to bore you, and promise I won't linger past one cup." His smile was broad and pleasant. He was a handsome man. She'd been aware of that all evening.

"Thanks, but I can't. I'm . . . well, I'm spoken for."

"The fellow who was in before?"

"Yes. Goodnight, and thanks for the applause and good requests. I enjoyed playing them."

She got her coat from her locker and left through a rear door that emptied onto a small employee parking lot. She didn't see the tall, handsome man in the bush jacket sitting in a car close to hers. In a dark green sedan next to his were two other men. The man in the bush jacket nodded and the others quickly got out and approached her. She was putting the key in the lock when she realized they were behind her. She turned and said, "Who are you?"

One of the men said, "Come with us, Ms. Black-burn."

"I will not. Who are you?"

The man who'd spoken stepped closer and grabbed her arm. When she opened her mouth to scream, the other man clamped a large hand over it. They dragged her across the lot to their car, tossed her into the back seat, climbed in, and drove away. The tall, handsome man in the bush jacket watched from his darkened car. When they were gone, he started his car, turned on the lights, and left in the opposite direction.

As the scene in the parking lot unfolded, Senator John Frolich and Elsa Jenkins lay side by side in a king-size bed in the Watergate's largest suite. It had not been as carefully choreographed an assignation as previous ones had been. She'd called him that afternoon at his Senate office and said they had to meet that night, that something was wrong.

She sat on the bed wearing a robe provided by the hotel, her knees drawn up to her chin, her long blond hair still damp from their lovemaking. Frolich, also in a robe, sat in a chair at the desk, his brow furrowed, shoulders hunched.

"What do we do?" she asked.

"I don't know," he said, rising and coming to the bed, where he sat down against a mound of pillows. "Obviously, we should have been more discreet."

"How could we have been? It's gone on too long to cover every moment, every minute."

"We knew Marshall suspected it a month ago, Elsa. Maybe that's when we should have called it quits."

She stiffened and faced him, her hand on his bare thigh. "You could do that so easily?"

"Easily? Of course not, but there are ramifications here for both of us that aren't pleasant. Tell me again what he said before he left for Rome."

She waved her hand in front of her face as though to brush away webs that were in the way of her thoughts. "We were packed and ready to leave when he said, 'You've betrayed me, Elsa.' He said my name with such scorn. I asked what he meant. I knew, of course, but hoped it was something else. He shook me—I fell back on a suitcase, his anger was so intense. He said, 'You and my best friend. You'll *both* pay.' "

"You're sure he said that?" Frolich asked.

"Yes."

"Did he use my name?"

"No, but . . ."

"I am his best friend, and as far as I know I'm the only one who's been sleeping with his wife."

"My God."

"What's the matter?"

"So cold, so matter-of-fact. Is that what you've been doing, sleeping with me?"

Frolich smiled. "As far as I know."

She scrambled from the bed and lit a cigarette near the window. He came up behind her and placed his hands on her long, graceful neck. "Calm down, Elsa. That won't help either of us." He could feel the anger in her body and slowly began to massage her neck and the tops of her shoulders. The feeling was intensely pleasurable and she actually cooed.

When he was through, she turned to face him. He undid the sash on her robe, did the same with his, and led her back to the bed.

Later he said, "How did he find out? I mean, for certain?"

"He's been having me followed."

"When did you learn that?"

"I suspected it a long time ago, but I became certain of it two weeks ago."

"Damn it, Elsa, why didn't you tell me?"

"Because . . ." She touched his face and tears glistened in her eyes. "Because I didn't want to lose this."

"We may lose a lot more," he said.

"But we'll have each other."

He didn't respond. His thoughts were on his wife, Henrietta. She knew, too, of his affair with Elsa—nothing tangible, just *knew*. She'd brought it up once. He'd denied it, and that was the end of any conversation about it between them. And there was Valerie, who had also known. *She* had had tangible evidence: She had seen it with her own eyes. He'd had no idea she'd been at the inn in Leesburg that same weekend he and Elsa spent a night there. Just one night, and his daughter had to be there to see them coming from their room, kissing, fondling in the hall, walking hand in hand until reaching the public area, where they parted with a curt, proper goodbye. But she'd seen it, and as he was leaving the inn to meet with Jenkins at his retreat, she'd confronted him about it. The look on her face had frightened him. He'd never seen her look or sound that way before, venom in every word, her eyes bright, glowing coals ready to be ejected at him.

As far as he knew, Valerie had never told her

mother, but it had hung over him ever since, a constant threat to the sort of family unity he so desperately needed, not only because of his presidential aspirations but for his own peace of mind.

"He will divorce me," Elsa said, which snapped him out of his thoughts.

"Maybe not," Frolich said. "I can talk to him. We can all have a talk."

She guffawed. "Don't be silly," she said.

"I don't consider myself silly, Elsa."

"I didn't mean . . . What does it matter? He comes back Friday. I'll be there to face him. You stay out of it, John. It is my indiscretion with my husband. I'll see that you aren't hurt by this."

He took her in his arms and whispered, "You're a remarkable woman, Elsa," but she knew what he was thinking: that he wanted to be shielded from any fallout of the affair. She also knew that he would be successful in avoiding it. Her husband would vent his anger on her, which was only proper. But between these two rich and famous male friends there would be only words, apologies, and then life would go on, deals would go forward, the fishing and hunting would never miss a beat.

She silently cursed that reality.

Chapter Twenty-eight

Potamos had intended to stay up for Roseann's call but the day's rigors had taken their toll. He awoke at seven in the morning, realized she hadn't called, and picked up the phone. There was no answer at her apartment. He was worried. An accident? Had she gone off with some jazz-musician friends for a jam session? Another man? He ruled that out. If there were, she wouldn't play it this way.

Which left an accident or a jam session. She wouldn't have gone off to play without calling him. That left only one possibility, an accident. He called MPD, identified himself, and asked for an accident report from that night. There had been a few, but none involved her.

He drove up in front of her place an hour later and knocked, peered in windows, looked for her car. "Damn," he said. He returned home to a ringing phone.

"Hello?"

"Mr. Potamos, this is Bob Fitzgerald."

"Yeah, Bob, how are you?"

"Sorry I didn't call last night, but I got tied up."

"Yeah?" He was concentrating on Roseann; Fitzgerald's words meant nothing to him.

"I saw Walter Nebel last night."

"Wait a minute . . . you know where he is?"

"No, but I saw him."

"Where?"

"In town. I went to a movie and when I came out, my friends and I felt like pizza, so we—"

"Get on with it."

"We were walking along and I saw him, by the kite shop on M Street."

"Was he with anybody?"

"Yeah, Anne Lewis."

"Did you talk to him, to her?"

"No. I saw them from a distance. I was with these friends, so it took a minute to explain why I was running off. By the time I went after them, they were gone."

Potamos's sigh said it all.

"I'm sorry, but I couldn't help it. Anyway, he's here in Georgetown, and Annie knows where."

"Why would she be with him?"

"Beats me, Mr. Potamos."

"Joe."

"Yeah, Joe. Want me to call her?"

"No, I will. What about Tony Fiamma? Find out anything about where he went that night?"

"No, except that a buddy of mine who tends bar said he saw him. I guess he came into the bar, looked around, then left."

Potamos's thoughts went back to the missing Blackburn. He said to Fitzgerald, "Okay, Bob, thanks. Good work. Keep in touch." He hung up.

The phone rang. He answered. "Mr. Potamos, this is Mary Hlavaty at the bank. That big check you deposited the other day—"

"Don't tell me, let me guess. He stopped payment on it."

"No, it was returned for insufficient funds in his account."

"No kidding. That . . ."

"Should I put it through again?"

"No, don't bother. I'll talk to him. Thanks."

"Sure, but you'll still be charged."

"For what? It's *his* bum check."

"Policy."

"Some policy. Get it from both ends."

"I'm sorry but—"

"Hey, not your fault. Thanks for calling. I appreciate it."

He dialed Bowen's Mass. Ave. number. "Mrs. Carlisle, this is Joe Potamos. Is he there?"

"He's in a meeting."

"Get him out of it. He gave me a bum check."

"He cannot be disturbed."

"Get him on the line or I'll come down there with a baseball bat and *really* disturb things."

"You are a crude, disgusting—"

"Yeah, and you're somebody's blue-haired grandmother. I want him."

She hung up.

He was just as glad. All he could do was sputter and threaten and then what? Go out and buy a bat? It didn't make sense, Bowen's writing him a bad check. He'd expected Bowen to stop payment on it, but a bum one? Maybe it was a mistake, maybe he forgot to balance his checkbook. He decided he'd deal with that later. Right now there was the matter of one person found, the other missing—Walter Nebel and Roseann Blackburn, in that order.

He called the Watergate Hotel and asked to be connected to the Terrace Lounge. Too early; call at 11:30.

He called Elite Music and got the redhead, asked for William Walters. Too early for him, too. "Have you had any contact with Roseann Blackburn?" Potamos asked. "You booked her into the Watergate this week."

"No."

"Thanks."

He considered calling her parents but struck the idea. No sense worrying them, at least not yet. There had to be a reasonable, logical explanation for it. Calm down, he told himself. She'll show.

When she hadn't by noon, he made another pass at her house, then went to MPD headquarters, where he found Peter Languth in his office. "Got a minute?" he asked.

"Yeah, come in. What do you need?"

"I need to know what's happened to Roseann Blackburn."

"Your girlfriend?" Languth shrugged. "What's the matter, she skip on you?"

"No, I don't think that's it. She never came home from the Watergate last night and I'm worried. I checked the accidents, but nothing there. I just figured since you've been on her case, you might know something."

"Not me, Joe."

Potamos sighed and slumped into a chair. Languth stared at him across the desk and said, "You look like hell. You want coffee?"

His offer surprised Potamos. "Yeah, thanks," he said. "Black, no sugar." Languth called out for two coffees. "If she doesn't show up today, Pete, I'd like it to go on the wire."

"Sure, happy to. Actually, I'm glad you stopped by, Joe. I want to talk to you."

"About what, my mother?"

"Your mother?"

"The FBI coming to her house in New York and turning it upside down."

Languth's expression indicated genuine ignorance of the event.

"You didn't arrange it?" Potamos said.

"Nope. What'd they find?"

"I don't know. There was nothing to find except a dozen crosses and lots of olive oil."

Languth pulled his bulky body up straight and propped his elbows on the desk. "The diary, Joe? Is that what they were after?"

Potamos shook his head and frowned. "You really didn't know about the bureau hitting my mother's place, did you?"

"I already told you that."

"Then who?"

Languth shook his head. "No idea." The coffee arrived. Languth tasted his, smacked his lips, and said, "It's getting better all the time."

"Pete," Potamos said, breathing in the steam from his cup, "I'm worried about Roseann. Somebody's pulling strings and getting people killed. I think whoever arranged for the FBI is the same person responsible for the murders, and for Roseann not coming home last night."

"Yeah? Who might that be?"

"You know more than me. Toss me a name."

"George Alfred Bowen."

"I wasn't thinking of him."

"Well, I was. I always am. That's what I wanted to talk to you about. I'm ready to make a move on him and maybe you can help."

"How?"

"The diary. I read those pages we found in your girlfriend's apartment. I get from them that Valerie Frolich and Bowen had quite a thing going."

"Maybe, maybe not. I read them, too, and you can take what you want from them, either an affair or a college girl's sexual fantasies."

"Come on."

"I mean it, Pete. She never said she slept with him."

"What about the rest of the diary?"

"What about it?"

"What more does she have to say about Bowen?"

"Pete, I don't know because I don't have it."

Languth curled his lip. "You did have it, Joe, or your girlfriend did. Was it at your mother's house?"

Potamos sipped his coffee and said nothing.

"All right, play it your way, but I agree with you—I think your friend Roseann is in big trouble and so are you. It doesn't matter whether you have the diary or not. The important thing is that you both read it. If it's loaded with damaging stuff about the high and mighty, having you two walking around with your heads full of what it said might be construed as unhealthy for the parties involved."

That thought had occupied Potamos all morning.

Languth hunched forward again. "Look, Joe, I don't need another murder on my hands, not with a lousy year to retirement. I got it all figured—where I'm going, what I'm going to do. This Frolich case, and now Fiamma, has sent my ulcers into war with my gut. I don't sleep nights, I eat like a pig, and my local liquor store is hangin' a plaque in my honor. I don't like these kinds of cases where the juicers, the big shots, are involved. Give me the drug pushers and the mob hits anytime. I want this over with. You must feel the same way, huh?"

"It doesn't matter to me anymore. They fired me."

"I heard."

"You and the rest of the world. The only thing I care about now is Roseann Blackburn. I just want to find her, get her back, and take off."

"With her?"

"Of course."

"What's this, number four?"

"Three."

"Guts, Joe, you've got guts. Once was enough for me."

Potamos looked at the wedding band on Languth's finger. "I figured you were still married, the ring and all."

"It was finished four years ago. I just never took it off."

Potamos was aware of the friendly nature of the conversation they'd entered into—two buddies comparing love lives over a beer. He said, "What do you want from me, Pete? I don't have the diary. The FBI does."

"From your mother's house."

"Leave her out of this. It doesn't matter. What do you want, for me to recite what's in it for you?"

"Just the Bowen stuff for now."

"You've seen it all, at least most of it. There was more stuff about making it with him, but nothing tangible."

"I don't need any more than I've got."

Potamos cocked his head. "Be serious. What's in that diary isn't going to give you a case against Bowen." As he said it, a happy fantasy flashed through his mind—Bowen being arrested, Bowen in court, the guilty verdict, the headlines, himself standing outside the courtroom laughing as Bowen was led away in cuffs.

"I have more than the diary, Joe."

"Yeah?" Was Languth about to tell him what it was?

"I've got his girlfriend, Julia Amster."

"What do you mean, you've 'got' her?"

"She's confirmed that Bowen had an affair with Valerie Frolich, and she's willing to testify to it."

Potamos had to smile. "Having an affair and committing murder don't necessarily go hand in hand."

"Lots of times they do."

"How'd you get her to tell you this?"

It was Languth's turn to smile. "An old technique, Joe. Get the tension going between a couple and one of them ends up wanting out of it. Anyway, it doesn't matter how. What counts is that I've got her. She gave me a statement."

Potamos checked his watch and thought about

Roseann. "Can I use your phone?" he asked. Languth nodded. Potamos dialed her number. Nothing. He said to Languth, "What do you want me to do? And if I do it, will you help me find Roseann?"

"Sure."

"Okay, lay it on me."

"Not here. Tonight, someplace outside. You know a joint in Alexandria called Rafters?"

"Yeah, lots of singles action."

"I wouldn't know about that. Meet me there at eight."

"Pete, I have other things on my mind. Why can't we just go get a cup of coffee and talk?"

"Too busy." He held up his beefy hands. "Hey, Joe, forget about it. I'll nail Bowen with or without you. As for your girlfriend—"

"All right, Pete, eight o'clock at Rafters."

"Right. Thanks for stopping by. And look out for yourself. You've got to be a hot item with Bowen and his crowd."

The people he made contact with at the Watergate had nothing to offer about Blackburn's whereabouts. She had played, as usual, and left on time. The bartender remembered Potamos's having been in earlier in the evening, and he mentioned the man with whom she'd talked during her break and just before she left.

"The guy with the bush jacket and gray Afro?"

"Yes. You talked to him, too."

"She leave with him?"

"No, unless she met him outside. She went through that door, and he left through the main entrance."

"He say anything to you?" Potamos asked. "You get his name? He use a credit card?"

"Nope. Cash, small talk."

"You ever see him before?"

The bartender shook his head.

The frustration welled up in Potamos. "Thanks," he said. "If she calls, let me know, huh?" He handed the bartender his card with his home phone on it.

"Reporter, huh?"

"Yeah, but this is no story. I'm worried about her. We're supposed to get married."

He left carrying the distinct feeling that the bartender viewed him as a jerk, a naïve guy in love with a beautiful female piano player—and everyone knows what *they're* like; probably made a date with the handsome guy at the bar who liked the way she played and looked and . . .

He called her apartment every five minutes throughout the afternoon, to no avail. By four, the worst possible scenarios had surfaced and he found himself pacing his rooms like a caged jungle animal, ready to kill anyone and everyone responsible for her disappearance.

He forced himself to momentarily put aside his grim thoughts and call Anne Lewis's house. A man answered, said she wasn't home, asked who was calling. "A friend," Potamos said. "Thanks, I'll call again." He hung up and realized he'd heard that male voice before. Who was it? He searched his recent experience and came up with

Steve McCarty, the former law student who was now a journalism student in Bowen's seminar. Why was he answering Anne Lewis's phone? He considered going there but ruled it out, at least for now. He had his date at eight with Languth. And Blackburn was supposed to start playing at eight in the Terrace Lounge. His worst fear was that he'd swing by there and she'd be sitting at the piano, as pretty as ever. She'd say to him, "Oh, Joe, I'm sorry but something came up, a wonderful chance to play with the biggest names, and I just couldn't resist. I would have called, but there was only this broken pay phone, and the other phone where we were playing was constantly busy and . . ."

He parked in front of the Watergate, slipped the doorman a buck, and ran inside. He could hear the piano before he ever reached the lounge. It stopped him in his tracks. "Bye-Bye, Blackbird," one of his favorites. On the piano in her apartment she'd shown him how she substituted chords for the simple ones that usually accompanied the melody—what had she called them, extensions and inversions? He slowly walked to the entrance to the lounge, afraid to see her there, more afraid of what he might say or do. He stepped inside. A black male piano player in a tuxedo flashed him a big grin and continued playing.

Potamos went to the piano, put a dollar bill in the tip glass, looked around the lounge, and wished he could speed up the metronome in the pianist's head.

The song ended. "Thanks," the pianist said, indicating the glass.

"Yeah, fine. Where's the girl who's been playing here all week?"

"Roseann? I don't know. Took a vacation or something. I'm just filling in."

"Who told you?"

"Who told me what, to play here? My agent."

"Oh, right, of course. You didn't talk to Roseann."

"No. I got a call this morning and here I am. Actually, I can't do the week, only tonight, but my agent got somebody to cover tomorrow."

"Your agent Elite Music?"

"For this gig, yeah." He laughed. "Got a request?"

"No, anything you like. I have to run. Who called Elite to tell them Roseann wasn't coming in?"

The pianist shrugged. "I guess she did," he said, launching into another song.

He arrived at Rafters forty-five minutes late and hoped Languth had stayed around. He had. He was at the long, handsome bar, hands clasped around a glass. The place was busy; a sign out front had touted Thursday as "Musical Trivia Night" with "Prizes for All."

He came up to Languth and said, "Sorry I'm late. I stopped to see if Roseann was at the Watergate. She wasn't."

Languth slowly turned and took him in with bloodshot, watery eyes. "How you doin?" he said.

He was sloshed, which didn't please Potamos. Then again, he reasoned, maybe it was better.

Drunks talked a lot. Maybe he'd learn more than if Languth were stone-cold sober. He sat down next to him and ordered scotch with a splash.

"She wasn't there, huh? Where do you figure she is?"

"I don't know. You said you'd put out an APB. You'll do that tonight?"

"First thing in the morning, Joe. First things first. Here." He handed Potamos an envelope.

His first thought was that he was receiving another check. He opened it and took out a piece of eight-and-a-half-by-eleven white paper with typing on it. "What's this?" he asked.

"Read it, then we'll talk." Languth told the bartender to fill him up again.

The bar was dimly lit and Potamos had to position himself to catch the light from a wall lamp behind him. There was a date in the upper right-hand corner, the previous Saturday.

> *Dear Joe,*
> *I thought because we are working together that I should let you know what I am doing. I just got a call from Professor Bowen who wants to meet me tonight down near the campus. I found out that he met Valerie the night she was murdered and I guess that's why he wants to talk to me. I don't have time to bring this to you but I wanted it written down in case something happens. I'll call you tomorrow.*
> *Tony*

Potamos dropped the paper on the bar and stared at Languth.

"How about that?" Languth said, his speech slurred.

"How about that, Pete?" Potamos said disgustedly. "Where'd you get it?"

"It was dropped off at my office. Nice, huh? Puts Mr. Bowen at the scene both times."

"Pete, you don't think this is legit."

"Legit? Come on, Joe, why wouldn't it be?"

Potamos shook his head. "In the first place, it isn't signed. In the second place, Fiamma would never have written it like this. He was pretty good, from what I saw—a lot better than this thing."

Languth looked straight ahead and finished his drink, plunked the glass down on the bar, and ordered another.

Potamos leaned close to him. "Level with me, Pete. Did you write this?"

"It was written on Fiamma's typewriter. I already had the test run."

"That doesn't answer my question. If you have the typewriter to test, you have it to use. Jesus, Pete, this is crazy. Why the hell are you showing it to me?"

Languth fixed Potamos with his large, watery blue eyes. "Because we can get that slime Bowen, Joe. You and me can settle scores with him."

"Pete, I—"

"I want you to come out with this note. You can write a story about it, anything you want, but just say that you found this in stuff Fiamma gave you."

"Like I said, Pete, this is crazy. *You're* crazy. What score do you have to settle with Bowen?"

Languth started to answer, stopped to yell at the bartender for his refill, turned again to Potamos, and said, "What'a you say, Joe?"

"No, and my advice to you is forget it. Of everybody in this town, I probably dislike Bowen the most, but I'd never frame him in a murder."

"It's not a frame, Joe. The kid wrote the note. We even got a print off the page."

"Great, then announce you have it and arrest Bowen."

"I can do that, but having it come from you would be better—no questions, you know?"

"Pete, what'd Bowen do to you?"

"He's a type, Joe. They use their jobs to get close to young girls in their classes and take advantage of them."

"That's all that's behind this? That you don't like college professors?" He couldn't keep the incredulity out of his voice. He watched Languth in his raincoat hunched over his drink, his face contorted from some inner anger, his breath coming in short, distinct, labored bursts. Potamos sensed that any further probing would result in a combative response, so he dropped the subject, finished his drink, and prepared to go, Fiamma's alleged note still on the bar. He suddenly realized that now *his* prints were on it. He said, "Pete, want me to take this with me?"

Languth turned slowly. "You'll do it?"

"No, and I don't think you should, either. Why don't I just tear it up and—"

Languth grabbed the paper from Potamos's hands, held it tightly, moved it up and down as though it were a club he intended to use. "You listen to me, Joe, and you listen good. You've got kids, right? What, two of them? They're both alive, right? You get to see them once in a while, talk to them, see them grow up."

"That's right."

The anger seemed to have flowed out of Languth. His big body sagged and his voice had an edge of sorrow to it. "I had a kid, Joe. Her name was Jane. My only kid, a good girl. My wife and I got along pretty good until Jane went off to college out in Michigan, Michigan State. We were really proud she got in, even got a scholarship. She was gonna be a teacher. She loved little kids, baby-sat for everybody."

It began to come back to Potamos now, a rumor three or four years ago that Languth had lost a kid. He hadn't seen Languth for months after hearing the rumor, and when they did meet up again, Potamos had either forgotten about it or declined to ask. Languth had never mentioned it, and it sort of faded away like most rumors.

"She was out there a couple of months, Joe, that's all, and then we get these letters that we couldn't understand. She got involved with some goddamn cult or something, and one of her teachers was in it, too, a crazy older guy who was into drugs. He got ahold of . . ." His voice started to crack and he fought valiantly not to break down. "He got ahold of her and she . . ." He blinked and inhaled, ran his hand over his eyes. "Goddamn," he said, turning away from Potamos and taking a large swig of his drink.

Potamos looked away to give him some dignity.

Had his daughter been killed by the professor he was talking about? He put his money on the bar and said, "You okay to drive, Pete? Want me to take you home?"

"No. I'm staying awhile."

"Can I suggest something?"

Languth didn't reply.

Potamos said, "Let me have the note. I'll keep it safe until tomorrow, until you've had time to think it over, really think it over. Maybe we can get together and talk some more, kick it around. How about dinner tomorrow night?" He'd forgotten for the last fifteen minutes about Roseann. When she took center stage again, he almost withdrew the offer. If he found her, they'd be together. The hell with Languth and his craziness.

"All right," Languth said, handing him the note.

"Yeah, good, Pete. I have to go. I'm still looking for Roseann."

"You think about it."

"The note?"

"Yeah. You've got plenty of reason to get him, too, and don't forget it."

"I won't. Will you put out an APB on Roseann if she doesn't show tonight?"

"Sure."

"I'll call you in the morning."

Languth drew a deep breath, slowly let it out, and wrapped his hands around his glass. Potamos touched him on the shoulder, said goodnight, and headed back to the city.

Chapter Twenty-nine

Potamos stopped at Bob Fitzgerald's apartment on the way home. He wasn't there. Potamos tacked a note on his door asking him to call at any hour.

His next stop was the Watergate, where Blackburn's substitute was still playing. He resisted having a drink and asking more questions; a waste of time.

He popped into his favorite newsstand on M Street to buy the papers and some magazines to pass the time at home. The new issue of the magazine Liza Dawson wrote for was prominently displayed. He thumbed through it until he found her column. There it was, the second lead, that he was writing a book on the Frolich murder. He had to smile; she'd tossed in a line just below it about Roseann Blackburn, a Washington pianist "poised at the threshold of jazz stardom." His smile faded as he thought of her. He paid and quickly went home, called her number. He gasped. Instead of a series of unanswered rings, there was the incessant drill in his ear of a busy signal. "Thank God," he said. He tried it again. It rang. No one answered. He tried again and again with the same result. You misdialed the first time, he told himself. Damn it, I thought . . .

The phone rang. It was Bob Fitzgerald. "I just got home and saw your note," he said.

"Yeah, good. Listen, Bob, how about getting over to Anne Lewis's house and seeing what the story is with Nebel?"

"You said you were going to call."

"I did call, but she wasn't there. I think Steve McCarty answered. Anyway, it occurs to me that you'd get a lot better reception than me. Make up an excuse, do whatever, but get in there, talk to Anne. Don't tell them when you call that you saw Nebel."

"I'll try but . . ."

"There's not much time, Bob."

"What do you mean?"

"Just take my word for it. Things are happening and I'm afraid we'll end up with somebody else dead."

"Who?"

"I'll fill you in when I see you. Get in touch with them and call me back."

"Hey, Joe, am I in danger?"

"You? Why would you be?"

"Because I'm in Bowen's seminar."

"I don't think so, but look over your shoulder. Talk to you later."

He sat in his recliner and tried to come up with some course of action, knew he couldn't just sit there all night and do nothing. He did the only thing available to him at the moment—phoned Blackburn's apartment every five minutes. He kept that up until midnight, then walked Jumper, took a shower to clear his head, put on his pajamas and a robe, and made a pot of coffee. He sat at the kitchen table waiting for it to brew. On the table in front of him was the note Languth had given him. He stared at it. It might work. He thought of Languth drunk in the bar at Rafters and couldn't contain a small smile. Languth actually might have done something worthwhile.

Potamos had George Bowen's unlisted home number but had never used it. He checked the kitchen clock: 12:30. Bowen might not be home, or, if he were, he might be asleep. Wait until morning? Impossible.

He dug out the number from a dresser drawer, returned to the kitchen, and poised to dial. He wasn't as filled with resolve as he had been ten minutes earlier. "The hell with it," he said as his finger found the first button on the phone. "What's to lose?"

His heart pounded as he heard the first ring on Bowen's end. It rang five more times before a woman answered.

"Is Mr. Bowen there?" Potamos asked.

"Yes, he is. Who is calling?" Had to be a maid.

He said, "Tell him it's . . . tell him it's Joe Potamos and it's very, very important."

"All right."

Potamos strained to hear what was in the background. Voices, laughter, music. A party. The bizarre thought hit him that whoever was playing the piano sounded like Blackburn, and that maybe Bowen had kidnapped her to perform. He rubbed his eyes and warned himself to stay rational.

Bowen came on the line after a long delay. "What do you want?" he asked angrily. "This is my home."

Potamos knew he'd probably have only a minute or less to get his message across, and had rehearsed it in his mind ever since coming up with the notion of calling Bowen. He said quickly, "One, your check bounced. Two, I have a piece of paper, and so do the police, that you're going to be damned unhappy over."

"What paper?"

"Paper that means big trouble for you, George, maybe enough to see you go to jail for the rest of your life."

Bowen laughed. "You're mad. Don't ever call me here again."

"I'll be at your office in the morning with a copy of the paper. And have a new check ready, plus what the bank stuck me for."

Bowen slammed down the phone, which made Potamos feel good. There was something satisfying in having upset America's leading columnist.

He weighed his next move. Chances were that since Julia Amster had come forward with a statement to the MPD, she wouldn't be attending Bowen's party. Potamos paused to consider whether Languth had been honest about Amster's action. He bought it, found her number, and dialed. Amster answered. She sounded breathless, as though she were hoping it was someone else, probably Bowen.

"Ms. Amster, I'm Joe Potamos of the *Washington Post*. Sorry to bother you this late, but it's important."

Her anticipatory tone suddenly changed to defensiveness. "What do you want with *me?*"

"I want to talk to you about George Bowen and the statement you gave MPD."

"How do you know about that? That was confidential. I've never—"

"Look, Ms. Amster, I'm not necessarily looking to write about it, but I thought you'd want to know that there have been other developments in the Frolich murder that involve Mr. Bowen."

"Other developments?"

"Yeah, and I'd like your reaction to them."

"Please, I have nothing to say in this matter. You say your name is Potamos. You're the one George has . . ."

"Has what, bad-mouthed?" He laughed, said, "Listen to this, Ms. Amster. This is a note written to me by Tony Fiamma the night he was murdered." He started to read.

"I don't think this is any concern of mine," she said.

Potamos kept reading, slowly and deliberately, pronouncing each word with care. Amster said nothing. When he was finished, she was silent for a moment, then said, "How do I know that's a legitimate note?"

"Call Sergeant Languth at MPD. It was written on Fiamma's typewriter, has his fingerprints all over it, and . . . and his signature checks out. Enough?"

Now her voice had lost its luster. She asked softly, "Why read this to me? What do you expect me to do?"

"Talk to me, that's all, any time, any place. You want me to come over now, I'll be there."

"No, please don't. I need to think about what you've said. I could call you tomorrow."

"Sure, if you want. Here's my number. I'll be here until eleven. Then I have a couple of appointments to keep."

"Eleven. Yes, I'll call you by eleven. Thank you, Mr. Potamos."

"Thank *you*, Ms. Amster. Have a good night."

He spent the rest of the night and early-morning hours pacing, talking to himself, alternating between despair and a rage that physically shook him. He dozed off a couple of times in the chair and was asleep when the phone rang at four. He had to shake himself into awareness before picking it up. It was George Bowen, who said sharply, "What the hell do you think you're doing, Potamos?"

"Protecting my interests and trying to find the woman I love."

"What does that have to do with me?"

"Lots, Bowen. You and your cronies are behind what's happened to her, and it's all bound up in Valerie Frolich and Tony Fiamma's deaths. I couldn't prove it before, but now I can, at least where Fiamma is concerned. Your girlfriend, Amster, call you?"

"How dare you slander me to my friends?" His voice had the tensility of carbon steel.

"Slander, hell," Potamos snapped back. "Want me to read the note I read your girlfriend?"

"That trash? It's a lie. I never arranged a meeting with Fiamma, nor did I see Valerie Frolich the night she died, except on the barge."

Potamos was feeling better all the time. The fact that Bowen was bothering to deny a note he hadn't even seen was positive.

"I told you I'd be by for a check, Bowen, and to show you this note. How about eleven? I've been up all night."

"You're a dead man, Potamos."

"Huh? You're threatening me?"

"Just listen to me, you demented slob. I'll have you buried ten feet deep in a grave you dug yourself. Don't test me, Potamos. Don't make my day."

It was Potamos's turn to pull back a little. He'd been certain that Bowen would agree to see him. Now there was only the threat that sent a chill through him. He glanced at the note on the table and wondered whether it might be legitimate. Maybe he'd dismissed Languth too fast. Languth hadn't flatly declared he'd written the note, just asked Potamos to help give it credibility. What if . . . what if Bowen was a madman who now had all the reason in the world to get rid of Roseann and him?

Potamos reacted from instinct, ignoring those thoughts. He said in a voice as hard as Bowen's, "The way I see it, Bowen, you're the one who's dug a grave. I'm going to the MPD with this. They think you did it anyway, and this is the spade that digs the grave deep enough, you pompous creep."

Bowen didn't respond, but Potamos could hear him breathing. Finally, he said, "I won't play games with you any longer, Potamos. Come to my office at eleven."

It took Potamos by surprise. All he could say was "I'll be there."

"And bring this so-called note with you."

"I'll have a copy."

The king-of-the-mountain conversation was over. Potamos poured himself a drink and took a half-hour to calm down. When he had, he found a pen, sat in the kitchen, and carefully signed the note: *Tony*. Satisfied, he tried Blackburn one more time and went to bed, setting his alarm for ten. He fell asleep not having any idea whether what he was doing would do anybody any good. But at least he'd done something. Any action was better than no action.

Chapter Thirty

Mrs. Carlisle was not at her desk, and the door to Bowen's office was closed. Potamos patted his jacket pocket containing the photocopy of Fiamma's note. Then he knocked. He heard a man's voice, then Bowen opened the door and stepped aside for Potamos to enter.

Potamos looked across the room to where another man stood. "Go on, sit down," Bowen said gruffly.

Potamos stood behind one of the visitors' chairs and placed his hands on it. The man by the window walked to the coffee service. Now Potamos could see his face and figure—tall, slim, with a carefully sculptured mass of gray hair and wearing a bush jacket and turtleneck. The one from the lounge at the Watergate. "What are you doing here?" Potamos asked.

Geof Krindler ignored him and opened a small can of orange juice that rested on ice in a silver bucket. He drank slowly from it as Potamos watched.

"You were at the bar," Potamos said, taking a step toward Krindler. "Do you know where Roseann is?"

"Sit down," Bowen said, taking his seat behind the desk and propping his feet on the edge.

"What's going on here?" Potamos asked. "What is this, some kind of a setup, a joke?"

Krindler went to the desk, placed a hand on a professional-quality Marantz cassette recorder, and said in a voice Potamos remembered so well from the bar, "We have a tape we'd like you to hear, Mr. Potamos. You will find it interesting. I'll play it when you sit down."

"A tape of what?"

Krindler glared at Potamos like a stern headmaster profoundly disappointed in a student. Bowen said, "Grow up, Joe, get smart and sit down. The games are over, for all of us. You've acted like an irrational jackass and it's time you stopped, realized that there are issues of far greater importance than one hack writer's need for fulfillment. Sit."

Potamos sat. Krindler started the tape, and a few seconds later Blackburn's voice came from the speaker:

"Joe, it's Roseann. Please don't worry, I'm okay. Nobody hurt me and they won't if you listen to what they have to say and do what they want. I'm sorry I put you in this position, but I couldn't help it. I'm fine, Joe. I'll see you soon." There was a hint of her voice cracking at the end, but Krindler abruptly stopped the tape.

Potamos leaned forward and said to Bowen, "I always knew you weren't wrapped too tight, Bowen, but kidnapping?"

Bowen smiled as Krindler went to the

window and leaned against the heating and air-conditioning duct, again becoming a silhouette to Potamos. Bowen said with a sigh, "It constantly amazes me how forgiving and understanding the American spirit is. Frankly, Joe, if I were holding the reins, I'd simply have you shot and hanged in Lafayette Park for all to see."

"Yeah, I don't doubt that. You kill a couple of college kids, what's another couple of bodies? Here, look." He angrily pulled the copy of Fiamma's note from his jacket and flung it at Bowen. Bowen picked it up from his lap, unfolded it, and casually perused it. Then he dropped it on the desk and sighed again, louder this time.

"Hey, you, what the hell is your name?" Potamos asked Krindler. Krindler didn't reply. Potamos said, "If she's hurt—I mean one hair, one inch of skin—I'll—"

"You'll what, Joe, be angry?" Bowen said. He turned to Krindler and said, "I have very little patience for this. Tell him what he needs to know and get him out of here. He turns my stomach."

Krindler took a chair next to Potamos. He crossed his legs, played with the medal dangling on his chest, and chewed on his lip.

"You kidnapped her?" Potamos asked, feeling increasingly helpless.

"She's been detained for national security purposes," Krindler said in a monotone. "Her well-being, yours, and the well-being of millions of citizens depend upon your cooperation."

Potamos laughed because he didn't know what else to do. He said, "Who wrote this script, Paddy Chayefsky?"

"Please drop the wise-guy act," Bowen said. "Go ahead, Geof."

"Geof? Geof what?" Potamos asked.

Krindler ignored the question and went on with his matter-of-fact presentation, still in a monotone. "The things you have been delving into, Mr. Potamos, involve extremely sensitive political and global issues. I know you don't realize that. Perhaps if you had, you would have reacted as a concerned citizen instead of a crusading reporter." Potamos started to say something but Krindler held up his hand. He said to Bowen, "I'm afraid I don't have the sort of patience you do. Coddling people like this, explaining things to them, is a waste of time."

"No, go ahead," Potamos said. "I want to hear. Hey, I may run off at the mouth sometimes, but I'm always willing to listen. Maybe that's been the point here, nobody's explained anything to me, just come down heavy, tried to buy me off." He smiled. "The American way. Everybody's got his price." He looked at Bowen. "Only the American way doesn't include bad checks."

Bowen said, "I did that deliberately, Joe, to see whether you were going to live up to your end of the bargain. Unfortunately, you weren't. I read Miss Dawson's column. Writing a book after taking my money and promising you'd forget the whole matter—that's very shabby, Joe."

"Yeah, well, talk about shabby, this mess is—"

Krindler stood, picked up the tape recorder from the desk, and said, "I'm leaving. I was against this from the beginning, and I think my people will now see the futility of it."

Potamos jumped up. "You guys have to be kidding. You want to talk about citizens. You've kidnapped a citizen, a piano player who pays her taxes and never did a damn thing except go out with me. I'll have you all arrested."

"Would you like to come with me?" Krindler said.

"Come with you? Where? For what?"

"For the education I've been ordered to give you and Miss Blackburn. I do it reluctantly, but I do have my orders."

"Where are we going?"

"To the reason for all of this."

"The condo."

Krindler went to the door. Bowen said to Potamos, "You've been invited to a weekend retreat, Joe."

"Huh?"

"A chance for you to have things put into perspective, heighten your civic consciousness, be at peace with yourself. A car will pick you up in front of your building tomorrow morning at eight. Pack an overnight bag, and don't tell anyone where you're going. Understood?"

"What if I don't want to?"

"Suit yourself. Remember Miss Blackburn."

"She's at this 'retreat'?"

"Yes."

"Jenkins?"

"Go with my friend here now. He has something to show you, and please don't be stupid. This has been a trying experience for so many people and it's time it was finished, in the past.

Please, Joe, make it easy for everyone. You'll be rewarded. This time the check will be even larger, and I assure you it will be good."

Potamos followed Krindler out the door and to the street. "My car's over there," Potamos said.

"We'll take mine," Krindler said.

"What do I do with mine?"

"Pick it up later."

"I'll go with you if I know your name."

Krindler walked away.

"Okay, okay, calm down," Potamos said, "I'm coming."

Krindler's car was a bright red Corvette that was immaculately clean. They got in and Krindler started the engine, glanced in the sideview mirror, slipped into first gear, and roared away from the curb.

"Nice car," Potamos said.

Krindler said nothing, just went through the gears like a knife in butter, nimbly passing everything on the road until approaching the condo in Georgetown. They walked past the trailer and to the rear entrance of the building.

"Where's Jim?" Potamos asked. "Jim Blake, the super."

"He has the day off."

"Because we were coming?"

Another cold shoulder. They opened the gate to the elevator and stepped inside. Krindler pushed a button and the slow, jerky, noisy ascent began. It wasn't until they reached the top and Krindler had opened the gate that Potamos began to experience fear. Here he was, fifteen stories up with a man he didn't know, who'd kidnapped a woman and had all the trappings of a weirdo who probably enjoyed pulling wings off flies and running down animals on the road. He almost didn't step off the elevator. His mind was racing: what to do in the event that . . .

Krindler turned and looked at him.

"I've already been here," Potamos said, still in the elevator.

"I know, but you didn't have the advantage of a good teacher. Come on, I want to explain twentieth-century political reality to you."

Potamos watched Krindler cross the broad expanse of concrete and stop at the edge overlooking the Russian Embassy. Potamos drew a deep breath and said, "Might as well." He stepped from the shaky elevator platform and slowly walked to where Krindler stood.

"What do you see down there, Mr. Potamos?"

"The new Soviet Embassy. What do you see?"

"I see evil. I see oppression, global expansionism. I see a threat to our way of life, to the democratic ideals this nation is based upon."

Potamos pondered how to respond. Was this the reason he'd been brought here—to receive a civics lesson from a guy in a bush jacket whose name he didn't even know? He decided to ask questions. "I know you won't give me your last name, Geof, but who do you represent?"

Krindler looked straight ahead as he said, "Your government."

"Mine? Not yours?"

Krindler narrowed his eyes against a chilly breeze that blew in his face. "It's *our* government,

Mr. Potamos, but some of us prize it more highly than others. There are those who simply enjoy its fruits, and those of us who devote themselves to protecting it, protecting the likes of you."

"What makes you so special? I love this country."

"You love what it can do for you, Mr. Potamos. My love for it isn't that narcissistic."

Potamos laughed. "I love guys like you, all full of yourselves and your patriotism, like the fate of America rests on your shoulders."

Krindler slowly turned, looked at him, and said without a hint of modesty, "That's exactly right, Mr. Potamos, exactly right. That's why when people like you insist on standing in the way of this country's survival, measures have to be taken to neutralize your threat to all of us."

" 'Neutralize.' That's an old CIA term."

Krindler again looked down at the Russian Embassy. Potamos did, too, for a second, then glanced over at him, saw his right hand go inside the bush jacket, saw the revolver slowly being drawn from a holster beneath his left armpit. What Potamos did next was as natural as blinking, or swatting an insect on his face. His right arm went out and he shoved Krindler. It took only a second, maybe less, for his body to disappear over the edge. Potamos didn't want to see it fall, but he did, fifteen floors to the ground, where it landed on its back, digging a foot into the earth. Krindler didn't say anything on the way down, and his body bore silently into the ground.

Potamos stepped back and started to shake. Then he ran to the elevator, pushed the button, and waited for what seemed hours before reaching ground level. He stepped outside and looked around. There wasn't a soul. Had any Russians in the embassy compound seen what had happened? Would they report it, come running over? He sprinted around the building to where Krindler's broken body was sprawled. The revolver was ten feet away. Potamos put it in his pocket. He stood over Krindler and felt he might vomit. Krindler's eyes were open and gazing up. His mouth was twisted, his gray Afro perfectly straight.

Potamos grabbed the dead man's arms and started to pull, realized that all the bones in them were broken. He shut his eyes tight against the rebellion in his stomach, opened them, and again started pulling Krindler out of his self-made hole and across the ground, around the building, and to the red Corvette. He dug into the corpse's pockets and pulled out his car keys and wallet, opened the trunk and managed to wedge the tall, lanky body into it, shut the lid and got behind the wheel.

He drove to his apartment, parked Krindler's red Corvette in the underground garage, and went upstairs. Jumper leaped all over him, he petted her, gave her fresh water. Then he stripped off his clothes and took a long, hot shower, dressed quickly, and sat down on the edge of his bed. It was the first time he'd taken a moment to think since it happened. It was too painful, too confusing. He jumped up, walked the dog, called a cab, and fifteen minutes later was on his way to where he'd parked his car near Bowen's office on Massachusetts Avenue.

Chapter Thirty-one

Potamos drove to a secluded overlook off the George Washington Parkway and took out the weapon he'd taken from Krindler. He'd found the dead man's last name in the wallet, which contained little else: a hundred dollars in small bills, a driver's license, an American Express card—nothing to link him to a government agency. That made sense. Whoever he worked for could be proud of his discretion.

Writing on the revolver indicated it was a French-made .380 Manurhin Automatic, which meant nothing to Potamos; he'd never owned a gun and had little interest in them. He made sure it was pointed away from him as he played with the slide and levers. He assumed it was loaded and would fire, but wasn't about to test it. He placed it beneath his seat, looked around to make sure he hadn't been observed, and left the overlook.

It was three o'clock. He drove without a destination until he decided he should hook up with Bob Fitzgerald and see if he'd found out anything.

Fitzgerald wasn't home, but as Potamos left the building and walked toward his car, Fitzgerald came running up the street. "Hey, wait!" he shouted. He reached Potamos and said, "Where have you been? I've been going nuts trying to find you. All kinds of weird things have happened."

"Don't talk about weird things to me," Potamos said. "What's up?"

"I talked to Walter."

"Nebel?"

"Yeah. I went to Annie's house and she let me in. I mean, I didn't think she would if Walter was there. We sat and talked for a couple of hours. Man, it was weird what he said!"

"Let's go somewhere," Potamos said as he saw an MPD squad car approach. He felt like a fugitive, a marked man. "Come on. I need a drink."

They drove up Wisconsin. Potamos spotted a parking space across from the Georgetown Inn and took it, locked the doors, and led Fitzgerald into the large barroom. The circular bar was empty. He considered sitting there but opted for a small table off to the side. "What do you want?" he asked.

"I don't know. I don't drink much."

A waiter came to the table. "A double ancient age for me, and give my friend a bloody mary."

"What's in that?" Fitzgerald asked.

"Most places vodka and some spiced-up tomato juice. In here, it depends on who's making it. You'll get vodka, plenty of it, but if there's some amigo in the back whipping up the juice, you'll get a transfusion."

"I don't . . . Okay, whatever you say. Where've you been, Joe?"

"Learning about my country. Tell me about Nebel. What'd he have to say?"

Fitzgerald blew air through his lips and looked nervously around the room. He leaned across the table and said, "Joe, I know who killed Valerie."

"Yeah? Who?"

"Sam Maruca."

"Says who?"

"Walter."

"How does he know?"

"Because . . ." More breath that carried a whistle with it, and more furtive glances over his shoulder. Now, closer to Potamos and a whisper: "Because . . . because Maruca told him."

"Come on, Bob, why would he tell anybody if he did it?"

"Joe, remember about Nebel asking Sam to provide him with an alibi?"

"Sure. Nobody bought it."

"Right. Walter didn't ask Sam for an alibi. Sam suggested to Walter that he'd need one because he'd had the fight with Valerie that night."

Potamos nodded. "So Maruca ended up with the alibi. He's not dumb, but why is Nebel talking about it now, and how does he know, *really* know, Maruca killed Valerie?"

"I told you, Sam told him. It was an accident."

"Accident?"

"Yeah. All Sam wanted to do was scare her, but he hit her too hard. I guess she really fought and he kept hitting her."

The waiter brought their drinks, which silenced them. When he was gone, Potamos said, "You're losing me, Bob. Start from the beginning and go slow. I've had a tough day."

It turned out that Fitzgerald had little more to

offer. What he did have, however, was a commitment from Nebel to talk to Potamos. "I convinced
him, Joe, that you were the only person he could
trust."

"When?" Potamos asked.

"This weekend."

"Too late. It has to be tonight."

"Why?"

"I have . . . I have a date tomorrow morning, a
country jaunt."

"Ah, come on."

"How's the bloody mary?"

"An amigo made it." Fitzgerald smiled. "Took
the roof of my mouth off."

"It's even better at Sunday brunch. Call Nebel,
see if we can get together tonight."

"He's still at Annie's."

"What do her parents say about him staying
there?"

"They're away on a long trip. She has the house
to herself."

"Convenient. Go ahead, call. Here's a couple of
quarters."

Fitzgerald used a lobby phone and came running back a few minutes later. "I have Annie on
the phone, Joe. She wants to talk to you."

Potamos went to where Fitzgerald had left the
phone dangling and picked it up. "Anne?"

"Yes. Look, Mr. Potamos, this whole thing is
getting wild. We have—"

"Who's we?"

"Steve and I and Walter Nebel have put together the whole story, every piece of it, some-

thing the police and you and everybody else couldn't do."

"I'm impressed, and I assure you, Anne, that I'm not looking to jump in and steal your thunder, but things have changed. My fiancée has been kidnapped, there's a CIA guy very dead in the trunk of a car, and I'm this far away from the end of a silencer. Let's not get hung up on who's got what, okay?" The operator cut in and asked for more money. Potamos swore and searched his pockets for change, found a quarter and inserted it. "Anne," he said, "did Bob tell you I'm doing a book on this whole mess?"

"Yes, and he said maybe we could all get involved. Is that true?"

"Yeah, it's true."

"If not, we'll just do it ourselves."

"Go ahead."

"We'd rather work with you because you have the credentials. Besides, there's a whole aspect of this that only you know about."

"You bet there is, Miss Lewis. But I'm running out of time, patience, and quarters. Tonight, at your house?"

"Yes, but late. Ten, even eleven."

"Your choice."

"Eleven."

"Nebel will be there?"

"Yes, and maybe Sam."

"Maruca? Why would he be part of this?"

"Because he's very frightened, Mr. Potamos. He never bargained for this."

"I'm sure he didn't. Neither did I. See you at

eleven at your house. Fitzgerald will be with me."

"Let's go," he told Fitzgerald as he tossed enough money on the table to cover the drinks.

"Where we going?"

"Some nice hotel where the world won't know where we are, someplace with a fancy restaurant and maybe a health club. I need booze, food, and a little steam."

Chapter Thirty-two

"I've never been in a steam bath before," Fitzgerald said as he and Potamos sat next to each other on a bench.

"All part of the learning curve," Potamos said. They'd had prime ribs with the trimmings in the hotel's dining room, and Potamos had ordered champagne, not to celebrate, more to blot out the unpleasant reality of the day. He couldn't rid himself of the image of Krindler's fall. Why had Krindler decided to draw the gun and kill him? Had he acted on his own, decided to dispose of Potamos and explain it later to his superiors? That would mean he had plenty of room for discretion—or just didn't care. Either way, Potamos could only hope that Krindler wasn't supposed to report back to someone. That could foul things up the next morning.

They'd had a massage from a big, burly fellow named Ed Kelly who looked the name. That was another first for Fitzgerald; he must have said "I never did this before" a hundred times to Kelly, who just laughed and kept digging deeper, bringing forth loud groans.

They returned to their room and prepared to

leave. Potamos had pumped Fitzgerald at dinner and in the steam room for every scrap of information he had, which turned out not to be much more than he'd offered at the Georgetown Inn.

"How do we play it at Lewis's house?" he asked Fitzgerald as they were about to leave.

"I guess just be as open with them as you have with me" was his reply. "They're scared, all of them, especially Walter."

"Lewis said Maruca was scared."

"I guess I would be, too, if I were in his shoes. You know what, though?"

"What?"

"I believe Sam didn't mean to kill her, just wanted to scare her off."

"Off from what?"

"From what she knew and was ready to publish."

"What is it she knew, Bob?"

"I don't know, but I guess we'll find out."

Anne Lewis answered the door looking considerably less calm and self-assured than when Potamos had had dinner with her at Martin's. She closed the door behind them and said hurriedly and in a lowered voice, "We're downstairs in the den. The housekeeper's in her room, so let's keep it down. I don't want her to hear anything."

The house was beautifully furnished. Paul Lewis's clients obviously paid him handsomely to manipulate the American governmental process in their favor. Anne led them through an

arch and down a wide flight of stairs to a pan-
eled room with a pool table, projection-screen TV,
sauna, and minigym. Steve McCarty was sitting
in a corner with a young man Potamos assumed
was Walter Nebel. He was Germanic in appearance, tall, and well built, his upper body defined
through a tight yellow T-shirt. His hair was short
and sandy-colored, his features sharp. There was
a certain feminine quality to his looks, pretty
rather than handsome.

Rock music played at low volume. A large
brown dog bounded across the room, sniffed
Potamos's shoetops, then ran up the stairs.

Fitzgerald introduced Potamos to Nebel, who
stood as an afterthought and shook his hand.
"Hello, Steve," Potamos said to McCarty. McCarty
nodded but said nothing.

"Mind if I sit down?" Potamos asked.

Lewis pulled three director's chairs into a semi-
circle around McCarty and Nebel. Potamos sat
down between Fitzgerald and Lewis. He looked
at Nebel for a long time before saying, "I understand you have a story to tell."

Nebel glanced nervously at the others. "I'm not
sure you're the one to tell it to."

Potamos sighed, looked at the ceiling, and said
to Lewis, "I thought this was worked out."

"There's really nothing to be afraid of Walt. You
didn't do anything wrong," Lewis said to Nebel.

"Except run," Potamos said. "How come you
did?" He leaned forward, his elbows on his knees.

"Because I didn't want to be involved" was
Nebel's response.

"With Valerie's murder?"

"Of course. You know I used to go out with her."

Potamos nodded.

"And that we saw each other after the barge party and got into a fight that other people saw."

"Right, but that wouldn't automatically make you a suspect. Okay, maybe I can understand panicking like that and taking off, but what's this about the false alibi you and Sam Maruca cooked up? Bob told me it was Maruca who suggested that you needed one, not that you asked for it. Is that right?"

"Yes." He was barely audible.

"Why did he do that?"

"Because . . ."

Lewis said, "Before we go any farther, Joe, I think we should talk about the arrangement."

"What arrangement?"

"The book you're doing. Bob told us that if we all work together, we can share in the credit and proceeds."

Potamos held his true feelings in check and said in a calm, well-modulated voice, "And that's the only reason you're coming forth with this?"

McCarty said, "No, but it makes sense. We've done a lot of work, a lot of digging. We know things that no one else does, including you. We could go to the police, but—"

"Which is exactly where you should be going," Potamos said, anger creeping into his voice.

"I don't want that," Nebel said, "at least not yet."

"Why not? You didn't kill anybody, did you?"

"No!" It was the first animation from him.

"Your buddy Maruca did?"

They all looked at each other. McCarty answered: "Yes, he killed her, but it was an accident. It wasn't supposed to turn out that way."

Potamos sat back, thought for a minute, then said, "What was it supposed to be?"

There was no answer.

"Hey, look," Potamos said, "I didn't come here to play twenty questions. I don't have much time. Who sent Maruca? You, Nebel?"

"No, I—"

"Her father?"

"Marshall Jenkins," McCarty said.

Potamos puffed his cheeks and grunted. "Proof?"

"That's what Sam says."

"Why would Jenkins send a college kid to scare a senator's daughter out of something?"

Lewis started to answer, but McCarty got up and cut her off. He stood in front of Potamos like a lawyer arguing a case and said, "I really think we should work out our agreement before we allow another thing to be said. Here. . . ." He handed Potamos an envelope. "It's a simple letter of agreement among us concerning anything that's written about the Frolich and Fiamma murders. We'll work as a team and split the money, fifty percent to you, the rest to us. You get the major by-line, but we get a 'With the help of' credit. Go ahead, look at it. I drew it up. It's only two paragraphs."

Potamos opened it and read the brief declaration of intent and terms. He was ready to leap from his chair and attack them all. Instead, he pulled a pen from his jacket and signed it, handed it back to McCarty, who was profoundly surprised at the ease of it.

Potamos ignored McCarty and said to Nebel, "Okay, Walter, let's get to the nitty-gritty. Why would a rich and powerful man like Marshall Jenkins hire Sam Maruca to scare his best friend's daughter? And no stutter-steps. Straight talk— nice, simple sentences with subject and a verb and the right punctuation at the end."

"It was because Sam worked for Jenkins. So did I."

"What'a you mean, 'worked' for him? Doing what?"

"Whatever he wanted, I guess. Sam got me into it. Mr. Jenkins wanted to get people to sell their houses in Georgetown at cheap prices and figured a good way to do that was to cause some problems in the neighborhood. At least, that's how it started."

"Demonstrations, things like that?"

Nebel shrugged. "Lots of street people, bikers, vandalism. He brought in kids from school to help him. That's what I did when Sam first got me involved."

There was silence. Potamos said, "And?"

"Then Sam started doing other things for Mr. Jenkins. There was this old guy who lived in a house that Mr. Jenkins owned someplace in Georgetown. Jenkins wanted him out, but the old guy wouldn't go, so Sam went there and . . ."

"And what, beat him up?"

"Yeah."

"He was a goon for Jenkins?"

"Yeah."

"You, too?"

"I never . . . I did some things for him like that."

"Jesus, a campus Mafia," Potamos said.

"It was nothing terrible," Nebel said. "I mean, we never killed anyone or—"

"Until Valerie."

"That was a mistake. It really was, Mr. Potamos. You have to believe me."

"Why?"

"Because . . . Look, I don't want any part of this anymore. I'm supposed to graduate, but now I won't. My folks are real upset and—"

"Nice of you to think of them, Walter."

Nebel slumped back in his chair and looked like he was about to cry. It was a crybaby generation, Potamos thought. Do your own thing, get your act together, snort and smoke and do whatever else turns you on until somebody catches up with you. Then, you cry, and hope daddy and mommy come to the rescue—which they too often did.

"Where's Maruca?" Potamos asked Lewis.

"We don't know."

Potamos said to McCarty, "Give me back that paper. No Maruca, no deal."

"He left," Nebel said.

"Where?"

"Europe."

"Just Europe."

"Spain, I think. At least that's what he talked about."

"Okay, let's get back to this business of Jenkins and his campus mobsters. No, let's get back to Valerie Frolich. I read her diary."

Everyone's eyes opened. Lewis said, "You did?"

"Yeah, that's right. Tony showed it to me. She indicated in it that she had an affair with Bowen. All of you know that?"

They looked at each other.

"So you all knew it. Now, Fiamma ended up with the diary and was going to write stories based on it. You knew that, too?"

More glances at each other.

"Come on, who knew in this precious group?"

"I did," McCarty said. "How could I miss? That's all he talked about, how he was going to make it big because of it."

Potamos looked at Lewis. "You knew it, too?"

She lowered her eyes. "Yes."

"Nobody thought to call the police?"

"That would have gotten Tony in trouble," McCarty said.

"You cared that much about him?" Potamos asked, his tone answering his own question.

"He said he was working with you on it," Lewis said.

"See what it got him?" Potamos said, not comfortable with his flippancy. He turned to Nebel. "Look, Walter, if you're telling the truth, you haven't got anything to worry about. Maruca's the one who's got to worry. What the hell is with you guys, running instead of facing things and working them out?"

"It was dumb, I know," Nebel said.

"It sure was," Potamos said, "and you know what it did? I still wonder who's telling the truth here, you or Maruca. Maybe it's the other way around. Maybe you killed Valerie and are laying it on your friend."

"I swear that's not it," Nebel said. "Sam was told by Mr. Jenkins to make sure she didn't talk or write about the real story behind the condo."

"Which is?" Potamos asked.

McCarty jumped in. "Which is, Mr. Potamos, that Marshall Jenkins is just a front for the CIA, like he is in lots of things—businesses, buildings. He has been for years. In the case of the condo, it's being built with West German money that's being laundered through him."

"Why West German?"

McCarty said, "It doesn't matter. It could be Arab money, or British or French. When the Russians started building their new embassy on Mount Alto, Senator Frolich was told by the president to come up with a plan to counteract their surveillance activities from it. Frolich has used Jenkins before. He's a silent partner in a big employment agency in New York that's really a CIA operation to get information on people. He's also behind a publishing company in New York that publishes books the CIA wants in print. This time, it was to get something tall built near the embassy so that we can put in our own electronic equipment and . . ." He looked at Anne Lewis. "And weapons."

"Weapons?"

"Yes, missiles aimed at the embassy."

Potamos shook his head. "If the Russians knew that, they'd raise hell."

"That's right," McCarty said. "It would make us look like fools, and with a summit coming up we'd be in a bad negotiating position."

Potamos sat back and chewed what he'd been fed. "Two questions," he said. "First, why would Jenkins build the condo with foreign money?"

Lewis said, "Because it had to be a purely private enterprise. There couldn't be any government money involved or it would look like the president was building a launching pad against the Soviets. Senator Frolich wanted Jenkins to raise private capital here, but he wouldn't do it. He had easy access to the German money and made a deal with them. They'd own a valuable piece of real estate here and we'd have what we wanted, a listening post and strategic advantage over the embassy."

"How come Jenkins calls the shots in something like this?" Potamos asked. "If it's a matter of national security, Frolich and the president should be making those decisions."

Anne Lewis looked toward the stairs leading up to the kitchen. Confident that the housekeeper wasn't there, she said, "Mr. Potamos, Marshall Jenkins *owns* Senator Frolich. The senator benefits financially from everything Jenkins does."

Potamos said, "Question number two: How do you know all this?"

"Steve and I . . ." She looked to McCarty for confirmation that she could continue. He nodded, and she said, "Steve and I have known for a long time about the condo. I picked up pieces of it from conversations my father had with Senator Frolich."

"Which you eavesdropped on," Potamos said.

"Yes. At the time I just considered it interesting. That was long before Valerie was murdered. You hear so much when you live in a house like this."

"Why'd Frolich discuss something so sensitive with your father? He's not a government official, he's a paid lobbyist."

She didn't respond.

"You don't have to tell me, Anne," Potamos said. "What is your father, in business with Frolich and Jenkins?"

She looked Potamos in the eye and said, "My father is involved with them financially. He has no connection with the murders. If I thought he did . . ."

"Enough said." Potamos looked at McCarty. "You got all this from what she heard her father say during conversations with Frolich?"

"No. We got most of it from Valerie."

"She talked about it?"

"Yes, but that was long before her murder. She wasn't telling tales out of school to hurt anybody, wasn't looking to use it, but she was disgusted with it. We'd sit around talking and every once in a while she'd get on the subject of how our government operates, *really* operates. When she was killed, Annie and I compared notes and realized why Valerie was murdered—to keep her quiet. Once things really got bad between her and her father, she started using what she knew to get even with him. She told us one night that she'd laid it all out for him, everything she knew about the condo and Jenkins and . . ."

"And what?"

"And his extramarital affairs, particularly with Mrs. Jenkins. That's been going on for years."

"Does Jenkins know?"

Nebel answered that one. "Jenkins had Sam follow her over the past few months. He told Jenkins about it."

"Which gives Jenkins an even greater hold over the esteemed senator from New Jersey," Potamos said, more to himself than to them.

"Like Mr. Bowen," Fitzgerald said.

Potamos snapped his head to the right, where Fitzgerald sat. "Bowen knows about the affair?"

"Sure." Fitzgerald turned to Lewis. "You were there that night, Annie, when Valerie got a little drunk at that bar and called her father a puppet for Jenkins and Bowen."

"That's right," Lewis said. "Bowen's always preaching to us about ethics in journalism, but we all know you don't get scoops like he gets without lots of inside contacts."

McCarty said, "I've been doing some heavy checking on Bowen and his relationship to Jenkins and Senator Frolich. He's got a financial piece of a lot of the businesses Jenkins has set up for the CIA, and he writes whatever Jenkins tells him to write. Some ethics, huh?"

"You can prove that?" Potamos asked.

"Yes."

"Okay, but did Bowen have anything to do with Valerie's murder?"

"We don't think so," McCarty said.

"Did he know Jenkins sent Maruca to warn her off?"

"We don't know that, either."

"The senator—does *he* know that his friend Jenkins is behind his daughter's murder?"

"We talked about that last night," Fitzgerald said, "and we decided he must know. How could he not?"

"That's a heavy load to carry around," Potamos said. He shook his head. "You've really come up with a lot of answers, but there's still a big question."

"Tony."

"Right, Tony Fiamma. Who killed him? Maruca, at Jenkins's behest?"

Nebel shook his head. "That's why he took off. I saw him for a couple of minutes just before he left. It was the day Tony died. He told me he'd had it, was through with doing what Jenkins wanted. He said they wanted him to do the same thing to Tony that he did to Valerie that night."

"Kill him or scare him?" Potamos asked. "Another accident?"

"I don't know," said Nebel. "I asked him if Jenkins told him to meet Tony, but he didn't answer me. The only thing he said was that he wasn't going to do it and was leaving. He said '*they*.' That, I'm sure of."

Potamos thought for a moment, then asked Nebel, "What other students worked for Jenkins, did his dirty work?"

"None that I know of. Sam was the only one until he brought me in. I needed the money and—"

"Knock off the rationalizations, Walter. It doesn't matter why you did it. What did Maruca think about your coming back here? You're a big threat to him. You've already blabbed about his being the one who killed Valerie."

"He told me that he didn't care what I did or said, because I was the only one who knew it was an accident. Right after I met up with Valerie that night and we had our fight, I went to Sam's apartment and told him what had happened. He asked me where she was, and I told him. When I asked why he wanted to know, he explained what Jenkins wanted him to do and figured that was as good a time as any."

Potamos smiled ruefully. "Some friend he turned out to be, Walter. He probably figured if something went wrong, you could be the patsy because you were with her."

Nebel looked at the floor. "I know. Sam always used me." He looked up at Fitzgerald. "You used to tell me that, Bob."

Fitzgerald nodded. He turned to Potamos. "What happens now?"

"I don't know," Potamos said. "I *do* know that everybody here had better lie low for a day or two. I have an appointment in the morning that might shed some light on the rest of it. I'll be back to you later tomorrow." He stood and took in each of their young faces. "I have to admit I don't like any of you much. I also have to admit you're probably all going to end up pretty good reporters. We have our deal, and I'll honor it. Talk to you tomorrow."

He went up the stairs, with Fitzgerald and Lewis at his heels. She opened the front door and said, "Don't think too poorly of us, Joe. We just happened to be here. None of us planned this."

"Yeah, I know. Neither did Valerie Frolich or Tony Fiamma. Talk to you tomorrow."

Fitzgerald went with him to his car.

"You stay here, Bob," Potamos said. "Keep everybody cool, make sure they don't decide to do anything else on their own. Oh, and one more thing."

"What?"

Potamos handed him a set of keys. "There's a red Corvette parked in my garage. These are the keys to it. If you don't hear from me by Sunday morning at eight, go to the police, give them the keys, tell them where the car is parked, and tell them to look in the trunk. Then tell them I went to Marshall Jenkins's retreat down in Leesburg, Virginia."

"That's where you're going?"

"Yeah, but that's between us. Not a word to any of them in there. Right?"

"Right. What's in the trunk?"

"A mistake, mine. Take it easy."

Chapter Thirty-three

Before Potamos went upstairs, he checked the garage to be sure the red Corvette was still where he'd parked it and that the smell of death hadn't begun to seep out of the trunk yet. Then he walked Jumper, made himself a grilled ham and cheese sandwich, opened a beer, and took deep breaths to relax at the kitchen table. The centerpiece was Krindler's .380 Manurhin. It was one o'clock Saturday morning. He was tired and craved sleep but knew that unless he took the time to sort things out, he'd just lie in bed, eyes open and thoughts whirling. He had to be organized: an hour of thought, five hours of sleep, an hour to prepare for the arrival of the limousine.

At eight, showered and dressed, the revolver in his waistband in back, the dog's needs satisfied, he left the apartment and went downstairs. The limo wasn't there yet. He sat on a bench in the lobby and looked out through the glass doors at the curb. Eight-fifteen . . . eight-thirty . . . Was it coming? He'd give it until nine, which he did, then went upstairs and called George Bowen's home number. No answer.

He went down to the garage, got into his car,

and headed for Route 7. Forty-five minutes later he reached Leesburg and drove down its main street, past rows of antebellum red brick buildings, until reaching a gas station at the edge of town. "I'm looking for Marshall Jenkins's house," he told the gangly young man who came out of the office.

The kid shook his head, then said, "I think it's out that way," pointing to a small paved road that jutted north from the main road.

"How far?" Potamos asked.

A shrug and painfully puzzled frown. "I don't know. Never been there, but it's out there some place." He grinned. "He don't hang signs, you know."

Potamos took the small road and drove slowly, looking left and right as the town faded away and the northern Virginia countryside turned rural. There were driveways off the road but few signs, and after a mile he began to curse. He'd never find it, wasn't even certain it was Jenkins's "retreat" that the limo was scheduled to bring him to. It had to be, he reasoned, and kept going, wondering whether he'd get lucky, see something that would give him a clue to which driveway to take. Ten minutes later he found it, a small mail truck making deliveries to roadside mailboxes. He pulled up alongside and said to the pretty young woman wearing a U.S. Postal Service uniform, "I really got turned around. I'm visiting Marshall Jenkins and lost count of the driveways."

She smiled and said over the sound of their engines, "You have a lot more counting to do."

"Yeah? I'm that far off?"

"A couple of miles. What directions did Mr. Jenkins give you?"

Potamos had hoped it wouldn't come to that, hoped he'd come off as someone who belonged at the Jenkins estate. He said, "He told me to come up this road for about a mile and then count from the boarded-up red house I just passed."

She looked at him as though she were making a decision. Potamos added pleasantly, "I'm already late for the meeting. You know him, he doesn't like his people being late for anything."

It brought a smile to her face. "You work for him?"

"Yes, public relations. Been on his staff for over a year now."

"And you've never been out here?"

Potamos was getting angry. Why was she being so protective of him? Was everybody in the greater D.C. area on his payroll? He kept his tone pleasant and said, "Big moment for me, getting invited to the old man's house. Looks like I'll keep my job for another week—*if* I ever get there."

She said, "You misunderstood his directions. He meant the second boarded-up red building on this road, about two miles farther, on your left. An old schoolhouse. Count from there."

Count how many? he wondered. He was trying to formulate a way to ask when she said, "Don't count the first road that looks like a drive-way. It goes nowhere. Skip that one and count five after it."

"I'm glad I ran into you. Thanks."

The dirt driveway's opening was small and

obscured by bushes and a stone wall. Potamos turned into it and traveled a few hundred yards before reaching a tall, metal fence with barbed wire coiled along its top. There was a gate manned by a young fellow wearing a red and black plaid shirt and jeans. A shotgun rested against a battered and peeling wood shed. The young man sat on a tree stump in front of it. As Potamos approached, he got up, laced his fingers in the gate's mesh, and waited for Potamos to say something.

"I have an appointment with Mr. Jenkins," Potamos said.

"What's your name?"

"Potamos, Joe Potamos. Mr. Bowen is expecting me, too."

The young man hesitated, then went into the shed. To make a phone call? He returned in a few moments with a question: "You're sure you're Joe Potamos? You have I.D.?"

Potamos's mind was racing as he pulled out his wallet. When the limo hadn't arrived, he'd been almost sure it was because Bowen and Jenkins assumed Krindler had done the job. He was positive now. His heart pounded as the guard scrutinized the I.D., glancing up at him to check his face against the photo on the press card. He handed the wallet back and returned to the shack. When he came out again, he picked up the shotgun and carried it to the gate. "You can go in," he said, using a key to free the padlock from the gate.

Potamos headed up a steep, winding road until he reached a circular drive in front of the red brick mansion. He stopped, turned off the ignition.

There were no other cars, and no one came to the front door. He climbed the steps and rang the bell. He was tapping the back of his hand against the revolver tucked in his belt when the door opened. George Bowen stood there. "Hello, Joe," he said.

Potamos cocked his head and leaned back a little, smiled and said, "You look surprised to see me, George. Did you think I wasn't going to make it?"

Bowen's eyebrows went up and he ran his index finger over his thin moustache, but said nothing.

"This is where the party is, isn't it?" Potamos asked. "I would have brought the hostess a gift, but . . ."

"Come in, Joe. As long as you're here, you might as well partake of the festivities."

Bowen stepped back and Potamos slowly entered the large foyer tiled in Italian marble, with bronze reliefs on the walls. "The house that Jenkins built," he muttered as Bowen closed the door. Potamos turned to face him. "Is Roseann here?" he asked flatly.

"I've met many fools in my day, Joe, but you take the prize. *You* are the most foolish of them all."

"Yeah? Well, maybe we'll see who's a fool after all this goes down, George. Where is she?"

Bowen's answer was to open a pair of heavy wooden doors off the foyer and invite Potamos in with a sweep of his hand. Potamos could see most of the room from where he stood. It was huge, all wood and leather and Oriental rugs, with a fireplace blazing at the far end. Standing in front of

the fire were Marshall Jenkins and Senator John
Frolich. Another man came briefly into view as he
started to join the others, then stepped back. Potamos recognized him: Paul Lewis, Anne Lewis's
lobbyist father.

"Hail, hail, the gang's all here," Potamos said as
he entered the room, not feeling nearly as cavalier
as his comment.

"You're Potamos," Jenkins said from where
he stood. It sounded like a proclamation, giving
Potamos his name at a baptism. "Why are you
here?"

"You invited me. Correction—your crony here,
Bowen, invited me, but the transportation never
showed. That's why I'm late. My apologies, for
being late and for being alive."

Frolich started to say something, but Jenkins
cut him off. "You're a troublemaker, Mr. Potamos,
a serious one, a constant, nagging thorn in everyone's foot."

"And you're a murderer," Potamos said.

The abruptness of the comment stopped Jenkins for a moment. He sighed and indicated a
leather chair near the fire. "Sit down, Mr. Potamos. George hasn't done a very good job of explaining the facts of life to you, but I assure you
I'll be more effective."

Potamos ignored Jenkins and looked at Lewis,
standing in the corner. "What's your act, Mr.
Lewis? You part of this? Your daughter's going
to be very disappointed with daddy if you are. I
was with her last night. Good kid, and she's done
her homework." He turned to Bowen. "You taught

your seminar students pretty good, George. They've been on the beat, digging, asking questions, and have come up with some serious answers."

Frolich spoke for the first time. His tone was syrupy, conciliatory. "Mr. Potamos, there have been some unfortunate misunderstandings about everything that has happened, beginning with the brutal murder of my daughter, Valerie. I would ask you to show some sensitivity and to give us at least the courtesy of a chance to explain."

"Explain what, senator? Why you hang around with the man responsible for your daughter's murder?" He looked directly at Jenkins. "That's right, senator, your close buddy here sent one of his henchmen, a college student named Sam Maruca, to take care of your daughter. He took care of her, all right—bashed her pretty head in. That's what you want to explain to me, senator? Save your breath."

Jenkins said, "That's a libelous accusation you've made. I trust you have proof."

"Yeah, I do. Sam Maruca didn't mean to kill your daughter, senator. He was supposed to scare her off from writing about the condo." He looked at the floor and guffawed. "Jesus, here I am explaining it to you. You know it all, damn it—the whys and the wheres and everything." He said to Jenkins, "Maruca's had it—he's all through doing your dirty work. He's in Spain, gave me the whole story on the phone last night. He's on his way back to testify. Good enough?"

There was silence.

"Where's Roseann?" Potamos asked.

"Safely put away," Jenkins said.

"Why?"

"For the same reason George has been making you offers any reasonable man wouldn't refuse." Until this moment, Jenkins's voice had been as flat and gray as his face and hair, but not now. He approached Potamos and glared at him, his hands tightened into fists. "This is America. This is my country and yours. There is a threat to it that could wipe out everything, for everyone. You, and your kind, will not be allowed to stand in the way of a vigilant and dedicated defense. What was done had to be done, without regard for—"

"For what," Potamos said, "your ability to make fortunes, Jenkins? You—all of you—are a bunch of hypocrites." He took a step toward Frolich. "What about you, senator? Are your White House dreams so desperate that you can close your eyes to your daughter's death?" Bowen was next. "And you, you mealy-mouthed psychopath, lining your goddamn pockets while you ignore the First Amendment!"

He took them all in before shouting, "I want Roseann Blackburn! Where is she?"

He never heard the person softly approaching behind him. Two things happened almost simultaneously. Potamos saw their eyes and realized they were looking at someone to his rear. Then a powerful forearm gripped his neck and his hand was whipped behind his back and wrenched upward until he gasped with pain. The force against his windpipe was so great that he thought he was going to pass out. He was pulled backward, across the room and through the same small door his assailant had used to enter. He was dragged down a long, narrow hallway, his physical protests sending him bouncing off walls. A table was toppled as he continued to struggle. The assailant stopped and reached for a doorknob with his free hand, opened the door, and tossed Potamos into the room like a sack of grain. The door was slammed and he heard a key turn, looked up at a small window with closed blinds.

Someone stirred in the opposite corner. He poised against another attack, then saw that the figure was on the floor, a blindfold over the eyes, a cloth around the mouth, hands tied in back. As he became more accustomed to the low light, he realized it was a woman. "Roseann?" he said softly, the words hurting his throat. "Roseann!" He scrambled across the floor and tentatively touched her leg. She turned and her eyes met his over the blindfold. He reached behind her head and untied the blindfold and gag. She blinked and swallowed. "What did they do to you?" he growled as he worked on the cord that bound her hands. When she was free, he sat next to her and took her in his arms. "I'm sorry," he said over and over, stroking her hair and feeling her silent sobs against his body. They stayed that way for a long time, until she'd calmed down and said, "Joe, I'm so glad you're here."

"Yeah, me too. What's happened? Why did they do this to you? Have you been like this since you disappeared?"

She shook her head. "No, nothing like this. They brought me here and—"

"Who brought you here?"

"I don't know. They brought me here and I've been okay. They've treated me well. I've had good food and they even let me play the piano. They talk to me."

"What do you mean, they 'talk' to you?"

"About . . . about what's happened, the diary, the murders . . . just talk, sometimes for hours."

"Who talks to you?"

"I don't know them. Two men. They . . ."

"They *what?*"

"They gave me a shot."

"A shot? A needle? Some kind of drug?"

"I think so."

"And?"

"Nothing. There were times when I lost track, you know? Just lost hours. But I'm all right. I really am." Her voice took on the sound of sudden panic. "Why are you here, Joe? You shouldn't be. They'll hurt you."

"No, don't worry about that. I know who killed Valerie Frolich. I know a lot of other things, too. We'll be okay, believe me. I just have to think for a minute." He sat up straight and his hand went to his back. The revolver was still there. "It didn't fall out," he mumbled.

"What?"

"This." He held the weapon in front of her face.

"No, Joe," she said, getting to her knees and kneeling before him. "We have to do what they say. They're right."

He leaned against the wall and stared at her. "They're right?" he repeated.

"It isn't like we thought, Joe. It wasn't a murder, not a real one. It was necessary to protect us."

He said nothing, continued to stare at her.

She took his face in her hands and said softly, seductively, "Joe, they aren't bad. We misunderstood, were in the wrong place at the wrong time, got in their way, that's all."

"Roseann—"

"Listen to me, Joe. They just want us to go away, to forget about what's happened and get on with our lives. They had a job to do, a difficult one but one that has to be done if we're going to survive."

"Survive? You and me?"

"All of us, Joe, the country, our way of life. It makes such sense, but you never took the time to listen."

"Roseann, they've done something bad to you."

She shook her head, and her voice took on added urgency. "No, Joe, no, they haven't. I told them that I understood and that I knew you would, too, once I had a chance to talk to you." He could see her smile in the dim light and he closed his eyes. "We can go away, Joe, just like we talked about. We can find a nice place to live away from here and forget about it." His eyes remained closed and tears welled behind the lids. "Joe, please listen to me. Everything is all right now." There was actually a touch of mirth in her voice. "Wouldn't that be nice, to go away together! Do you still want to marry me?"

His eyes opened. He reached out and crushed

her to him, rocked her like a baby. He heard a sound in the hallway, saw a shadow, continued to rock her, the revolver still in his right hand. A key was turned and the door opened slowly. A man stepped inside and quickly shut the door behind him. Potamos started to slide out from under Blackburn and brought the gun up so that it was pointed at the man's abdomen.

"Mr. Potamos," a voice said.

"You make a move at us, you're dead," Potamos said, getting to his feet and holding the weapon up, catching light from the window. He squinted, said, "Maruca? Sam Maruca?"

"Yeah. Hey, put the gun down. I won't hurt you."

"You bet you won't. You won't hurt anybody ever again."

Maruca put up his hands and said, "Please, give me a minute, that's all I ask. I'm sorry I had to do that to you, but if I didn't, they'd—"

"*You* had me by the neck? I ought to—"

"Please, hear me out. I'm here to help."

Potamos paused, then said, "Get over in the corner, on the floor. Put your hands behind your head and spread your legs. You got it?"

"Why . . . ?"

"Just do it, damn it!"

Maruca did what he'd been told. Potamos squatted on his haunches, the revolver held in both hands and pointed at Maruca's head. "You'd better talk fast, Maruca, and it had better make sense. She and I are walking out of here and I don't mind doing it over your body. I've already . . ." He looked at Blackburn, then said, "How do we get out? How many people are around—Jenkins's goons, guards, anybody else?"

"Just a few—the guy at the gate, a guy who patrols the grounds, that's all. I'll go with you."

"Come on, Maruca, you're one of them and you'll drown with them, buddy. You're all going down the tube, every last one of you."

"I . . . Mr. Potamos, it was an accident that Valerie died. I—"

"So I heard from your puppet, Walter Nebel. Big deal, Maruca, she's still dead."

"I know. How do you think I feel? I never wanted anything to do with it. The things I did for Mr. Jenkins were never that heavy. I told him no, but . . ."

"But he dangled an apartment and cash in front of you. What the hell do you think that does, get you off the hook, make you some kind of a hapless dupe? Try that on a judge."

"It's the truth, and when he asked me to do it again, I said no."

"What are you talking about, Tony Fiamma?"

"Yes. I didn't kill him."

"Who did?"

Maruca hung his head and muttered something.

"What? I can't hear you," Potamos said.

There were footsteps in the hall, and the door was flung open. The guard from the front gate stood there, the shotgun leveled at them. Potamos gripped the revolver and slowly raised its muzzle, his hand and the gun's butt on the floor. His mind was short-circuited by a barrage of conflicting thoughts: Would the guard fire the shotgun even if Potamos's bullet caught him in the stomach? Who'd die in the room? Blackburn? Himself? His finger gently tightened on the trigger as he tried to make a decision.

There was a commotion from another part of the house. The guard turned and looked down the hall in the direction of the study. Voices. What was one saying? " . . . a warrant." He heard his name. "Potamos. Where is he?"

The guard with the shotgun disappeared in an opposite direction. Potamos stood and pulled Blackburn to her feet, the revolver still on Maruca. "It's Languth," he said to her. "The police."

Maruca stood but remained against the wall, his hands raised. Potamos went to him and pressed the muzzle of the gun under his chin. "You got thirty seconds, Maruca, to tell me your life story. Tell me good and I'll help you. Tell me bad and I'll do the taxpayers a big favor."

Chapter Thirty-four

Potamos pushed Maruca ahead of him up the hall, with Blackburn behind them. They entered the study, where Frolich, Jenkins, Bowen, Paul Lewis stood facing Pete Languth, four uniformed police officers from Loudoun County, and the students from Bowen's seminar: Bob Fitzgerald, Anne Lewis, and Steve McCarty.

"What are you doing here?" Potamos asked of everyone.

Languth said, "We're here to arrest you, Joe."

"For what?"

"For murder."

"What are you talking about?"

Fitzgerald said, "I'm sorry, Joe, but I couldn't help it. I told Annie and Steve about the keys you gave me and we decided to go to your place and see what was in the trunk of the car." He closed his eyes and shook his head. "Boy, it was awful! We took a vote and decided to go to the police."

"Beautiful," Potamos said. "You really listened to me, didn't you, you—"

"Joe, who's the guy in the trunk?" Languth asked.

"He's . . . Hey, wait a minute, that doesn't matter.

Right here in this room are the murderers of Valerie Frolich and Tony Fiamma."

"Yeah?" Languth said, looking directly at Bowen. "Tell me about it."

Potamos drew a deep breath, then said, "This one here, Sam Maruca, killed Valerie Frolich, only he didn't mean to. It was an accident, and there's another witness to corroborate."

Languth looked at Maruca, who said, "He's right. I didn't mean it, but—"

Potamos jumped in. "He was sent to do it, Pete, by Marshall Jenkins."

Languth turned to Jenkins. "That's nonsense," Jenkins said.

"Save your breath, Jenkins," Potamos said. "You're as cut-and-dried as they come. Now, Pete, we get to the interesting part. Who killed Tony Fiamma?"

Paul Lewis stepped from behind his friends and went to his daughter. "This is terrible," he said.

"Daddy, if I could have—"

"Shut up," Jenkins said to Paul Lewis.

Lewis spun around and said, "It's over, Marshall. Finished. Can't you see that? The end is here."

"Fool," Jenkins said. He faced Potamos. "Do you really think you'll manage to topple the institutions that protect this nation against the Communist threat? Do you want to? That's traitorous. You'll hang for it."

Potamos stared at Jenkins incredulously. He was a madman, certifiable, warped beyond any boundaries of rational thought.

"Go on," Languth said to Potamos.

Senator Frolich stepped forward. "Sergeant, I'm John Frolich, United States senator."

"Yes, sir, I know that," Languth said. "We don't mean to bother you, sir. We're here for Potamos on a warrant."

"Then I suggest you take him under that warrant and deal with his wild accusations at a more appropriate time."

"Why?" Potamos said, coming around Maruca and standing a few feet from Frolich. "Because you'd just as soon not have to deal with the fact that you murdered Fiamma?"

"Hey, Joe," Languth said, "you're getting—"

"Shut up, Pete," Potamos said. He still had the revolver in his hand and he waved it at Frolich. Languth shouted for him to put it down, but he refused, saying to Frolich, "You're the worst of the bunch, senator. You knew your best friend had ordered the murder of your daughter, but you didn't do a damn thing about it, because he pulls all the strings, doesn't he? What'd he do, promise you the White House if you went along with him? Some president you'd make, Frolich. Even Nixon didn't murder anybody."

"Joe," Languth said, approaching Potamos. Potamos pointed the gun at him and said, "In a minute, Pete. Just a minute, that's all." Again to Frolich: "Your buddy here, Jenkins, tried to get Maruca to take care of Fiamma the same way he took care of your daughter, but he wouldn't— he'd had enough. That left you guys in a bind, didn't it, a young journalism student running around with Valerie's diary and ready to make his mark on the world by writing everything he knew about that condo that's so precious to you. Couldn't have that happen, could we? So Jenkins left it up to you. Was it an accident, senator? Did you just mean to talk to him, maybe hit him once or twice with a rock like Maruca did to Valerie, 'scare' him? Probably not. By this time you probably figured you might as well just kill him and get it over with. Kill everybody who could get in your way, in *his* way." He pointed the gun at Jenkins. "You know what just happened, Mr. Jenkins? America just got saved from you and your protégé here."

Frolich maintained his calm demeanor. He said to Languth, "You've got a very sick person on your hands, sergeant, and he has a gun, if you haven't noticed."

Languth said to Potamos, "Come on, Joe. I know where you're coming from, but Sheriff De George here looks like he's getting itchy. It's his county, Joe, and they do things different."

Potamos lowered his gun and said in an almost pleading tone, "Pete, the murderers are right here, Maruca and the senator, with Jenkins calling the shots."

Languth looked at Bowen. "What about *him?*" he asked Potamos.

"I don't know. Look, let's go and talk about the guy in the Corvette, but don't leave it at that." He turned to Maruca. "Am I telling it straight, Sam?"

Maruca nodded. "He's right."

"He's cooperating, Pete. He's a good kid, just

got wrapped up with the wrong types. His buddy's a witness, too, Walter Nebel."

"Put down the gun," Sheriff De George said.

"Yeah, sure." Potamos dropped it to the floor.
Two of De George's deputies came around behind
and slapped cuffs on him.

"What about them?" Potamos asked, nodding
toward Jenkins, Frolich, and Bowen.

"They're not going anywhere, are you?" Languth said. He came to Maruca. "You want to come
with me and make a statement?"

"Yes," Maruca said sullenly.

"And Roseann, too," Potamos said. "They kidnapped her."

"That true?" Languth asked.

She hesitated, looked at Potamos, then said,
"Yes."

"This is preposterous," Jenkins said. "I caution
you, sergeant, to walk easy. You're dealing with
the next president of the United States."

Potamos looked at Frolich and said, "You're not
the next president, senator. You're a murderer, the
world's worst father, and an adulterer to boot." He
said to Jenkins, "You don't even care, do you, that
he's been sleeping with your wife?" He laughed
and started toward the door. "You're all rotten,"
he said. "Rotten to the core."

Chapter Thirty-five

Potamos and Languth sat in Martin's Tavern. It was noon, a Saturday, a full week since the events at Jenkins's retreat in Leesburg. They'd both ordered the Tavern Treat—lump crabmeat on an English muffin with hollandaise—and beers.

"I still don't understand what's going on with the Krindler thing," Potamos said. He'd spent the previous Saturday night in jail, was released Sunday afternoon.

"He fell, an accident," Languth said, shoving a large portion of food into his mouth.

"It was no accident, Pete," Potamos said. "I told you, I pushed him."

"It doesn't matter. We were told to list it as an accidental death. End of story."

"Who told you to do that?"

"Come on, Joe, lay off. Sometimes when guys like Krindler get it, their people take care of things, nice and quiet, no hassles, no public airing."

"Who're 'his people'?"

"Beats me. I just take orders. Eat. It'll get cold."

Potamos took a bite and washed it down with the cold beer. He watched Languth finish, drain his glass, and wave for a waiter. "Pete," Potamos said, "do you think the charges will hold up against everyone?"

Languth nodded, belched, excused himself, and leaned back, his arms up on the back of the booth. "Yeah, Maruca's got Jenkins crucified. Dumb kid. Blew a good future."

"It'll go light on him, though, won't it? He's a friendly witness."

"I suppose so. We're talking to the D.A. about it."

"What about Frolich? It's Maruca's word against his, a U.S. senator."

Languth grinned, reached into his jacket and pulled out a sheet of paper, handed it to Potamos. He unfolded it and read:

> *Dear Joe,*
> *Sorry—can't make it tonight—got a call from none other than Senator John Frolich—wants to meet me tonight to talk about Valerie's murder and the diary—meeting him at ten down near campus—call you tomorrow.*
> *Tony*

"Pete this is . . ."

Languth leaned forward and said, "Joe, this is real. It's even signed."

"But . . . you know something, Pete, it crossed my mind that you weren't smart enough to come up with that phony note on your own. I wondered whether there'd been a real note, only without Bowen in it. Is that what happened, this note triggered the other one?"

"I'm an officer of the law, Joe. I'd never falsify evidence."

"Right, and I'm Jack Anderson. One question, Pete. This note from Tony *reads* like he wrote it. Why didn't you just copy it and change names?"

Languth took the note from Potamos and frowned at it. "This is lousy writing—just dashes, no commas or periods. The kid was a journalism major. I figured . . ."

"That's what this city needs, a literary critic for a cop," Potamos said.

"Hey, what this city *don't* need is a reporter playing cop. Finish your lunch. This beer's on me."

"What about the first one?"

"On your expense account."

"I don't have one. I'm unemployed."

"You're writing a book."

"Maybe. First I'm getting married. I'm taking Roseann up to meet my family, sort of a reunion party at my mother's house."

"Going for number three, huh?"

"I think so. She hasn't said yes yet, but I think I'm winning."

"Good luck." Languth started to get up.

"Pete, I just want to say that I'm sorry about what happened to your daughter. I didn't know. I'm really sorry."

"Well . . . I ought to thank you for keeping my head straight. I really would have gone after Bowen."

"I know. I think we're all lucky."

They were on their way out of Martin's when the bartender yelled to Potamos, "Joe, a call for you." Languth said he'd keep in touch and left. Potamos took the phone from the bartender and said, "Hello."

"Joe, George Bowen. I thought I'd find you in some bar."

"What do you want, Bowen?"

"A chance to get together and talk. You know, Joe, we're sitting on the political scandal of the past hundred years, maybe of all time. I'll be breaking it over the next couple of weeks nationwide, which steals some of your thunder with the book. I'm willing to work with you, strike a deal, do it together—your writing, my name. We're talking megabucks, Joe, a lot more than you alone will come up with."

Potamos held the receiver away from his ear and looked at it, screwed up his face, blinked, and shook his head.

"Joe, are you there?"

"Yeah, I'm here, George. That's a very generous offer, but I don't think it would work."

"Why?"

"Because when I'm done with you in the book, you'll be lucky to get space in Marv Goldson's *Georgetown Eye.*"

There was silence, then a confident laugh. "Still thinking you can topple institutions, huh? A thickheaded Greek, a hack. I'll bury you, Joe."

"No, George, the funeral's on me. And don't worry, I'll be there at graveside, me and Sergeant Peter Languth, maybe the only ones, but we'll be there. In the meantime, shove your phone up your ear and start clipping coupons. You'll need them."

Later that afternoon, Potamos and Blackburn sat in a New York Air plane as it taxied for takeoff to New York.

"How're you feeling?" he asked.

"Fine. You?"

"Terrific."

"Joe . . ."

"What?"

"Will your mother . . ."

"What, ask if we're getting married?"

She laughed. "That, too. Will she?"

"Probably."

"What should I say?"

"Say whatever you mean."

"Will she like me?"

"Nah. You're not Greek."

"Then . . ."

"Just play the piano good—classical music, no jazz. My father liked opera."

"That's why I'm invited."

"Absolutely. Every party needs a piano player." He smiled, took her hand, and kissed her on the lips as the aircraft broke the bonds of gravity and lifted into the overcast sky above Washington, D.C. "So do I," he said.

"So do you what?"

"Need a piano player."